W9-CKU-786

MONUMENT

OTHER NOVELS BY HOWARD OWEN

Littlejohn
Fat Lightning
Answers to Lucky
The Measured Man
Harry and Ruth
The Rail
Turn Signal
Rock of Ages
The Reckoning
Annie's Bones

WILLIE BLACK SERIES

Oregon Hill
The Philadelphia Quarry
Parker Field
The Bottom
Grace
The Devil's Triangle
Scuffletown
Evergreen
Belle Isle
Jordan's Branch

A WILLIE BLACK MYSTERY

MONUMENT

HOWARD OWEN

THE PERMANENT PRESS
Sag Harbor, NY 11963

For information, address:
The Permanent Press
4170 Noyac Road
Sag Harbor, NY 11963
www.thepermanentpress.com

Library of Congress Cataloging-in-Publication Data

Owen, Howard, author.
Monument / Howard Owen.
First edition.
Sag Harbor, NY: The Permanent Press, 2021.
Series: A Willie Black mystery; 11
ISBN: 9781579626471 (cloth)
ISBN: 9781579626518 (trade paperback)
ISBN: 9781579626495 (ebook)
1. Mystery fiction.

PS3565.W552 M66 2021 (print) 2021025826
PS3565.W552 (ebook) 2021025827
DDC 813'.54—dc23

Printed in the United States of America

To Karen

CHAPTER ONE

Saturday, May 30

This time, Cindy doesn't have to wonder where the hell I've been. The story that's been consuming my last few hours has taken place right below our living-room and dining-room windows, six floors down.

"What a clusterfuck," my beloved observes.

Indeed. The clock in the hallway where she meets me says it's five minutes until three. In the morning.

Outside, in Monroe Park, they're still raising hell, but this blaze in a city one of our political pundits used to call "a hotbed of rest" seems to have burned down to embers for the time being.

It all started out as your generic demonstration. People were a tad pissed off after seeing a young Black man being nonchalantly choked to death for almost nine minutes by a Minneapolis cop last Monday. That woke people up even in staid old Richmond.

We figured, and I'm sure the cops figured, that folks would chant and march awhile and then get bored and go home.

Not exactly.

Nobody, for now, is sure when a peaceful demonstration turned into a riot.

I wasn't even part of the coverage until about ten o'clock. That's when Callie Ann Boatwright, sent over to the park to get a few quotes from the aggrieved, called in to say we were going to need a bigger boat.

Who knows who threw the first stone? Who knows if some overzealous cop inspired the protesters with a little pepper spray? Hell, we didn't expect much of a turnout, with Virginia Commonwealth University's student body dispersed by COVID-19. How can you have a decent riot without college kids?

However it happened, Callie Ann was sounding a little overwhelmed.

"They're setting shit on fire," she told Sally Velez. "Broad Street's like a war zone."

I was out the door before Callie Ann got off the phone.

We already had a photographer there, but Sarah Goodnight, our adult supervision, was able to scramble two more. There were only three other reporters in our desiccated newsroom at that time last night, and Sarah gave them their marching orders.

"What the hell are we supposed to do?" Jack Clatterbuck asked. "I'm just a sportswriter."

"Say bye-bye to Toyland," Sarah informed him.

I told the other three where to go—one to Monroe Park, one to Arthur Ashe Boulevard, where we had a report of a fire, and Clatterbuck and me to different ends of an eight-block parcel of Broad Street that seemed to be Ground Zero.

Clatterbuck rode with me. Before I dropped him off, he asked me what he should look for.

I could hear the chanting, sirens, and occasional breaking of glass from Grace Street a block away.

"Don't worry," I told him. "You'll know it when you see it."

I put on my coronavirus mask and ventured out. It wasn't easy getting past police lines. It never is. I spied my old flatfoot pal Gillespie standing guard half a block off Broad. He looked frazzled.

"Jesus," he said, lifting up his face guard. "We got a mess here."

He had on enough riot gear that I almost didn't recognize him at first. The other cops I saw were armored up like it was go time in Baghdad. We have often wondered why the police dress like they're going to war when they show up for what starts out as a little steam release. I asked L.D. Jones, our hardheaded chief, about it once a few months ago. He said you never know when you're going to need it.

Sometimes, I told him, if you come expecting a war, that's what you get.

He told me, as he often does, that I was full of crap.

Making my way down the street, I saw things I didn't really expect to ever see in Richmond.

There was a Pulse bus, one of those fancy new ones that zip you across town almost as fast as a car, blazing away near the intersection of Broad and Arthur Ashe. I saw people of all races running out of stores carrying whatever they could find. How heartening, I thought, to see Black and white citizens united in something: looting.

And, as I got near police headquarters, I saw that the cops were in something of a Custer vs. Native Americans situation. The crowd, which now could appropriately be called a mob, was throwing anything that wasn't nailed down in the general direction of L.D. Jones's domain. I heard a report that somebody in a car had been shot.

The police were outnumbered, but they weren't outgunned, a fact that eventually became evident to their attackers, who finally backed away.

I saw two guys loaded down with clothing from a store on Broad hop into a Lexus, which sped away, dodging the protesters. Farther up the street, a fire had broken out in one of the apartments that had been hacked out of old abandoned buildings along Broad, and some of the geniuses in the crowd were blocking a fire truck. While I was watching, the cops managed to clear a path, and I found out later that a family inside had been rescued.

I found Callie Ann standing there as close to the fire as we could get.

"This is nuts," she said. "What are these people thinking?"

I'd seen it happen before, but not on this scale.

At some point, it's like all these individual people morph into one entity, and that entity's collective mind is hardly ever on the side of peace and harmony.

I WAS there, a few years ago, after the cops shot and killed a teenage boy over in Creighton Court because he had driven away from a traffic stop and then tried to hoof it when they finally snagged him at a roadblock. They swore he was reaching for a gun when one of the city's finest plugged him four times. All he had in his pocket, when they searched him, was a cell phone. The cop later was reprimanded severely.

The crowd, maybe a hundred people, was still outside when I got there after they'd taken the body away. Four cop cars and eight policemen, looking a little uneasy, were huddled.

"Why you shoot Latrese for?" I heard a Black woman shout.

More yells followed.

And then I saw one of the cops, who was standing under a streetlight and thus was visible to everyone, shake his head, smile, and say something to his partner.

"They laughin' at us," I heard a young man scream. "They think it's funny. Ain't funny, motherfucker."

Then the first rock flew. It occurred to me, as I stepped back far enough to be out of any crossfire, that many of the Creighton Court residents probably were well-armed, so throwing a rock might have been an act of kindness, relatively speaking.

But the cop closest to the rock started walking toward the crowd. And then the crowd started walking toward him, in step like some vigilante army.

By the time they were through, one cop car was overturned and set on fire and the eight cops crowded into the other three vehicles and got the hell out of there with rocks banging against the windows. At that point, the crowd, now jacked up, just stood there, screaming and demanding justice.

Some of them caught sight of me. Being half white and holding a notepad, I was the closest thing to The Man they could find. Just when I thought I was going to pay the price for some cop's homicidal stupidity, I heard the booming voice of Big Boy Sunday.

"Leave that man alone," Big Boy said. "He ain't doing no harm. He's one of us."

They didn't de-escalate right away, but when Big Boy made his oversized way through the crowd, parting it like the Red Sea, to stand beside me, I was saved.

After they had cleared out, leaving only the other Black women to comfort Latrese's mother, I thanked Big Boy.

"Ain't nothing," he said. "I might need a favor from you sometime."

Right then, I'd have given Big Boy Sunday the contents of my bank account if he'd asked for it.

I remarked that it all happened so fast.

"Yeah," Big Boy said, "it happens that way sometimes. People get tired."

I asked him tired of what, although I pretty much knew.

He looked at me like I was the stupidest cop reporter he'd ever seen.

"Tired of people's shit."

Big Boy, whose drug-dealing minions have induced a few dirt naps themselves, obviously felt that if anyone was going to do any shooting in his neighborhood, it better not be some interlopers in uniform.

As I was leaving, he leaned into the open window on the driver's side, pretty much filling up the space.

"Sometimes," the big man said, "people get tired of asking politely. Sometimes they get tired of knocking at that same old door. Sometimes, they just kick the motherfucker in."

WHATEVER THE flash point was, it definitely set off a shitstorm the likes of which Richmond has not seen in my adult lifetime.

As we compared notes via cell phone, I learned that somebody set fire to the Daughters of the Confederacy headquarters over next to the Virginia Museum.

Someone apparently had an epiphany, realizing perhaps for the first time that there was a Daughters of the Confederacy and that this was their headquarters. Where the hell else would it be? This is, after all, the former capital of Dixie.

But it surprised me. Wasn't this supposed to be about a Black man in Minnesota who was murdered by a white cop? How did ghosts of the Late Unpleasantness get pulled into this?

I managed to file what I saw and what I could learn, although not for our actual ink-and-paper product. That was locking up about the time Callie Ann called us. But there was plenty to impart to the insomniacs who get their news online at three A.M.

The four of us posted what we could. Sally and Sarah gave our epics a cursory glance before sending them into the ether. Hell, with most of our online stuff, we're lucky if any editor sees it before it goes public.

I called to see if Sarah needed anything else.

"Nah," she said. "That's good enough for the website." Although Sarah's young enough to have been a mentee of mine before she became my boss, she still sees the actual newspaper, the one that slaps down in your driveway in the morning, as something more serious than what we send to dot-com land, bless her heart.

"You sound like you need a nap," I observed. "Maybe a little jet lag? Or maybe you're just not used to being in an upright position for so long."

Sarah and her newly minted husband, Jack, just got back from their honeymoon in Hawaii five days ago.

She told me to mind my own business and be prepared for another long day today.

I told her I was thinking about calling in sick.

I heard her laugh.

"You wouldn't miss this shit for the world," she said. "You're a junkie. If you're not here, champing at the bit, by noon, I'll kiss your ass."

I observed that that was quite an inducement to stay home.

"You know what I mean."

"Well," I said, "I know I won't be alone. Takes a junkie to know one."

Cindy sometimes wonders why I keep opting for the banana cream pie management throws in my face every chance it gets.

"You mean they expect you to be there, what, nine hours from now? And are you getting overtime for this?"

She knows the answer to that one.

"It's all I know how to do," I explain, not for the first time.

"Bullshit. You could get one of those government jobs where you come in at eight and punch out at five. You said even that guy Baer, the one you couldn't stand, got one of those."

Yeah, Mark Baer, who left us involuntarily when he was caught pimping for a congressional candidate who never got seated, finally landed on his feet after being off them for about nine months. He's flacking for one of the state's many little governmental fiefdoms now, no doubt drawing a bigger salary than I am.

"I wouldn't last a week," I assure her.

"Well, this shit has got to stop. You're sixty years old, and the way you treat your body, it's probably more like eighty."

Cindy's a little testy lately. While I'm perhaps working too many hours, and definitely too many unpaid ones, she's going stir-crazy.

Old Mr. COVID-19 sent all the kiddies and their teachers on early vacation back in March. Cindy still gets a salary, which I find ironic. She gets paid not to work. I work and don't get paid, at least not after my forty hours run out. But Cindy's a woman of action. Our apartment has never been cleaner, and the home-cooked meals have been a bonus, but she needs to be, as she says, "doing something other than being a maid and chef."

She's looking into tutoring, and she's making grocery runs for some of our more aged residents of the Prestwould, where we rent our unit from my third ex-wife. Plus there are the online yoga classes.

"All I'm saying is, this crap is going to catch up with you. And I don't want to be drawing your pension any sooner than necessary."

I tell her not to think too much about the pension. With the Grimm Group as captain of our own personal Titanic, the pensions probably will go the way of raises, overtime pay, and Christmas bonuses.

"You're starting to depress me," Cindy says. "Let's get you to bed."

"I'll drink to that," I concur as I head for the liquor cabinet.

CHAPTER TWO

Far before it should have, the phone rings. I resist the urge to throw it against the wall.

"Willie," Sarah says, "they've found some bodies."

"Can this wait?"

"I don't think so. There's a press conference at eleven."

That would be in a little over an hour. I ask Sarah if she can be a little more specific about the corpses who are important enough to justify waking me up.

"It's a family, a man and woman, and there was a kid there. They had one of those walk-ups on Broad Street. And it apparently happened last night, when all hell was breaking loose."

OK. She has my attention now.

"I don't know much else," Sarah says. "I just heard about it fifteen minutes ago. I can send someone else if you'd like."

A sane person would like that. A sane person would like to roll over and go back to sleep.

"I'll be there."

Cindy has been listening, half-awake.

"You are an idiot," she says and rolls back over.

No time to shower and shave. I find a clean pair of pants and a shirt that passes the smell test. The fancy coffee machine makes me a cup, which I then pour into a go-cup, and I'm on my way.

On the elevator down to the lobby, I briefly wonder how the hell Sarah Goodnight has better sources than I do. I'm accustomed to being the one telling my editors about news, not vice versa.

Several Prestwouldians are on the front steps facing Monroe Park, surveying the aftermath of last night's excitement.

Actually the park looks fairly normal. Hard to believe we had a riot out here last night.

Many of my neighbors are elderly. Some of them might have participated in anti-Vietnam War rallies back in the 1960s, but their rebellious youth is a fast-fading image in the rearview mirror, and from what I hear from them, they don't like change so much anymore, at least not the kind that keeps them up half the night.

Feldman, aka McGrumpy, is holding court, wondering why we don't have a full-time guard stationed at the desk all night to protect us from "those people." He has no doubt conveniently forgotten that he led the charge two years ago to stop paying a rent-a-cop to sleep here seven nights a week, to shave a few dollars off the ruinous condo fee.

Clara Westbrook is leaning against her walker. Wearing the damn COVID-19 mask isn't helping her breathing any, I'm sure. Now that she's outside the front door, she's slipped it down around her neck. Clara's well past eighty now, and she's lost a step or two but has hung on to her sense of humor.

"Lord, Willie," she says, "this was the most entertainment I've had in a long time. Do you think they'll be back tonight?"

I tell her that her guess is as good as mine.

"My daughter, out in Bon Air, called and said they were going to come and get me. She's the one that has the assisted-care places on speed-dial. I told her to mind her own business."

She smiles.

"It's good to see young people get excited about something for a change."

THE PRESS conference is at City Hall. The mayor and the chief are front and center. I see Pechera Love standing a few steps behind L.D. Jones. Usually Peachy, who once was an honest journalist, gives me a heads-up on impromptu press conferences. Maybe she figured alerting my boss was good enough. Or maybe she just didn't want to wake me.

L.D. enlightens me, along with a trio of bleary-eyed TV types and the guy from the African American paper that's somehow still in business:

An hour after I left the scene this morning, a couple of policemen went inside one of the buildings that apparently had not been looted. They went in because the front door was cracked open. On the ground floor was a secondhand bookstore, Remainders of the Day. I've been in there a couple of times, browsing. The owner even explained to me what a remainder was. From the price I saw on a couple of hardcovers, the guy was practically giving shit away. Evidently books are about as indispensable in the twenty-first century as newspapers.

They poked around inside and didn't see anything unusual. They were about to leave when one of them noticed that there was a light coming from a door in the back of the shop. They could hear a TV in the distance.

So they walked back and saw that the door led to stairs. They walked up, not knowing what to expect. At the top, they realized they were in a hallway outside an apartment.

Another door opened to the apartment itself. That's where the light and the TV noise were coming from.

They went inside, guns drawn no doubt, and that's when they found them.

The man and woman were both bound and gagged, tied to two chairs in the living room. They both had been shot once in the chest, once in the head. There was no sign of a struggle.

"They were just sitting there, like they were watching TV or something," L.D. says. "There were beer bottles and chips on the table." It was more information than the chief usually gives. I could see that, even with all the hell breaking loose around Broad Street, this got to him.

They searched the house and didn't find anything or anyone else, except the baby, who was in the bedroom not ten feet away from where her parents were killed. The cops said she didn't cry until they opened the door and found her.

L.D. says they estimated she was less than a year old.

They can't release the names of the victims, since they don't at present know them and then will have to notify the next of kin.

I ask if there is any chance that the man might have been the proprietor of the bookstore. He says he can't tell me.

The mayor jumps up to the mic then and makes all the usual noises about how he understands the pain people are feeling about the guy in Minneapolis and all, but that nobody is allowed to destroy our fair city. He promises that order will be restored.

I don't know. That crowd last night didn't look like a one-night stand to me. The weird thing: Here in Richmond, we like to think of ourselves as the new, improved South, where ebony and ivory mix into a smooth, peaceful blend. But usually you go into a restaurant or a bar, and it's mostly one or the other.

Last night, though, there was a true coming together. About half the folks I saw screaming through their masks were Black and the other half were white.

Black or white, the ones I saw looked like they were pissed off. I'm not sure the mayor understands the level of their anger just yet.

I catch L.D. as things are breaking up.

"Do you think I could see a picture of the victims?" I ask him.

"Why?"

"I think I might know the guy."

The chief sighs.

"You probably do," he says. "You know every damn body else."

I ask him if I can accompany him back to police headquarters.

"Let's walk," he says.

It's about eleven blocks from city hall to L.D.'s domain. It's a nice day for a stroll, carnage notwithstanding. My only regret: I can't smoke a Camel through this damn corona mask.

We are serenaded by chain saws. Proprietors are putting up plywood in front of their windows, many of which already have been shattered. Some of them are writing or painting "Black Lives Matter" on the plywood. A cynic would wonder how much of it is heartfelt sentiment and how much is self-preservation, blood-of-the-lamb stuff.

"Can you believe this shit?" L.D. asks rhetorically.

Up ahead, there are the charred remains of the Pulse bus that was torched last night. A few cars were sacrificed as well.

The chief tells me that the headquarters of the Daughters of the Confederacy building is still standing, although it's going to need some major, um, reconstruction.

A white shop owner comes out to greet the chief as we walk by, although "greet" is probably not the right word.

"Where the fuck were the police?" he asks after he pulls down his mask. Behind him, a couple of friends are helping him salvage what is left of what was, until last night, a semi-upscale clothing store. "They just took shit and ran with it. Nobody stopped them."

L.D. tells the guy that the cops couldn't be everywhere. Hell, a bunch of them were back at headquarters, trying to save their own building.

The man stops yelling long enough for the chief to tell him that the cops will do everything in their power to keep the peace tonight.

This doesn't cut much slack.

"Little late for that now," the guy says. "I guess that the old rules are out the window when 'Black Lives Matter.' "

I can tell this really eats L.D. up. As an African American police chief in a city where half the population and nowhere near half the money is Black, he's used to getting it from both sides. If he weren't such a hard-headed media basher, I'd feel sorry for him. He's both The Man and the guy his white critics say is soft on African American crime.

"I guess you bastards are going to have a field day with this," he says to me.

If we had later deadlines, I tell him, it'd be even worse.

"Do you think you could get the protesters to start tearing stuff up a little earlier?" I ask, although neither one of us thinks that's very funny right now.

I ask L.D., off the record, if he thinks the Richmond police might have been a teensy bit overzealous on occasion in the past. I mean, can all this be about one dead Black guy half a country away?

He looks like he's ready to hit me. Then he takes a deep breath.

"You've been there," he says at last. "You've seen some of the shit we have to put up with. Hell, we've got some Rambos out there, and we rein 'em in the best we can. But do you know how hard it is to find a good prospect and turn him into a good cop?

"Damn, as soon as we get one up and running, the goddamn counties hire him away. They'll pay them more for a hell of a lot less aggravation."

I let it slide. I could bring up a ghost from my past, one of L.D.'s lieutenants who broke all the rules and damn near killed me in the process a decade ago, but it doesn't seem like a good time to mention David Junior Shiflett.

Police headquarters looks like a war zone. Lots of plywood going up there, too, and they're putting up barriers around the front.

"Must have been rough last night," I observe.

"It was crazy. Hell, you saw it, right? Those kids must have been on something. They kept throwing bricks and water bottles. If we'd have let them, they would have taken the building. Even tear-gassing them didn't slow some of them down."

We get to L.D.'s office. He reaches into a file and comes out with photos from the killing. The chief doesn't often let me have this kind of access, and whatever I see is off the record for now. He's letting me have a peek because he thinks I can identify the victim.

The guy's lifeless eyes stare up at me. His head's a mess.

"Yeah," I say after a couple of seconds. "That's him."

"Him who?"

"The guy who owned the bookstore. I only knew his first name. William. Wife's name was Susan, I believe. I think somebody else owns the building."

"Did you ever see his wife or girlfriend?"

I did once or twice, but I can't be certain that's her, but since the two of them were up there together late on a Friday night, you'd have to assume that the woman was Mrs. Bookstore Proprietor.

He says he will find out the man's name, find out if the woman is his wife or girlfriend or what.

"And the kid?"

"She's with protective services. God, what that poor kid must have seen."

I'm about to leave when the chief gives me one more tidbit of information.

"None of this is for print until we ID and notify," he warns me, "but there was something else about the kid."

"What?"

"Well, you saw the parents. Pretty pale, wouldn't you say?"

"Yeah, pale as an Oregon Hill corpse."

"Well, the baby, she wasn't."

"Wasn't . . . white?"

"Darker than you," the chief says.

With a long-gone light-skinned African American father, I often pass for maybe Greek or Italian, but I'm dark enough.

I ask L.D. what chance the cops have of figuring out who took the trouble, in the middle of a riot, to go inside a bookstore and murder two people.

"Hell, we don't know if it was somebody from outside. Might have been domestic."

"So, what? The guy ties up his wife, shoots her two times, then ties himself up and shoots himself twice?"

I don't have to tell the chief how dumb that sounds, but L.D. doesn't like to say anything's true until he has it nailed tighter than those storefront windows down the street.

The chief says that some of the shops on that block have cameras, and the cops are checking to see if (a) any of them were working, and (b) they caught anybody coming out of the bookstore.

If this gets on the eleven o'clock TV news or anywhere else before I get the names of the deceased for print, I promise L.D. that he will be on my shit list forever.

The chief usually isn't amenable to threats from nosy-ass reporters. All this upheaval, though, seems to have shaken him.

"Don't threaten me, you asshole," he says, but without the usual piss and vinegar. "I've got bigger fish to fry than you today. You'll hear from me when you hear from me."

The chief looks tired.

I wish him luck and make my way down to the paper, taking the mask off long enough for a little nicotine fix.

I DON'T make it in until a quarter past noon. Sarah declines to pay up on her bet.

"What'd you find out?"

I tell her what I know, and what I can't print.

"Hopefully, they'll get back to me by deadline. What is deadline now, sunset?"

Sarah doesn't think it's all that funny. None of us do. We lock the paper up at ten most nights. With half the circulation of our salad days and all that technology that was going to make our lives better, we go to press three hours earlier than we did when I started working here, back in the Stone Age.

I hear a commotion coming from the vicinity of what's left of our copy desk. Enos Jackson, one of the few dinosaurs here who predate me, is throwing a shit fit about something.

I hear Sarah sigh behind me.

"Blacks."

I opine that I didn't know Enos was a racist. My impression was that he disliked humanity in general.

Sarah explains.

The Associated Press has made a change. And like most white Richmonders, Enos hates change. The AP Stylebook, the newsroom's Ten Commandments, has decreed that Blacks, as in African Americans, will henceforth be capitalized. And that racial groups in our fair country will be freed from hyphens. Yesterday, I was at least marginally black and African-American. Today, I am Black and African American.

"I feel much better," I tell Sarah.

I stroll over for the show.

"How's it going to look," Enos asks anyone who'll listen, "when we write that lowercase whites and uppercase Blacks went on a rampage last night and damn near burned down the police station? It just looks weird."

James Pettis, our only Black copy editor, has been sitting quietly, ten feet away.

"Well," he says when Enos stops to take a breath, "you know what Sam Cooke said."

"No," Enos replies. "What the fuck did Sam Cooke say?"

"He said it's been a long time comin'."

A couple of other staffers start clapping. Enos snorts and goes back to mumbling under his breath.

From the size of the crowd that's reportedly gathered in Monroe Park, it seems obvious to everyone that tonight will be eventful. Last evening, from all we can gather, was the kind of spontaneous outburst that happens sometimes when the social justice pipe springs a leak.

This time, the people who got everyone's attention last night know they have the floor, and they're not going to take a seat willingly.

Shortly after seven, L.D. has Peachy Love give me a call with the information and confirmation I need. The chief offers aid and comfort to the news media about every total lunar eclipse, but he did owe me one.

In the meantime, I've already gotten the name of the bookstore proprietor. William Keller. I knew he had a wife, Susan, who I assumed was the other unfortunate soul the cops found. Peachy confirms that and gives me a few more facts for tomorrow's story. The Kellers had lived in Richmond for more than five years and opened Remainders of the Day four years ago. They moved here from Durham, North Carolina. And they adopted an African American baby seven months ago. Her name, Peachy says, is Aurora.

"But nothing about how it happened?"

Peachy says it appears they were killed by an intruder. A couple of the stores nearby did have cameras that survived the festivities last night, but the police haven't found anything useful yet.

"Well, call me if anything else comes up."

Peachy assures me that this is probably the last gratis info the chief is going to send my way. That's what I expected. Peachy is my main source when L.D. goes into lockdown mode, which is almost all the time. It's strange for her to be giving me information over the table for a change.

I know much of what Peachy told me already, since I was pretty sure who the victims were. I have already found a photo of the couple that went with a story the business desk did when the bookstore opened. William and Susan Keller, who died at thirty-three and thirty-one, respectively, look even younger than they would have been in 2016.

Susan was quoted as saying that they "loved Richmond and looked forward to being part of the thriving community downtown."

I bang out a few hundred words and then start to head over to Broad Street.

Before pandemonium sets in, I check the websites of our network TV stations. Three don't have shit, but the fourth one has it all. They even have pictures of William and Susan.

Dammit.

It appears that somebody in videoland got out and worked a little on a Saturday. Either that or somebody in our local constabulary gave them what they needed. Or they just lifted it from our website, where it was posted half an hour ago.

There are a hell of a lot more questions than answers right now. On top of a pandemic and Black Lives Matter, we now have a double murder. A tragedy wrapped inside chaos enclosed in a plague.

The next time I'm bored, I wish somebody would kick my ass and remind me to be thankful for the quiet times.

Mal Wheelwright, our chief editor and Sarah's immediate boss, comes out of his office as I'm leaving to report on the latest excitement.

"Be careful out there," he advises. He's already had to pull Chuck Apple in to cover whatever other crime might be happening in the city tonight so I can cover the mayhem.

I ask him if the paper offers hazardous-duty pay.

He tells me to be careful, again.

CHAPTER THREE

Sunday, May 31

Since the pandemic has made indoor dining impossible, the brunch bunch has traded the back table at Joe's for an alfresco experience. We've opted for folding chairs in Peggy's Oregon Hill backyard.

We all have our thermoses of coffee and Bloody Marys. We brought our own breakfasts. R.P. McGonnigal and Andy Peroni each let McDonald's do the cooking. Cindy, bless her, made ham biscuits for us and Custalow. The McMuffin crowd looks covetous.

Peggy and Awesome Dude have joined us, which seems fair, since it's their yard. Their breakfast appears to be a box of Krispy Kremes. Awesome offers everyone a toke, which R.P. and Andy accept while the rest of us stick to vodka and coffee.

One advantage this place has over Joe's is that we are definitely not in a no-smoking zone, whatever you're smoking.

"Did you hear that come July 1 they won't give you nothin' but a twenty-five-dollar fine for possession?" my old mom asks. "Hell, you get more than that for parking in a no-parking zone."

I agree that there is at least some good news today.

There wasn't much last night, if you were a fan of peace and quiet.

WHAT STARTED as a loud but orderly demonstration went to hell in a hurry after sunset.

A couple of fires in the general vicinity of the university, everything from frozen-yogurt shops to running-gear stores looted, and a general feeling that the old rules didn't apply led to Richmond's finest arresting more than two hundred citizens. Some of them were damn near as old as me, and it looked to be about even between Black and white.

Everybody's pissed at the cops, and the pepper spray and tear gas didn't help. Some of it was administered, best I could tell, as a preemptive strike.

I interviewed a middle-aged Black woman whose unambiguous sign read, "Fuck the Police." She said she was tired of it all.

"When they killed that man on TV," she said, "that was the last straw. I ain't puttin' up with no more shit."

It is hard for me to understand how so many people came to the same conclusion at the same time. For the sake of law and order, it doesn't happen that often. Maybe it was the way the Minnesota cop looked right into the camera, like, "Yeah, I'm killin' him. Whatcha gonna do about it?" I don't know. Like anybody in this part of the world with an ounce or two of African American blood, I've had to bite my tongue 'til it bled a few times. If anybody could predict when the lid was going to blow off, I guess they'd be a little more sensitive about murdering people and other such rude behavior.

A white guy who probably was somewhere between twenty and thirty years old took umbrage at my notebook and called me a pig and a lackey of the state. When I asked him where he was from, he told me to fuck off. Everyone was cranky.

I'd never gotten a whiff of tear gas before, and I can't say that it was a pleasant experience. Somebody gave me some water to douse my eyes.

An older white woman wearing a "Black Lives Matter" T-shirt said she was just trying to show support.

"I've never been to one of these before," she said as we moved back from the fumes. "It's kind of exciting."

L.D. and the mayor seemed, yesterday morning, to want us to think this was the work of outside agitators. That's always a good way to call for tough action without blaming your own community.

However, everyone I talked to last night was from Richmond or the suburbs. I wondered how much crazier things would have gotten if they hadn't sent the VCU students home to their mommies and daddies when the pandemic hit back in March.

I saw Gillespie standing amid a clump of cops in front of police headquarters. He and his buddies seemed a little dazed, although it was hard to tell, with all that body armor.

With everyone wearing masks, and the crowd throwing rocks and bottles and the tear-gas canisters that had been shot at them, the whole scene did look like newsreels from one of those places where they have juntas and shit like that.

It sure as hell didn't seem like Richmond.

I sent in a story and a sidebar, interviewing a woman who said her son was killed in a police shootout fifteen years ago. Couple that with the story on the two apparent murders, and I earned my salary yesterday. I think it came out to about thirteen cents a word.

"Didn't anybody do anything to the cop that did it," the woman said. I wished I'd had time and resources to do more than ascertain that her son did indeed die from police gunfire, but sometimes you just have to go with what you've got.

It was well after one when I got home. Cindy was awake.

"It was pretty wild down in the park," she said.

Tell me about it, I said.

We shoot the bull in the backyard for a couple of hours, with my longtime buddies pumping me for information about last night's excitement. But it's getting hot outside. As I'm packing up the tailgating chairs, I get a call.

I don't recognize the number, but it's local.

"Willie," she says, "it's Jeanette."

My first wife doesn't call me very often. She's moved on and, I hope, forgiven me for the grief I caused her before and after I let Little Willie lead me astray, leaving her to raise Andi by herself.

I step as far away from the group as I can in a small Oregon Hill backyard.

"It's Adam," she says.

Adam would be Jeanette and Glenn Walker's youngest. I do the math and figure he's nineteen now. I remember that Andi, his half-sister, said he's a freshman at VCU.

I ask her to explain.

"You haven't seen the news?"

I explain that all I've had time to do is catch a few hours' sleep and go to brunch.

"They put it on Channel 6's website. One of our neighbors called me."

What I finally learn is that the cops did find something they could tie to the double killing. One of the cameras caught a young man coming out of the bookstore. The time was 3:32 A.M. Saturday. They also caught him entering the store at 3:20 A.M.

"It was him," Jeanette says. "He looked right at the camera. I even recognized the shirt I bought him for Christmas."

I ask her if the police have figured out his identity yet.

"I don't know, Willie. I'm just calling you because I thought, you know, you might be able to help. I know you're right in the middle of all that stuff."

"Let me check it out. I'll call you back."

Cindy walks over and asks me what's wrong.

"Wife trouble," I say, then explain that the wife who's having trouble is three wives ago.

"What's going on with Jeanette?" she asks. Cindy, although she can exhibit a smidgen of jealousy on occasion, knows both my first and third ex-wives, and they don't seem to have any animosity toward each another.

"What did you all talk about?" I asked Cindy after she had come back from having a get-acquainted coffee with Jeanette.

"You," she explained.

I check my emails and find one from Peachy, telling me that the police have released a photo of a suspect in the killings. She sent it an hour ago.

An email from Andi came thirty minutes ago, pretty much telling me what Jeanette just imparted.

I go to the TV station's website and take a peek.

Yeah, that's Adam.

He looks like a deer in the headlights, but then Adam always looks like that. They say he's "on the spectrum," which means he's functional, but his brain seems to be missing the part that helps you tell the difference between appropriate and shut the fuck up.

Last Christmas, according to Andi, he asked Jeanette's mother, who is Stage 4 and doesn't have much time left, if she was going to die soon. He didn't mean it in a bad way, Andi said, and everybody knew it was just Adam being Adam, but he can try your patience. At least he tries mine. I've only met him I think three times. The first time, and he was probably twelve or thirteen, he asked me if I was the one that abandoned his mother. Again no ill will. He's just missing that filter that stops most of us from speaking the unspeakable.

He apparently has good grades. At least they were good enough to get him into VCU.

Jeanette says that he's been living at home, in eastern Henrico, since the semester was suspended, and that he'd gone back into town on Friday to take part in the demonstration.

She hasn't seen him since he left that afternoon.

So now I have a bit of a problem. Do I tell L.D. Jones and his lads that I'm pretty sure who the suspect is, that he's the son of my first wife? Do I write about it first? Or do I forgo my roles as responsible citizen and reporter and let the police figure this one out on their own? When somebody else fingers him, both L.D. and my editors are going to want to know why the hell I didn't tell them it was Adam.

This sounds like a lose-lose-lose to me.

"You've got to do something," Cindy says.

Maybe, I say, but let me think about it first.

When I say "think," I mean if I stall a little bit, maybe the situation will take care of itself.

THERE'S NO rest in the middle of a clusterfuck. If I don't go in on my day off and write about what happens tonight,

Callie Ann Boatwright, Leighton Byrd, or some other whippersnapper will be glad to take over.

So I go into the office a little after two. Sarah is there already. I ask if she slept at her desk last night.

"Do I look like I slept at my desk?" she asks.

Nope, I answer wisely. You look fresh as a daisy. Never better.

"Did you see the pictures on the Channel 6 website?" she asks me. "We've already put them on ours too."

Nope, I reply. Too busy enjoying my Oregon Hill brunch.

"Yeah," she says, "you've got tomato juice on your shirt."

"Weird-looking dude," she says. "I don't know how serious a suspect he is, but he's the only one they saw going out of there."

I'm headed for my desk to check in with either the chief or Peachy when she says, "Wait. Here's something. They've apparently ID'd the guy."

"Already?" I say.

"Yeah. His name's Adam Walker. He's at student at VCU."

I feign surprise and ask to see the picture.

"Holy shit. That's Jeanette's son."

"Your first wife?"

"Yeah. Damn. I better call her."

Sarah looks at me with something like suspicion in her eyes.

"I'm surprised she hasn't called you already."

"We're not that close, as you might imagine."

"Still I'm surprised."

I let it pass and head back to my desk. I actually pretend to have a conversation with Jeanette and then call the chief's private cell number.

He's in his office. If my days are long, L.D.'s are longer. Both sides of the aisle are screaming for his head. The cops are either doing too much or not enough.

"Something you need to know about Adam Walker," I tell him.

"What?"

"He's family, once-removed."

I explain Adam's tenuous relationship to me, careful to add that I didn't see the photo until a few minutes ago, or I would have alerted him at once.

I hear him snort.

"Yeah. I'm sure you would've. Have you talked with his mother or anyone else?"

I lie that I've just called Jeanette, who doesn't have any idea where he is.

"Do you know where he is?"

I swear that I don't and tell the chief I've only seen the boy maybe three times ever. I tell him that he might be maybe a little semi-autistic.

"Well, we've sent somebody out there. If you're involved with hiding the suspect, you know your ass is mine."

I assure L.D. that I'd never do anything to put sand in the gears of justice and endanger our loving relationship.

While I have him on the phone, I ask about the two hundred or so protesters who were arrested last night. He says they've all been charged and released.

"What kind of penalties are they looking at?"

He sighs.

"Off the record? We'll probably drop everything eventually, except for the three who actually did assault police officers."

I wonder out loud how much you can assault a man wearing more protective gear than an NFL linebacker if you've only got rocks and water bottles for weapons.

"It's the principle of the thing," L.D. says.

"Do you think any of your folks might have gotten a little overzealous and maybe thrown the first stone, so to speak?"

"You mean the pepper spray and tear gas? We're looking at the video. For the record, the police used only appropriate force to protect the peace."

I wish him good luck tonight. Maybe, I suggest, Sunday will be a day of rest. The mayor has upped the ante by issuing an eight P.M.-to-dawn curfew and the governor has called in the National Guard.

"Not counting on it."

I MAKE another quick call to Jeanette to tell her what she probably already knows. The cops have ID'd Adam and will be knocking on their door soon.

There isn't much to do other than to tell her I will find out what I can.

I call Andi, who says she has a campus address for Adam, but since no one's been on campus for more than two months, that doesn't help much. She gives me the name of a friend of his who has an apartment, but when I track down the friend, he says he hasn't seen him lately.

"Dude," he says, "Adam wouldn't hurt a fly."

I take a short nap in Wheelie's office and go out about seven P.M. to see what the new night brings.

Up until then, things had been peaceful. The only change, and it seems to be a rather meaningful one, is that the protest pivoted. Somebody or bodies figured that, if Black lives really do matter, it might be time to start addressing the overabundance of Confederate statuary in our fair city.

Protesters gathered at the statues to Robert E. Lee and J.E.B. Stuart, demanding what would have been unthinkable a few days ago: Monument Avenue without monuments. Our city is not without its share of committed graffiti artists, and this could be the best opportunity they've ever had to let their creativity flow. By the time I get there, the Lee statue is covered to fifteen feet up in colorful scribbling, much of it obscene or unintelligible. The police don't seem interested in doing anything much except keeping the peace.

Now as eight o'clock approaches, the crowd around Marse Robert's monument doesn't show any sign of going home.

I have a tough time convincing the cops that I'm allowed out after eight, being a reporter. Gillespie sees what's happening and tells the hardhead who's hassling me that it's OK, that I'm "harmless."

Then just minutes before the witching hour, one of the guys in uniform can't wait any longer. It seems clear to me that many in the assembled mob are already headed to their bikes and cars when the tear gas hits. If the intent is to scare the protesters, it fails spectacularly.

Suddenly we're in riot city again. People come rushing back toward the statue. This time the tear gas doesn't sting so much. Maybe I'm building up a resistance.

Then the crowd, through some signal unseen by me, suddenly starts marching eastward. They're like a flock of birds or a swarm of angry bees, all pulled in the same direction for no apparent reason. I follow along the best I can, occasionally interviewing a protester.

By nine, they're at the VCU Medical Center, for some reason, and they're met with more tear gas and pepper spray. Then some of them head back west, toward Monroe Park.

There isn't a hell of a lot of vandalism, maybe because the smarter business folks have cornered the market on plywood along with Magic Markers to assure the crowd that they believe Black Lives Matter.

One kid with the local public radio station gets tackled and pepper-sprayed, so I guess my evening could have been worse. At one point, I run into Leighton Byrd. She seems put out that no one has bothered to use tear gas on her yet.

Keep plugging, I encourage her. Everybody ought to get gassed at least once.

By the time the evening's over, I figure I've walked a good four miles, stopping occasionally to lean against a building and send some sterling text to Sarah.

"For God's sake," I implore, "make sure you read this crap before you post it."

She says she'll do the best she can, but she and one copy editor are handling sometimes incoherent snippets from four other reporters, plus the occasional citizen journalists who volunteer their pearls of wisdom.

Robert E. Lee looks kind of sad up there on Traveller. If statues could talk, I think this one would be urging somebody to put him and his horse out of their misery.

By the time I stumble back into the building, it's after one in the morning. As pissed off as the crowd was, it did run out of steam shortly after midnight, with promises to return.

I have time to make another call to Jeanette, who says the police have come and gone.

"They didn't believe us when we said we didn't know where Adam was," she says.

Well, I reply, you are his mother.

"Willie," she says, "I know that boy. He has never harmed a living soul. But I'm just afraid, you know, that when they get him . . . well, he doesn't make a good first impression."

Or second, or third.

I assure Jeanette that this will all work out, somehow. I tell her that I even know the name of a pretty good lawyer, if it comes to that.

CHAPTER FOUR

Monday, June 1

In late morning, Cindy rides with me out to Jeanette and Glen's place, east of town off Route 5.

"What the hell else am I going to do?" she asks.

I tell her how fortunate she is to be getting paid to stay home. In our newsroom, it doesn't work that way. The Grimm Group told everyone back in early May that they have to take a couple of weeks of furlough between now and the end of June.

"Do we get paid?" one of our younger staffers asked Benson Stine, our publisher. BS didn't laugh, but pretty much everybody else did.

I'll get around to taking my unpaid vacation when things calm down.

"Like they ever do," Cindy observed.

Hell, I'm not even getting paid today. Sundays and Mondays are my alleged off days. But I'm not letting this story get poached. Besides, this is family, sort of.

We pass shuttered restaurants. Many of them were just dipping their toes back into solvency when the protests hit. Now I see boarded-up storefronts all through the Bottom. We drive past Millie's and wonder if we've had our last crab enchiladas.

Cindy asks me what kind of kid Adam Walker is. I explain his general quirkiness, along with the fact that his mother and his friend say he's harmless.

"Well," Cindy says, "somebody sure as hell was pretty damn harmful."

Yeah, there is that. Whoever tied the couple to their chairs and then shot first one and then the other, with their little girl in the next room, was not a very nice person.

"Do they know which one was killed first?"

I look over at my beloved.

"What the hell difference does it make?"

"I just think it would be terrible, you know, to have to watch someone you loved murdered right in front of you, knowing you're next."

I opine that there isn't really any good way to be a victim in a double murder.

My phone, which is of course in my pocket, starts playing "I Heard It Through the Grapevine." I pull over in the parking lot down by the river at Rocketts Landing.

It's Peachy, with news.

"We got him."

Richmond's finest nabbed young Adam at nine o'clock this morning, she tells me. He was hiding out at another friend's place in the Fan. They caught him walking down to the local market.

"He didn't really resist," Peachy says, "but he damn near got his ass shot. The officer who stopped him said that, when he told the boy to put his hands up, he reached into his pocket. Fortunately the guy was one of our smarter cops. He told me that he's never had to shoot anybody in twenty years on the force."

They've taken Adam to the lockup. I tell Peachy that I am on my way to talk to the boy's mother, and I'll break the news to her.

"Why are you talking to his mother?"

I explain that Jeanette is my ex-wife.

"Ain't everybody," Peachy replies.

So I need to be headed two places at the same time. We need to put something on the web about Adam Walker's capture, and I really need to talk to Jeanette.

I call the paper. Sally Velez answers. I tell her that they've caught the suspect in the double murder, and that I will post something and come in when I can.

There are three cars in the Walker driveway when we get there. It's a nice Colonial in a neighborhood of nice Colonials. Glenn, Jeanette's husband, never went to college, but he's made a good living, she assures me, as an electrician. Jeanette, who used to teach, sells real estate. Glenn opens the front door and lets us lead ourselves inside.

Jeanette and Glenn Jr., aka Buddy, are sitting on the couch. Nobody's wearing a mask, so we leave ours off, too, and try to keep our distance. They're watching the noon news. There's Adam, looking like a lost puppy, being led into the jail.

Jeanette is crying.

"We've got to get down there and see him," she says. "We can do that, can't we, Willie?"

I tell her that they might have to wait a day or two on that.

"How in the world can this be?" she asks. She's wringing her hands, and I'm hit with a terrible flashback. She wrung her hands that way the day I told her I was leaving.

Cindy sits down beside her to comfort her.

Buddy seems kind of put out by the whole affair. I know him about as well as I know Adam. He's twenty-one now and is, Andi tells me, making some kind of living driving for Uber. I don't guess he needs to make much money, since he lives with his parents and is probably driving the car they bought for him when he graduated from high school.

Glenn asks us if we want anything. I could use a Miller, but I remember that Glenn and Jeanette don't drink.

"She said you knew a lawyer," Glenn says.

I tell him that I'm on pretty good terms with Marcus Green.

"That colored guy that's on all the TV ads? Can we afford him?"

Well, at least he didn't use the N-word. I think he feels a vague discomfort being with his wife's first husband, and maybe more discomfort because she married a man who wasn't lily-white.

"Yeah," I tell him, "although I think he prefers Black or African American."

"Whatever," Glenn says.

I promise him and Jeanette that I'll talk to Marcus today, and that Marcus doesn't always charge an arm and a leg, especially if he can get some good publicity out of it.

I ask them if they want to say anything that I can put in the paper.

"Hell no," Glenn says.

Jeanette puts her hand on his forearm.

"Just say we believe he is innocent," she says.

Back in the car, I light up.

"You're never going to get a damn cent for this car," Cindy says.

I point out that the resale value of Honda Accords with well over 200,000 miles on the odometer is pretty tiny to begin with.

"Well, you might have to pay them to take this one."

She won't let me smoke in her car, which is why we never take it on long trips.

"He was a strange-looking kid," she says.

"Who? Adam?"

"Well, the other one wasn't exactly Mr. Personality."

I apologize for not taking Cindy to lunch.

"Well, hell," she says. "We're in Phase One now. Can't we get something to go?"

The city has loosened the coronavirus gag enough to let restaurants take your order over the phone or online and then either deliver it or let you pick it up onsite from some kid wearing a moon suit. The recent unpleasantness, though, has been a disincentive for most places to stay open even at this level.

The best we can do is the McDonald's on East Broad. She drops me off at the paper and takes the car home.

"Maybe I'll get it vacuumed," she says, wrinkling her nose as she moves into the driver's seat.

Nobody seems to be taking the day off in the newsroom. I even see a couple of furloughed wretches working away.

"What the hell else am I going to do?" Jack Clatterbuck asks. "Cover a Flying Squirrels game? Maybe go up to DC and do a feature on the Nationals? Oh, right. They're not playing. Nobody's playing."

The sports guys have been reduced to writing "remember when?" pieces. They've just about exhausted all the great moments in Richmond sports history already, so Sarah and Wheelie have drafted them to cover "real" news.

I make a call to Peachy and get a statement about the arrest of Adam Walker. They're just calling him a "person of interest," but there aren't any other people of interest in lockup, so our readers are drawing their own conclusions, as they often do.

The news I called in en route to Jeanette's home already has eight comments online. I should never read the comments. They reduce my IQ a good ten points and make me want to call in an air strike on the metropolitan area.

Six of the eight smell conspiracy.

"White dude murders two other whities b/c they got a Black baby," one of them opines, and five others start riffing on the same theme.

"Are you shittin' me?" replies another deep thinker. "How many folks breaking into buildings were white? What are the odds?"

The eighth guy says the couple got what they deserved, for going "outside their race."

I make myself look away, much as I would avert my eyes from the aftereffects of a head-on collision. I know that every one of those flamethrowers will draw another ten replies, who'll draw another ten, and so on.

After writing what I know and posting it, I make a call to the august law offices of Green and Ellis.

Marcus is the lawyer every city of any size has at least one of, the one with all the TV ads full of piss and vinegar, promising to free the innocent, and sometimes even the guilty. Kate Ellis is my third ex-wife and our landlady.

The secretary switches me to Marcus.

I tell him what I'm calling about.

"That kid is Jeanette's son?" he exclaims. That he remembers her reminds me of just how long I've known him. "Damn, Willie. What the hell happened?"

"I don't know much more than you do, but I know he needs a good lawyer."

"He needs to be in a jail about two counties away," Marcus says. "The brothers are already trying to make this sound like it's a racial thing. He won't be safe in jail."

"Do you think you can help him? Not much money in it, I'm sure."

"Aw, Willie," Marcus says, "you know my only concern is seeing justice done."

He takes offense when I break out laughing. He does agree, though, to meet with Adam, and to set the wheels in motion to get him moved to a lockup where he's less well-known.

In the meantime, I need to talk to L.D. Jones.

THE CHIEF is not in the best of moods. He is at the mouth of a crap funnel. He is worried about his job, the one he's had now for more than a decade. The current mayor can be something of a political weather vane. And the winds are blowing in the direction of change.

He doesn't want to see me, which is his default mode. I assure his aide that this won't take long, and I have pertinent information about his "person of interest."

That gets me in the door. L.D. has his elbows on his desk. A bottle of Tylenol sits near his right hand.

"What the fuck do you want?" he asks. "Don't I have enough trouble already? I'll be lucky if these bastards don't burn the building down."

I explain that I've just visited the suspect's parents.

"They're a little worried," I begin.

"Hell, they ought to be. He's the only son of a bitch that went in or came out of that door where those folks were killed."

"They think he's not safe in the city jail," I say, transferring Marcus's concerns to them. I add that I'm concerned, too, giving the chief the short version of what our readers have been posting online.

"They think it's racial?" L.D. asks.

I nod.

He shrugs.

"Hell, could be. We don't even know for sure if he did the deed, let alone a motive."

"But if he gets beat up, or worse, in your jail, that's going to be a big headache for you."

"Like I need another one."

Something the chief just said rings a bell.

"You said he was the only one. Was Adam Walker the only one the camera caught leaving the building?"

He looks at me for a long minute, weighing whether to give me a scrap of useful information.

Then he nods his head.

"How about entering the building? Anybody else there?"

He shakes his head.

"Not after ten P.M. anyhow. You can see how we might be thinking that he had something to do with those two dead bodies."

OK, so maybe even Marcus Green can't fix this problem. If the boy did it, I don't even want it fixed.

That's when I tell L.D. who is likely to be taking the kid's case.

He slams his fist on his desk. One of his awards falls off the wall.

"That's fuckin' great. That's just about all I need now. That ambulance-chasing son of a bitch. I suppose you put him up to this."

"It's Jeanette's kid, L.D. What'd you expect me to do, just stand by and let it happen? And what if he didn't do it? Hell, what if he did and he gets his ass handed to him in the city jail?"

After he's calmed down a little, the chief says he'll consider moving Adam to one of the county lockups, but that he's in a solitary cell right now.

"About the only thing they can do is hurt his feelings," he says.

He claims he's got a meeting in five minutes. I ask him if he has anything further to say about the alleged improper use of tear gas and pepper spray.

"Yeah," he says. "I do."

And then L.D. does something he almost never does. He admits that he was wrong.

Earlier he backed up his lieutenant's claim that people in the crowd incited the cops by throwing anything loose at them, that they didn't fire until they were fired upon, so to speak.

"That wasn't quite right," he says now. "I'm going to have Peachy send out a press release, but I'll tell you now. A couple of our young knuckleheads got a little carried away. They will be disciplined."

The confession surprises me, but the facts don't. I've seen policemen attacked by angry crowds, often angry about something that had nothing to do with the cops themselves. Nobody likes to be called a pig or be spit on. Sometimes people lose their tempers.

Still it doesn't make L.D. look good, having to backtrack like that.

I thank him for his honesty.

He looks at me.

"What was the big news you said you had for me."

"Just thought you would want to know the kid might be in some danger. And that Marcus Green is his lawyer."

"Get the fuck out of here."

CINDY ASKS me if I shouldn't maybe take at least a night off.

"You look a little run-down," she says. "Following a mob across Richmond half the night is tough work for a two-pack-a-day man."

I inform her that I'm down to a pack a day, if that. Hell, I can't smoke in the apartment, I can't smoke at work, I can't smoke while I'm wearing a goddamn corona mask. The pisser of it is, I need a cigarette now more than ever.

If it weren't for the great outdoors and my Camel-scented car, I'd have to go cold turkey.

Cindy shakes her head.

“What a shame that’d be.”

I go back to the newsroom long enough to write my second story for the electronic version and tomorrow’s paper, one reporting the chief’s admission that his lads and lasses got a little bit carried away last night, and that the guilty parties will be properly punished.

Ground Zero at the moment seems to be the Lee Monument. The woke are now agitating for a clean sweep of Monument Avenue. No more Lee, Jackson, Stuart, Davis, or even old Matthew Maury, who always seemed like he was more of a navy man than a dedicated Confederate.

I go home for a quick dinner and then go over to the monument.

I get there about seven. A peaceful if graffiti-crazed crowd has been gathering there all day. I talk with a few of those in attendance. One older white lady who lives in one of those big-ass mansions on Monument Avenue itself mourns the general tackiness of the recent unrest, without expressing any great empathy with the Confederacy itself.

A Black grandmother from the East End says she’s been waiting all her life for this. I ask her why she thinks it’s all happening now. They put Lee and his horse up there 130 years ago as a nineteenth-century real estate gambit. You lost the war, white folks, but we’ll sell you a new house out here by Marse Robert, and you’ll feel better.

She frowns.

“It wadn’t possible before,” she says. “Now it is.”

Simple as that. I’m thinking that killer cop in Minneapolis opened a lot of doors. Racism, you might conclude, has turned out to be its own worst enemy.

Over near a couple of guys giving out free water bottles, to either drink or throw, I see a familiar face.

My cousin Richard Slade is standing there, sipping water, accompanied by his nephews, Jeroy and Jamal. Like most of the crowd, they're wearing their corona masks, which are making all of us a little cranky.

He looks older than his fifty-four years, but the mirror says I'm not looking so good for sixty either.

We shake hands. He says he wanted the boys to be here, to see "that things don't always have to turn out bad, that there's good here too."

He says Chanelle is at work. She's a nurse, "worried sick about getting that damn virus."

I speak to the boys, who seem to vaguely remember me. Richard orders them to shake hands. They are in their teens now and are as tall as Richard and a good bit heavier. They seem vaguely bored by it all. Jamal asks their uncle, not for the first time, who "the white dude up there is." He patiently explains.

Richard either was born with a forgiving spirit or grew one spending much of his life as a guest of the state, incarcerated for a crime he didn't commit.

I comment on his equanimity.

Richard Slade looks off into the setting sun. He shrugs.

"You can either let it eat you up or you can let it roll off your back."

He turns to me.

"Sometimes, though," he says, "it does get to be too much."

About twenty minutes before the eight o'clock curfew, shit happens again.

This time, it might have been one of the state police or National Guard guys. Whatever, I saw it with my own eyes this time, before I couldn't see anything much because of the tear gas.

Soon the air is heavy with it, and a crowd that seemed happy to hang out on a warm early June night and give Robert E. Lee and Traveller a paint job instantly turns into a mob.

Some of them are retreating from the gas, and some of them are charging into it, mad as hell. The corona masks seem to work in their favor, maybe making them a little less susceptible to the fumes.

It's a pitched battle for a while. I am amazed that it doesn't turn into Kent State. All of the cops and a few of the protesters are locked and loaded.

Things ebb and flow. Eventually the crowd backs down a little and the cops do the same, but the rest of the evening is a little tense.

This time, it doesn't take long for the authorities to understand that tear-gassing the citizenry is not cool. By nine o'clock, the mayor has released a statement on Twitter apologizing. Most of the crowd isn't reading tweets at the moment, though, and eventually many of its members go marching east, then west, winding up back at the Lee Monument after midnight.

This time I don't join them. After dousing my eyes with water a couple of times, I let Leighton Byrd and a photographer do the leg work. Leighton did get her first whiff of tear gas, which she no doubt will turn into a life-threatening experience for our breathless readers.

I hang around the monument, posting, and chatting with the ones who have remained, along with some of the cops, the ones who will talk to me.

"Man," one lieutenant I've known for more than a decade says, "this has turned into a shit show."

He says it like he doesn't understand what everybody's so mad about.

CHAPTER FIVE

Tuesday, June 2

After a three-byline day, I looked forward to sleeping in this morning.

"Willie," Cindy says, as she shakes me awake. "It's Marcus Green."

I'd left the cell phone in the living room in hopes of avoiding a moment like this. We've finally become the last people in America to ditch the landline after being annoyed by one too many robocalls. But Cindy, who apparently needs less sleep than I do, was in the kitchen making coffee when she heard Marvin Gaye's signature number.

"I thought you'd want to talk to him," she half-whispers.

She's right, but it takes me a few seconds to regain enough consciousness to concede that fact.

"Rise and shine," Marcus booms. "Want to go for a ride to the city lockup?"

He's meeting Adam Walker this morning, having agreed to be his attorney. I guess Marcus decided he could get enough free publicity to make this worth his while. I hope Jeanette and Glenn didn't have to take out a second mortgage to make it happen.

The bail hearing is set for this afternoon at two.

Marcus is supposed to be at the lockup at ten, which doesn't give me a hell of a lot of time to shower, shave, and get dressed.

It's a nice day, spring on the calendar but early summer in reality. I walk down to Marcus's office. He's waiting for me, noting that I am five minutes late.

"And you forgot your mask."

So shoot me. I figured I wouldn't infect anybody in the four-block walk between the Prestwould and the Franklin Street office of Green and Ellis. He loans me one of his.

I hear a baby crying and go exploring. Marcus says we're going to be late, but he'll have to wait.

Kate is inside her office, bent over a crib that's been installed by her desk, trying to placate little Marcus Junior.

The kid is almost four months old now, born back in February. Like me, he will have to deal with some ambiguity when he's old enough to fill in the "race" box. Unlike my younger self, he lives in an at-least marginally more accepting world. By the time he's grown, this country won't be majority anything.

I offer young Marcus a finger, which he grabs and tries to put in his mouth.

"Maybe he's hungry," I opine to my third ex-spouse.

"He'd better not be," she replies. "He's just about drained me dry."

"Is he big for his age?" I ask.

"Yeah," Marcus says from behind me. "Just like his daddy. Now come on. We're supposed to be there in twenty minutes."

I disengage my finger and give the kid one last look. We do share something of a relationship, Marcus Junior and I. It isn't every guy who gets to be godfather to his ex-wife's child. When Bootie Carmichael, our boozy sports columnist, heard that, he offered the unsolicited opinion that I need to divorce a woman in order to get along with her.

This did not sit well with me, perhaps because the truth hurts. When I told Cindy what Bootie said, she said that my getting along too well with any of my former wives might be hazardous to my health. I reminded her that she is friendly with both Jeanette and Kate.

"I'm good with that," she said. "You're the one that better remember what 'ex' means."

We cross into the Bottom and take Eighteenth Street up to Fairfield Way. The city jail is strategically placed so that African American mothers in the projects don't have to go so far to visit their incarcerated sons. How thoughtful. Separated from much of the city by Interstate 95, it feels like another world.

It reminds me a little of the Oregon Hill of my youth. The state prison was just across US 1 from the Hill back then, and the joke was that the mommas hanging their wash could wave at their boys down in the pen.

We are led back to Adam. As promised, he is isolated from the general population.

The boy looks even more emaciated and unhinged than I remember. He could pass for fifteen instead of nineteen. He just stares at us when I introduce Marcus and tell him that he's going to be his lawyer.

"You're the one that left my mother," he says, like he's just figured out who I am.

Yes, I confess, but I'm here to help.

He looks around him.

"I need some help," he says.

Marcus pulls up a chair so he's sitting across from Adam.

"Tell me what happened," he says. "What happened that night, when those people died at the bookstore."

"William and Susan," the boy says. "Somebody killed them."

Marcus gives him his best pissed-off Black man stare.

"Did you do it?"

Adam looks shocked.

"Of course not," he says. "Hell no. Are you stupid? I wouldn't kill William and Susan. They were my friends."

I've already told Marcus that his new client is not famous for his social skills.

Marcus sighs.

"So tell me then, just what happened. Tell me everything."

"Are you going to get me out of here? My parents are going to be so pissed at me. And the food here sucks."

"It all depends on what you tell me, and whether you're telling the truth or not."

Adam seems offended.

"I always tell the truth."

That's quite possible, I'm thinking. The boy seems not to have that sense that most of us develop sometime in adolescence, the one that lets us know when to lie out of sheer self-preservation.

So Adam tells his story.

He went downtown, he says, because he wanted to be part of the demonstration.

"What they did to that Black man, that wasn't right," he says. "I wanted to let them know it wasn't right."

He says somebody on the street gave him a beer. And then some kids shared some of the wine they'd looted from one of the stores that got hit.

"I got kind of messed up," he says. "And then everybody started breaking stuff, and somebody said they heard gunfire, and I got a little scared. Then I saw William and Susan's store. So I went there, and their door was open."

Marcus holds his hands up.

"Whoa. Back up a minute. How did you know the Kellers?"

It turns out, according to Adam, that the couple had befriended him back during the fall, in his first semester at VCU.

"They'd let me hang out and talk about books and all," he says. "They were nice to me."

Marcus points out that 3:10 in the morning was not the time people usually come calling on anyone, friends or not.

"But their light was on," he says, "and the door was open. And sometimes they didn't mind if I came by late."

"Did you think it was weird that the door was open?"

Adam shrugs.

Marcus and I look at each other, wondering how a couple with a baby would have been receptive to a visit from a college nerd in the wee hours.

Adam seems to read our minds.

"They were good to me," he says. "William said I reminded him of his little brother. They let me babysit for them sometimes. Aurora liked me."

He looks up.

"Where is Aurora now?"

I tell him that she's being taken care of.

"Man," he says, "that poor kid."

Marcus pushes him along with the story.

He says that he heard the TV playing, but nobody answered when he called up to them.

"And then I walked up there, and there they were. I tried . . ."

He's struggling a little. We give him some time.

"I tried to wake them up, but they were . . . they were tied up, and they were dead. There was blood everywhere."

It's the first time I've seen him show any emotion, and it sure as hell looks real.

"Did you check on the baby, on Aurora?" I ask.

He takes a deep breath.

"She was crying. I tried to make her stop, and finally she did. But then I got scared. I should have took her with me. But I wasn't feeling so good. It freaked me out. So I ran."

He says he threw up in an alleyway and then went back toward the campus. He crashed on the sofa of one of his few acquaintances at VCU.

The next morning he says he realized what he'd done.

"I didn't tell Chad or any of them in the house about it. But then it was on TV Saturday night, and I guess one of Chad's housemates turned me in."

He sighs.

"I wanted to get caught anyhow."

He bangs his head on the table until we make him stop.

"Stupid. Stupid. Stupid," he repeats.

Marcus asks him if there was any sign that anyone else had been there.

"Well obviously somebody had been there. They didn't kill themselves."

"But did you see anything, or hear anything that maybe you didn't tell the cops about?"

He shakes his head no.

"I told them everything I knew. But they didn't believe me."

"Did they try to get you to confess?"

He laughs, but just with his mouth.

"About a thousand times. They must really be dumb, to think I'd confess to something I didn't do."

Marcus and I both know that people confess to things they didn't do all the time. Give a good interrogator enough time, and he could make me admit to the Lindbergh kidnapping.

"Did you ask for a lawyer?" Marcus asks.

Adam shakes his head.

"No. I didn't need a lawyer. I didn't do it."

"Well, young man, you're wrong. You damn sure do need a lawyer, and I guess I'm it, if somebody's willing to pay me."

The boy looks at Marcus.

"My dad can't afford you. The police guy who questioned me said they'd get the court to appoint one."

"That's not the kind of lawyer you need," Marcus says. "You need a lawyer that makes sure you don't spend the rest of your life in prison."

He sighs.

"I'm sure your father and I can come to some kind of agreement."

Adam nods. He looks a little freaked out, like maybe this is all starting to hit him, twenty-four hours after his arrest.

"My dad is going to kill me," he says, then thinks to ask when he can see his parents.

Marcus says he'll speak to the authorities about that.

"We're also going to try to get you moved to another jail."

"Why?"

Marcus explains that there are people who believe he killed the Kellers because they were a white couple with a Black baby.

"Why would that matter? Why would anybody kill them because of that?"

Either Marcus or I could do a seminar on that, but Marcus just tells him that there are some bad people out there, and stupid people, and sometimes bad and stupid come in one package.

Adam looks at me.

"Mom said your father was Black," he says.

"That's how I got this great tan."

"Well, I don't give a shit what color people are. You're still an asshole, though, for hurting my mom."

The way he says it, about race, you tend to believe him. After spending a few minutes with Adam, I am more inclined to think that, unlike most people I know, lying is not in his DNA.

"Was there anything you told the cops that I should know, if I'm going to try to get you out of this?" Marcus asks.

The boy thinks for what seems like a long time.

"There was one thing," he says.

What Adam noticed were shoe prints.

"They went a few steps, and then they just stopped. I think there was blood on them."

"What did the cops say about that?"

"They said they were probably mine, but they weren't."

He said they went from the chair where William died, away from him toward the back of the apartment.

"But then they just stopped."

Marcus asks him if there's anything else. The kid says no.

"Well, if you think of anything, whether it's something you told the cops or not, let me know."

Marcus tells him that he will be with him this afternoon for the bail hearing.

"Can you get me out of here?" Adam asks. "You need to do that."

Marcus says he'll try. He also says he'll check into the shoe prints. He promises to do his best to get Adam out of the Richmond jail and somewhere that might be a little safer, even if bail is denied.

He also says he will get Jeanette and Glenn in to see him as soon as possible, pointing out that he's sure they'll be in court this afternoon for the arraignment.

The kid calls out to us as we're escorted out.

"Don't forget about me."

On the way to the car, I ask Marcus what he thinks.

"I can't say for sure," he replies, "but he doesn't seem like much of a bullshitter, does he?"

I concur.

"The thing is," Marcus says, "I don't want to get that boy up in front of a jury. He seems like he's got a way of rubbing folks the wrong way."

After Marcus drops me off at the Prestwould, I call Jeanette and tell her about our meeting this morning. She says Glenn and she know about the arraignment hearing and will be there this afternoon.

"Well, please tell him to do something for Adam," Jeanette says. "I'm worried about him. He's always seemed young for his age. I can't bear to think of him in there with hardened criminals."

She is slightly reassured when I tell her that he's being kept in solitary, and that they might be moving him to one of the county prisons, where he might not run into quite so much animosity from his fellow inmates.

I have time for lunch with Cindy and Butterball, her insatiable feline who never misses a meal, then head over to the courthouse for the arraignment hearing.

The courtroom is almost full when I get there. A handful of the spectators seem to have an agenda.

"Justice for the Kellers," reads the sign that a deputy finally forces one heavyset guy to put under his seat. Like the crowds raising hell in the streets, the Keller contingent is of many different hues.

I find Jeanette and Glenn sitting near the front. Marcus is kneeling in front of them, no doubt explaining what it's going to cost to get Richmond's most high-profile lawyer to represent their son.

Glenn doesn't look happy, but they shake hands before Marcus goes back to stand beside Adam. The boy looks back at his parents once and waves before the arraignment starts.

The judge, one who's been on the bench here for longer than I've been on night cops, isn't exactly in favor of public hangings, but he is, as they say, tough on crime.

Adam, swallowed up inside an orange jumpsuit and handcuffed, is asked how he pleads to the murder of William and Susan Keller. He has to be prompted by Marcus to say, "Not guilty," adding after another prodding, "your honor."

Marcus puts on a spirited show for the judge, pointing out Adam's spotless record up to this point and his youth, which is evident to all. I wonder if the boy even shaves yet.

The prosecutor, a guy who keeps his job by winning every case, no matter how flimsy the evidence, points out in graphic detail the brutal way in which the Kellers were dispatched and what beloved citizens of our city they were. He is loudly endorsed by the slain couple's supporters, who are threatened with eviction.

Looking around I see an older couple sitting in the back. I know without even having to check. They have to be either William or Susan's parents. They wear their pain and shock like a neon sign.

As I suspected, the judge denies bail. Adam is escorted back to the jail. Jeanette and Glenn never get a chance to speak with him.

Marcus, who said a few words to the boy before they took him away, comes back to speak with his parents. While he is reassuring them that they will be able to talk with their son soon, I head to the back of the courtroom.

I catch the couple from the back row halfway to their car.

There isn't any delicate way to ask.

"Excuse me, but are you related to the deceased?"

They seem shocked at first. The wife jumps back a half-step and the husband moves in front of her.

I quickly explain that I am not a mugger but rather engage in the slightly less-odious occupation of journalist.

They look at each other and then the husband speaks.

"William is . . . was our son," he says.

I try to draw them out, telling them that I want to write something about the victims. They give mostly very short answers. William's parents are from Durham, where William grew up. The dead couple had been married seven years. They both graduated from a small college down in North Carolina. The bookstore was their dream. Susan, the father says, is from Minnesota. Her father's dead and her mother's in poor health.

I ask if they know what will become of Aurora.

"Who? Oh, the little girl," the father says. He shakes his head.

Pretty soon, William's father says they need to get on the road. The mother seems to be mostly trying to keep from crying in public.

As they're about to leave, I ask if either William or Susan had any enemies that they know of.

The husband turns.

"You mean other than that little bastard that killed them?" he says.

Mrs. Keller then speaks for the first time.

"Nobody that knew them up here," she says.

Her husband turns and gives her a look, and she doesn't say anything else. When I ask for enlightenment, William's father moves far too close to me and says, "Leave us alone, goddammit."

I write something about the arraignment, noting that the parents of the accused and those of one of the victims were in court. I make a note to myself to contact William's folks, who have endured a loss that every parent prays to be spared.

AND THEN it's off to the carnival.

Today it's L.D. and the mayor who are sitting in the dunking booth.

A crowd of more than a thousand has an angry tête-à-tête with the police chief and hizzoner at the state Capitol. The governor wisely has chosen to be elsewhere. The mayor tries to quell the multitude with his charm and sincerity. The crowd does not appear to be swayed.

"Where were you?" one woman screams over and over as the mayor holds on to the microphone and looks like he'd like to be just about anywhere else.

She and many others are pissed off. Things have reached the tipping point, where all the schmooze in the world won't work, at least not right now. They want to burn it all down. There's nothing like getting tear-gassed a time or two to raise your social consciousness.

L.D. looks about as comfortable as a deer hunter at a PETA rally. The chief is no politician, and it's probably just as well that he lets the mayor do most of the talking. I'm a little concerned for L.D. though. Hizzoner would like to someday be ensconced in the governor's mansion, and his approval rating is just above COVID-19 level right now. He needs a scapegoat. The chief is growing horns.

The crowd finally calms down a bit, and the mayor slips away. Later on he walks with the marchers from the Capitol down to the Lee Monument, but he can't win, at least not today. When he leaves at seven fifteen, pleading that he has to get back before curfew, he gets roundly booed again.

I am able to have a few words with L.D. back at his office between the clusterfuck at the Capitol and the march to the monument. There are Humvees around police headquarters. They're putting up Jersey barriers to keep the disaffected from storming the Bastille. My press pass doesn't do much good until Peachy intercedes.

Once inside what now seems like a damn fortress, I catch the chief walking toward his office and promise an "off the record" free pass if he'll talk to me.

He is not a happy man.

"What the fuck do they think I'm supposed to do?" he asks rhetorically. "I can't control every knucklehead out there every minute, not when these shitheads are calling us pigs and spitting on us."

I ask him if he thinks his job is in danger.

He bangs his fist on his desk.

"Of course my fucking job is in danger," he says, lowering his voice enough that his subordinates can't hear him. "Have you seen how that smooth son of a bitch passes it all off on me, like he was just an innocent bystander? Who was it, two days ago, getting all law-and-order and promising that the police wouldn't put up with this shit?"

L.D. can be a bit of a lightning rod. He also is loyal to his troops, sometimes to his detriment. This could be one of these times. He has promised that there will be no more firing tear gas at peaceful demonstrators, but he emphasized "peaceful."

I ask him what else if anything his minions have learned about the Keller murders.

He looks at me the way he often does, like I'm an idiot.

"What the hell else do we need to know? Goddamn, that little fucker went into the apartment at 3:10 A.M. He came out just after 3:30. Nobody else went in or out. Our men found their bodies just after four. Even you ought to be able to figure this one out. I don't think even that shitweasel Green can get him out of this.

"And we're still off the record."

I point out that Adam Walker had, until last Friday night, a spotless record. Not even a speeding ticket.

"First time for everything. He looks like he's not quite hitting on all cylinders. Maybe he just snapped. Who the fuck knows?"

I ask again if it is possible to move Adam to another jail, a little farther from Richmond. Every time he gets mentioned in a story, dozens of geniuses weigh in. Most of them think he's a racist who took umbrage to a white couple adopting a Black baby, and the city jail's population is decidedly on the dark side. Of course, they are rebuked by other mental giants who stop just short of dropping the "N" word on them.

In what the goddamn home-repair people and car salesmen on TV keep calling "these troubled times," we don't need anything else to inflame the masses, who already are spontaneously combusting.

"He's going to stay right damn here," L.D. says. "And you can quote me on that. We will keep him isolated from the general population. I've got bigger headaches right now than keeping murder suspects all comfy and safe."

As I'm leaving, he calls me.

"Be damn sure that's all off the record," he says, "especially that last part. I don't want to sound insensitive."

Perish the thought.

After the mayor leaves the Lee Monument, the night is calm, relatively speaking. There are no fires. No stores are looted. Nobody tries to burn down police headquarters.

Good news these days is relative.

CHAPTER SIX

Wednesday, June 3

L.D. is toast.

The mayor waited until this morning to hold the press conference, probably just to fuck with the paper for not kissing his butt enough recently.

Nah, that's not fair. With our sundown deadlines, we wouldn't have gotten it into today's paper even if he'd broken the news last night.

Hizzoner announced it at ten this morning. I tell Cindy that I might as well just set the alarm at seven every day, because I'm sure to get dragged out of bed by one damn thing or another.

They haven't fired the chief, just suspended him until the mayor's crack team can "do a thorough study of how exactly our law enforcement team is failing us."

The mayor, sensing a rising tide, says that he is lifting the curfew. He also says he would not be opposed to seeing the Confederate pantheon along Monument Avenue removed and will urge city council to approve such removal.

Almost in tandem, the governor steps up and declares that the Lee Monument, which is the state's problem, needs to go. Hell, it needed to go about two days after it went up in 1890, if you ask me, but you couldn't have gotten elected dog catcher for espousing that until Black Lives Matter seized the agenda.

I go straight from the presser to L.D.'s house. I've known his wife, Lucille, almost as long as I've known the chief, which is why she lets me in while telling a couple of good-hair TV types and their camera goons to "get the fuck off my lawn."

The man himself is in his den. He looks like he's getting ready to file his taxes, with papers spread everywhere.

He doesn't seem to know I'm there until I ask him what the hell he's doing.

He looks up.

"Covering my ass," he explains.

When I ask for further information, he says I'll know soon enough.

"That baby-kissin' son of a bitch isn't going to get away with this," he says. "He thinks he walks on water. Well, I'm about to take his damn life preserver away."

L.D. won't tell me anything else.

Trying to put the best spin on things, I remind the chief that he is suspended with pay, meaning that he can look on this as an extra vacation. When I then express my regrets over the way he's been treated by the mayor, he laughs.

"Hell, you're probably happy to see me go. But I ain't gone yet, you can bet your ass on that."

Whatever he's planning, I wish him the best. As someone who has been handed a cigarette and blindfold a time or two, I always have a soft spot in my head for the condemned.

I assure L.D. that he'll land on his fallen arches.

"Damn right I will," he says, then gives me a printable quote for the paper, one that stops short of calling the mayor a back-stabbing, buck-passing pussy. He gets the point across anyhow.

Amazingly the BLM protests and calls for the removal of our open-air Confederate sculpture gallery have seeped into the suburbs. Demonstrations have occurred in just about every county in what we grandly call our greater metropolitan area.

Callie Ann Boatwright had a story this morning about a gathering in Midlothian, a former village that is now more or less an anchor for the ever-expanding western burbs. Yes, even a place whose modern-day early settlers included much of the white flight antibusing crowd back in the 1970s is now throwing shade on Marse Robert.

Of course, not everybody is on the woke train. We've been filling up the editorial pages for the past three days with letters from both sides of the aisle. There is a sense of resignation, though, among the old guard, whose missives tend to bemoan inevitable change rather than vowing to fight to the death over their heritage, whatever the fuck that is.

After posting the sad story of the apparent demise of L.D. Jones, I walk back to the Prestwould and have lunch. I've been eating at home a lot in "these trying times." Butterball is grateful for the occasional scraps that fall from the table.

The governor has let Richmond take a step toward normalcy, meaning that restaurants can do something other than bring a bag of food out to your car. Unfortunately they can only seat you outdoors, and most of my favorite joints don't have any outside space other than a public sidewalk. Perly's, Joe's, the Bamboo, and other more urban dives aren't really set up for the alfresco crowd.

I hold my breath and hope they can stay afloat until the plague passes us over.

I do call ahead and then pick up a takeout pastrami and Swiss from Perly's for my newsroom supper, assuming I have time to eat.

I check with Marcus, who is pondering filing some kind of motion to have Adam moved from the city jail. Now that L.D. is at least temporarily relieved of his chiefdom, we both are a little uneasy about the boy's safety.

A call to Peachy helps to reassure me that the interim chief, a white guy who's been working his way up the ladder for twenty years and probably has at least achieved his proper level of incompetency, won't throw Adam to the wolves.

"He's harmless," Peachy assures me.

I ask her if she thinks L.D. is gone for good.

"I hope to hell not," she says. "Morale is about six feet underground here. Everybody hates us."

She says she will try to arrange an interview with the acting chief but can't promise anything.

I phone Jeanette and try to reassure her that her son is safe, at least for now. Her phone has been disconnected. I try her cell.

She says they've been getting a lot of hate calls, and that Glenn is finally dropping the landline. She says they can visit Adam at the city jail later today.

"How can people be so mean?" she asks.

I don't know, I tell her, but from my sad experience, they just are. I remind her that most of her neighbors aren't bastards. She concedes that several members of their Baptist church have come by to offer condolences and casseroles.

"God, Willie," Jeanette says, "it's like somebody died. Oh, damn. I know that's insensitive. I know somebody did die. That was awful. But it couldn't have been Adam that did it."

Wheelie calls me into his office sometime after two.

"Do you think you're too close to this story?" he asks. Everybody knows by now that the suspect is the son of one of my former wives.

"Damn, Wheelie," I tell him, "if I had to recuse myself every time a former wife was involved, I'd be back to doing that Richmond History bullshit again."

"Don't mention that," he says. "Never mention that." It was a painful episode in my sterling journalistic career, I must admit. Condemned to write local historical pieces every day a few years ago, I got creative, which is never a good idea when you work for a newspaper. Only a bit of blackmail aimed at our then-publisher saved my job.

We agree that we should note, every time I mention Jeanette in a story, that she is the writer's former wife. I argue him out of having to run a disclaimer every time I mention Adam. I also talk him out of taking this story away from me, no doubt to the distress of Leighton Byrd.

Not much happens, by this week's standards. A march that was supposed to start at a fading mall out in Chesterfield gets foreshortened by the heat. Daytime demonstrations in June in Richmond are seldom a good idea.

Peachy does get me in touch with the acting chief for a telephone interview. I wanted to drop by, but the new boss is a little busy putting out fires and getting ready for the next one.

James ("call me Jimbo") Stefanski is a man of few words, or at least few words he cares to dole out to a nosy-ass reporter. After we've dispensed with the biographical shit and I've managed to squeeze a little information from him about police plans for the near future, he says, "L.D. told me about you."

"Did he tell you how fair and honest I am?" I inquire.

"Not exactly," Stefanski says. "No, I don't think he used either of those two words. No, I'm pretty sure he didn't. I think he used the term 'pain in the ass.'"

I remind the acting chief that it is possible to be a fair and honest pain in the ass.

"Well," he says, "my ass is in enough pain as it is. I don't really need any more."

On the subject of Adam Walker, the man is mum.

There's plenty to write. I do a piece on the acting chief and a sidebar on the life and times of L.D. Jones. Leighton gets to do the story of the mayor and the governor joining ranks in calling for a new day on Monument Avenue. And that's before the sun goes down and it's showtime again.

Before I head to the BLM scene, I eat half that pastrami and Swiss and put the rest in the newsroom fridge, a very dangerous place to leave edible food. Then I do something I meant to do yesterday and just ran out of time. I walk over to the building on Broad Street that used to be a bookstore.

The usual yellow crime tape is over the front door, and plywood still covers the glass storefront. Nobody much is around now. Most of the action is apparently down among the monuments themselves, a few blocks west. Only a few shop owners are visible, trying to shore up their properties or maybe just paying a visit. A stray black-and-white cat sits in front of the building where the Kellers died, looking somewhat lost and hungry. It gazes up at me as if I might be its salvation. Good luck, kitty.

I walk down the narrow alleyway that separates the two-story building that housed Remainders of the Day from the used-clothing store next door. There are no windows on the side I'm on.

In the back, there's a public pay parking lot that opens to Grace Street. It needs repaving, and the lines don't seem to have been painted in this century. The rear of the building looks even worse than the front. No vandalism back here, just the result of a century or so of neglect. A deck on the second floor might or might not hold my weight, and the outdoor stairway leading to it looks like an accident waiting to happen. There is a back door at ground level. I'm about to try it when I'm interrupted.

"What the fuck are you doing back here?"

I jump six inches and almost swallow my cigarette.

A fat man in a purple knit shirt is standing the requisite six feet from me. He's wearing a corona mask, which makes him look like an overweight robber. He is holding a big-ass gun.

I explain, quickly and without making any sudden moves, who I am and what I'm doing.

The guy turns out to be the owner of the building.

He lets me show him my state press card. This mollifies him enough to take the option of shooting me off the table for the time being.

"Hot damn," he says, pulling down the mask. "You're that Willie Black, ain't you? I thought you looked familiar."

It turns out his partner in the slumlord business is R.P. McGonnigal's first cousin. Two degrees of separation.

He scratches his belly and looks mournfully at his property.

"Tell me what the hell I'm going to do with this building now? Anybody who'll risk renting down here is out of his fuckin' mind. And then they'll find out this is the place where two people were murdered. Might as well just have a little Jewish lightning, you know?"

His anti-Semitic reference to arson might be more than a bad joke. The place is a wreck. I could suggest that maybe replacing the stairs and deck and paying somebody to sandblast the graffiti off the side of the building might make the joint more desirable, but he is still holding that gun.

I tell him that I'm curious about the killings. It isn't often that somebody goes straight from a clean record to murder.

"Who knows?" the fat guy says. "You get all kinds around here. Hell, it all seems nuts to me. The looters didn't even take anything, although I guess that makes sense. What the fuck are they going to do with books?

"That couple, the Kellers, they seemed like good folks. Paid their rent on time every month, early even. They even painted the walls inside. Of course I bought the paint. But I didn't know much about 'em. Who knows what went on? Maybe some kind of kinky sex or something."

He looks back at me.

"The kid that did it looks like a nut, from his picture in the paper."

"Can we get inside?" I ask. "I'd like to look around."

I'm expecting him to either say no or hell no. He surprises me.

"Don't know why they didn't put that damn crime tape around the back door too," he says. "But, hell, it's my building. I guess I'm entitled to go into my own building."

He takes out a key and opens a door that is so weather-beaten that I'm not sure I couldn't have kicked it in.

"Knock yourself out," my host says.

I don't know what I'm looking for. This is often the case.

The back door opens to a storeroom with books even less desirable than the ones in the main room. The place has that old-book aroma to it. Our hallway at the Prestwould is starting to smell like that. Cindy loves to read, and she's managed to line the place with bookshelves, which she is filling at an alarming rate.

"They must of bought every book in every yard sale in Richmond," the fat guy says, shaking his head. "Hell, I bet the library wouldn't even take this stuff for free."

I walk up to the second floor, with the owner behind me. The stairs are creaking so loud that I wonder if they'll hold both of us.

The room where they were killed is off-limits, with more crime tape. I can see the bloodstains on the floor.

I am able to get a good look at the scene of the crime. Looking down the hallway, I can make out those shoe prints Adam told us about, the ones that lead nowhere.

"Is there any other way in here?" I ask the fat man. "I mean, other than the front door and the back door."

"Well, you got the upstairs back door, leading out to the deck."

I walk to the back of the apartment and see that it's locked from the inside.

I'm about to go outside and smoke a Camel when the guy adds, "and there is the basement, but nobody ever goes down there."

The basement is accessed via concrete stairs on the other side of the building. The fat man and I walk around there and make our way down the urine-scented steps, holding on to a rickety metal railing.

"I guess I ought to replace that sometime," the owner says. He says it in a way that indicates "sometime" will be right after hell freezes over.

Down at the bottom, there is indeed a door.

"I don't even know where the key is," he says. "Haven't stored anything in there in years."

It turns out we don't need a key. The door is unlocked.

"Son of a bitch," he says. "When the hell did that happen?"

I take a couple of pictures of the door, open and closed, on my iPhone camera.

He remembers where the light switch is, and one puny-ass light, miraculously still working and hanging from the ceiling, comes on.

We feel our way through whatever was stored there a million years ago and get to stairs that seem as shaky as the ones leading up to the second floor. I try not to imagine what's scurrying around in the recesses of that basement.

"You go on ahead," the fat man says. "I'll wait down here."

I don't argue. I really don't think the stairs could sustain my two hundred pounds plus his three hundred.

At the top, I try the door, which also is unlocked. It opens onto the storeroom.

I wonder why L.D.'s men didn't check this door in the back of the storeroom or walk around the building and find out the basement door was unlocked. Hell, I guess they've been too busy keeping the masses from burning down police headquarters.

When I make my way back down to the basement, the fat man has gone outside and up to street level.

We both light up.

"I need to get a lock for that door," he says, then checks himself.

"What the fuck am I talking about? Who's going to break in there and steal books? Aw, the hell with it. This place is toast. Might as well just take the plywood down and tell 'em to have at it."

As he shambles off, I feel fairly certain something in that basement is going to spontaneously combust in the near future.

Well, it might not be anything, but the cops can't claim any more that young Adam was definitely the only outsider to enter the building last Friday.

A chat with the interim chief seems to be in the offing, plus a call to Marcus Green.

WITHOUT A curfew to break, the protesters seem to have calmed down. Is there a lesson here?

A few hundred folks gather at the Lee Monument, and more of them are over in Carytown, which has no historical artifacts to my knowledge, and at the Virginia Museum of Fine Arts, which recently unveiled a very large statue of a Black guy on a horse, kind of a "kiss my ass" to the Confederate monuments.

It's pretty damn hot, which might also have tamped down the rebellion a bit. The National Guard and the state police are over at police headquarters, giving our men in blue a little backup.

I see my flat-footed friend Gillespie leaning against one of the jersey barriers at headquarters and ask him if he's tear-gassed anybody tonight.

He wipes the sweat off his brow.

"You'll be the first," he says.

I put in a call to Peachy Love at home.

"Did the cops know anything about there being a basement door to that bookstore where the couple was killed?"

"Not that I heard of."

I tell her what I found.

"Damn. It was unlocked? I guess normally we'd have found it, but this ain't exactly normal times."

"But don't you think your new chief would like to know about that other door? I mean the whole case against Adam rests on him being the only one that could have been inside when they were killed."

I hear Peachy sigh.

"Hell, Willie. I don't know if he'd really give a shit. I mean, that door could have been unlocked for a year for all we know. What are the odds of that having anything to do with those killings?"

"Well, just so you know: I'm going to let Marcus Green know about that door, and I'm bound to put something in tomorrow morning's paper, so this guy, Stefanski, he's going to be hearing about it soon enough."

"Oh, man. That's gonna be one more nail in L.D. Jones's coffin."

Yes, I concede that somebody under the aegis of our suspended chief didn't do his homework. It's understandable, considering that all hell was breaking loose along Broad Street when they found the bodies, but it'll be one more thing for the mayor to lay on L.D.

Still, how hard would it have been to do one lap around the goddamn building and check all the doors?

I tell Peachy that I'm sorry to put this one on L.D.'s overflowing plate of crap, but it can't be helped.

I ask her what's happened with the kid.

"I don't know," Peachy says. "Social services has her in their grasp for now. It kind of breaks my heart, Willie. They let me see her. She's old enough to know something really bad has happened, but she's not old enough to understand that her momma and daddy aren't coming back."

I call Marcus. Kate answers. I can hear Grace, her seven-year-old, chattering away nearby as Marcus Junior squalls in the foreground.

"Sounds like you're having a lively evening," I observe. She replies with some heat. I warn her about cussing in front of the children. She calls Marcus to the phone.

"They did what?" he exclaims. "All this shit about my client being the only one there, and they didn't even check all the doors?"

It seems that Grace and little Marcus will just have to get used to a certain amount of foul language from Mom and Pop.

He thanks me for the information. I tell him that the building's owner was there, too, and saw what I did.

"Did you go inside?"

I tell him I'd rather not say, but that if I had gone inside, I surely would have found that the door from the basement to the first floor also was unlocked.

"OK, I get it," Marcus says. "You don't want to be accused of impeding justice by walking all over a crime scene."

"If I'd been there," I add, "I would also have seen those shoe prints the boy mentioned."

"Damn," Marcus says, "this could get interesting."

Indeed.

AFTER CHECKING in with the demonstrators, I go back to the newsroom and write most of what I found. Sally Velez, my immediate editor, wonders how important that basement door is. Like Peachy, she figures it could have been unlocked forever.

"Probably bums sleeping there," she says.

"But wouldn't the Kellers have heard somebody down there and rousted them out if some vagrants had been homesteading in the basement?"

She concedes that point and says to give our readers ten inches or so on the unlocked door, after I've written about the night's activities around Monument Avenue. That story's not too sexy, since the night was relatively quiet. No news might be good news, but it has been my experience that good news is not what our readers most crave.

ON THE way home, I have to detour off Grace down Second Street to Broad, because the police have barricaded the block around their building.

As I pass the bookstore on the other side of the street, I slow down and look over. I see something that makes me do an illegal U-turn at the next intersection.

Sure enough, it's that goddamn cat. He's still there at the door. He's lying down. When I walk over, he gets up, but it seems like it takes a lot of effort.

"Can't you catch a damn mouse or something?" I ask him. "Show a little initiative." He mews, somewhat piteously.

I'm thinking maybe I can drop him off at a no-kill animal shelter tomorrow.

"Well, come on then," I say to the feline as I walk back to my car. I'm half hoping he won't follow, but, sensing a possible meal ticket, he does. He even works up enough energy to hop into the back seat after I open the door.

I'm thinking that maybe we can put the beast in the utility room to feed him and keep Butterball from killing him. Then, first thing in the morning, Cindy can take him to the shelter.

When I look in the rearview mirror, he looks like he's sizing me up, wondering if I'm his salvation.

"Not a chance, pal," I inform him.

CHAPTER SEVEN

Thursday, June 4

No good deed, blah-blah-blah.

I didn't count on two things when I brought the world's most pitiful cat home last night: Cindy and Butterball.

When I carried the critter into our unit, my beloved was still awake. She said she knew it was in bad shape. Otherwise a cat would never let a stranger carry him around like that. Hell, Cindy, who treats Butterball like royalty, has been scratched on both arms at one time or another.

My opinion was that the animal was just trying to make a good impression.

Whatever the case, Cindy fed him some of Butterball's cat food, and our guest must have drunk a quart of water.

"It's a wonder he's not dead," she said, stroking his fur as he inhaled Fancy Feast. "How long did you leave him out there?"

Not long enough, I was thinking. I smelled bonding. But I wasn't too worried. I had yet to see another four-legged creature with whom Butterball could get along, and this one was, for the time being, living in "her" abode and eating her cat food.

This morning, I was sure, would be his swan song in the Prestwould.

WRONG AGAIN.

Cindy goes out early to buy another litter box.

In the interim, Butterball senses another mammal in her domain. When I get up, she's standing at the utility-room door. I can hear meowing on the other side.

"Leave him alone," I command our porcine feline. "He won't be here long."

Butterball just looks at me with the disdain she usually displays unless she thinks I might be about to feed her. Then she meows back. It's like they're talking to each other.

I leave them like that, chatting through the door. When Cindy gets back, she sees what's happening and immediately opens the door. I brace myself for flying fur.

Instead the black-and-white walks out and, I swear to God, rubs noses with Butterball, who purrs. Prior to this, the only thing that has made her purr, in my presence, was pouring a little gravy over her cat food.

They go walking down the hall like old friends.

"Well," Cindy says, "I've never seen that before."

Trying to head off a problem before it becomes one, I remind Cindy that the Prestwould has a rule about having more than one pet.

"Oh," she says, "don't worry about that. We're not keeping him for good, just until we can find him a good home."

"Isn't that what the animal shelter is for?"

She reminds me of the odds of an abandoned cat being adopted.

"He'll wind up spending the rest of his life in a smelly cage."

I note that at least he'll get fed a couple of times a day.

"You have no heart," she says.

I remind her that I was the one who brought the creature here in the first place.

"Yes, you did," Cindy says and gives me a kiss. "You did a good thing."

I am far from sure about that.

THE INTERIM chief does not seem that impressed with the information in this morning's paper about the unlocked basement door.

"We would have found it," he says when I finally get in to see him at ten thirty. "We just hadn't had time to really investigate yet. You make us look like crap. And that damn lawyer friend of yours, Green, has already been jerking my chain."

I mention the bloody shoe prints.

"Who told you about that?" he says, raising his voice a bit.

"The kid. He was there, remember? Have you even checked to see if the shoes that tracked all that blood are his size?"

"We're working on that," he tells me. "Now get the hell out of here so we can get some work done."

When I tell him he reminds me a lot of L.D. Jones, he does not seem to take it well. Closing the door on his verbal abuse, I give Marcus a call. Any hesitancy he had about the case seems to have dissolved.

"They've got him convicted before they even started investigating," he says. "That new chief, I think he's over his head. I think they're stonewalling about moving him to another jail just to be dicks about it."

He says he's talked with Jeanette and Glenn and "worked something out" about paying for his services. He will go with them when they visit Adam today.

"I hope you didn't skin them too bad."

"Hey," Marcus says, "lawyers gotta eat too."

I have time to stop by Peggy's before clocking in.

She and Awesome Dude are eating sandwiches on little TV trays and watching some talk show that is best viewed stoned.

I ask my old mom if she's being careful, COVID-wise.

"Oh, hell," she says, "I don't ever go anywhere anyhow. Just made a trip to the grocery store to get some stuff yesterday. They got all huffy when I didn't have no mask."

I opine that a mask might not be the worst idea.

Peggy is on the short list of those who might be taking a coronavirus-induced trip to the morgue. She's seventy-eight years old. She has smoked enough marijuana to ensure that her lungs might, post-mortem, make an interesting science experiment.

"I don't like that thing," she says. "I can't breathe with it on. And don't ever put one on after you've ate garlic spaghetti. Phew."

I stress the need to be careful.

"Hell, something's gonna get me eventually. I ain't gonna live forever."

I WANDER over to the Lee Monument, where a small crowd has gathered. It's hard to tell, as I walk around, who's waiting to take the statue down and who's waxing nostalgic for Dixie. Black families take each other's pictures at the base of the edifice, now more or less completely covered with graffiti. Old white folks stand back a little and take photos, like they're saying farewell to an old friend.

There's a feeling of inevitability about it all. What seemed impossible a few days ago now seems impossible to prevent. The tide is coming in, and I sense that it will be a tsunami.

Callie Ann Boatwright asked me yesterday how I felt about the possibility of the Confederate monuments coming down.

"Didn't it bother you, growing up?" she asked.

She did make me think. There were a lot of things that bothered me, growing up in Oregon Hill.

People who didn't know me (and some who did) calling me "nigger" or "half-breed" bothered the shit out of me. Going into a bar or two, even in the early eighties, and knowing immediately that I was not welcome, bothered me. Getting stopped a couple of times for walking while Black in my own neighborhood bothered me.

Learning that I was more or less a non-person to my mother's family because I wasn't white as Minute Rice? Yeah, that still sticks in my damn craw, when I let it.

The monuments, though, hell, they were just there. I didn't ever feel like those statues were old white Richmond's way of saying, "You beat us once, but we're still here, and we still rule the roost." Maybe they did represent that, to some, but I wasn't seeing it that way. To me, they were just part of the scenery.

Maybe, if I'd been a little blacker, been harassed a little bit more, I'd have been more resentful.

That being said, I am glad that the end appears to be near. I'm happy for folks like Richard Slade and my other Black cousins. I'm happy for that old African American lady I saw yesterday, standing there at the base of the Lee Monument and smiling like it was Christmas. I'm happy for

Artie Lee, the dad I never really had, wherever he is in the afterworld. I'll bet he's smiling too.

So I told Callie Ann, who is idealistic enough at twenty-four to believe that change can come just by taking down statuary, that I'm glad the clock is ticking on our Confederate icons, even if I didn't do a damn thing to hasten their demise.

As I'm walking from the Lee Monument down to the one sanctifying J.E.B. Stuart, a familiar voice calls my name.

"Willie Black! Damn, ain't it a small world?"

I haven't spoken to Jimmy Deacon in probably five years. Amazingly he doesn't look a day older. Jimmy's always seemed younger than his true age, which must be somewhere between mine and my mother's. He's still Jumpin' Jimmy, the world's biggest sports nut. He once enabled me to win one of those cheap state press awards by helping me find out why somebody was killing off the former members of a nondescript minor-league baseball team.

If there's a sports event in town, Jumpin' Jimmy's there. He's been a scorekeeper, groundskeeper, general go-fer, whatever anybody with a pro, college, or high school sports team needed him to do. I'm told he still referees high school football and basketball games on occasion. I'd like to see that.

At one time, VCU got him a broom-closet office right by the basketball gym, but they had to finally end that deal when they learned that Jimmy was basically living in his "office." The cot and the refrigerator were what tipped them off.

I see him every once in a while, usually from a distance. I should have kept in touch, but Jimmy can kind of jangle your nerves. He's a nonstop chatterbox, and if you tied him to a chair and made him sit still, I think he might explode. And he does this weird thing where he refers to himself in the third person.

He's always lived alone, although not on the VCU campus anymore, and I wonder if he talks to himself when there's nobody else to listen.

"Man," he says, looking around, "Old Jimmy can't believe this shit. The old town is jumping, ain't it?"

He's actually hopping from one foot to the other, like a man who's half an hour overdue to take a piss.

"Not much for Jimmy to do, with the Squirrels not playing. Getting tired of watching all them reruns on TV."

I commiserate with the man. He's attached himself to the Richmond Squirrels, our minor-league baseball team, for the last nine years. Bootie Carmichael told me last year that they even had him wearing the mascot's uniform when the guy who usually wears it got sick. The mascot is a squirrel named Nutsy, which seems pretty appropriate for Jumpin' Jimmy.

He goes on for ten minutes, seemingly without taking a breath, mostly agonizing over the prospect of no high school or college football this fall. He's wearing his pandemic mask, and I'm transfixed watching the mask go in and out like a bellows as Jimmy yaks away.

When he finally has to stop and catch his breath, I look at my watch and take a step backward, ready for my escape.

He grabs my arm.

"Wait a minute," he says. "Wait a minute. Old Jimmy just remembered. I got something to tell you."

If any cub reporter gave enough of a shit to take the advice of a sixty-year-old hack like me, I'd tell her to let the ears work. Listen. Even when the source is an aging gasbag with nothing to do but bore the shit out of people, sometimes you learn something.

What Jumpin' Jimmy wants to tell me makes me pull that foot back and get out my notepad.

Jimmy, who probably hasn't read an entire book in his life, because it would have entailed an attention span longer than a lightning bug's, knew the book-loving Kellers.

"Yeah, they was a nice young couple," he says. He's standing as still as Jimmy ever stands, like he knows this is important.

He says he sometimes stopped at their store just to talk. He'd walk by there many days between his apartment over on Grace Street and the VCU gym.

"Some people, they don't want to give you the time of day," he says, "like they just want you to shut up and go away."

Imagine that, I think as I nod my head.

"But William and Susan, they wasn't like that. They acted like they were glad to see ol' Jimmy."

Maybe it was because Jimmy Deacon has no sense of social propriety, never thinks twice about asking questions most humans would consider as invasive as kudzu. Maybe Jimmy opened up enough about his strange life that Susan and William felt the necessity to reciprocate.

However it happened, they told him something.

"I don't think William wanted me to know, because he kind of tried to shush her up. But Susan, she told me anyhow."

What she told him was how William and Susan Keller came to move to Richmond five years ago.

The way she told it to Jimmy, events led them to decide it would be best to leave the greater Durham area and the state of North Carolina.

They were working down there, him in one of those big chain bookstores and her as a nurse, saving their money and probably dreaming of having their own store somehow, although from what I've seen, plowing money into a bookstore seems like a good way to empty your savings account. People seem to be buying books about as enthusiastically as they're renewing newspaper subscriptions.

"And then there was that wreck," Jimmy says.

When William realized that Susan was going to tell Jimmy all about it anyhow, he stepped in.

He said he'd had only a couple of drinks. As a longtime pro-level imbiber, I know it's always "a couple of drinks," but that was William's story.

He said that it was a rainy night, and he was headed for the farmhouse they were renting north of Chapel Hill when he came around this curve on some dark country road, and there was a car "like it came out of nowhere."

He said he figured later that the driver must have just turned onto the road from the parking lot of a little convenience store, and that it seemed like the driver was almost stopped.

At any rate, he was going too slow for William to avoid ramming the back of the car and sending it and its occupants into the ditch.

"He said he tried to get out and help them, but their car door was jammed, and the other side was pinned against the ditch, lying at a forty-five-degree angle. And then it caught fire."

A man, his wife, and their two children, ages five and three, were inside. Only the mother survived. William said he watched them burn to death.

"He was crying when he told me," Jimmy says. "He said he couldn't do nothing. Said he burned his hands trying to get the door open."

Things got a little dicey after that. Susan started to tell Jimmy more, but William told her they'd talked enough about it, that they'd like to let bygones be bygones.

"He said he wasn't drunk. He said that two or three times."

Whatever happened after that wreck apparently sent the Kellers north to our fair city.

"William said he did some community service," Jimmy says, but he doesn't know anything else about it.

"And now all this happens. I feel so bad for that little girl. She was a sweet little thing. Don't know what's going to happen to her."

He stops talking for a few seconds.

"But I hear they got the fella that did it," he says. "Man, Ol' Jimmy hopes they fry his ass."

I offer that I hope they've got the right man.

"Oh, they got him, all right," Jimmy says. "I seen that kid hanging around a couple of times. He was strange, like he had a screw loose."

Jimmy stops, probably remembering from newspaper and TV accounts that I have a slight connection to Adam.

"No offense," he says, "but he didn't seem like he was quite right to Old Jimmy."

What Jimmy Deacon told me sticks with me. It makes me remember something William Keller's parents said the only time I met them.

"Anyways," Jimmy says, "I thought you'd like to know, since you're writing about it and all."

I thank him for telling me and say that we should get together soon. When Jimmy says, "Just name a time," I say I'll call him later.

EVERYBODY'S HOPPING on the Monuments Must Go bandwagon.

The governor officially announces that the Lee Monument is coming down "as soon as possible," whatever that means. City council gives its support to taking down

Stuart, Jeff Davis, Stonewall Jackson, and even Matthew Maury.

"Whoever the fuck he was," Sally Velez says.

All this bending to their will does not deter the protesters. Actually the news flash that they are being heard probably encourages them. At any rate, a few hundred of them march from Monroe Park to Fourth Precinct headquarters over on Chamberlayne, but they eschew trying to burn the place down. Others gather around the monuments and demand what has already been promised.

Their wish list has grown. Now they want charges dropped against everybody who was arrested over the weekend, and they want a civilian police review board.

Leighton Byrd covers the city council meeting, which of course runs too late for tomorrow morning's edition. I get a couple of decent quotes from the governor, who more or less remembers me from my salad days on the Capitol beat, when he was the delegate from East Bumfuck. That was before I drank and smart-mouthed my way onto the night police beat.

I get a call from Jeanette, thanking me for helping get Marcus Green to defend Adam. She said that she and Glenn did get to talk to their younger son down at the jail. The news about the unlocked basement door seems to give her some hope.

"He just seems so helpless," she says, but Adam is still isolated from the other prisoners. From the crap I'm reading from our enlightened readers who post on our website, that's good. A lot of them seem to think this was all some kind of racial thing, killing white folks for adopting a Black baby.

"Adam isn't like that," Jeanette says. Then she lowers her voice a little.

"Glenn isn't either, really. He's got Black friends. He just doesn't know why they have to tear everything up."

It's a long story, I tell her, and promise to keep digging.

Chuck Apple, who's covering for me on night cops, says it was a quiet night. Depends on where you were, I tell him. Maybe Black Lives Matter is proving to be a relatively harmless steam valve for the homicidal set. It's hard to protest injustice and shoot people at the same time. Hard, but not impossible.

I make a note to myself to do some checking on a six-year-old car crash tomorrow.

I'm home not too long after midnight. In younger days, I'd have used my early escape as an excuse to hit Penny Lane for a pint or three, but Penny Lane is shut down, like most places serving liquid refreshment. The pandemic has been bad for the bars, good for the ABC stores.

Cindy is up, as is Custalow, the third part of our G-rated ménage-a-trois. Abe, who is the only thing keeping the Prestwould from crumbling into Franklin Street, excuses himself shortly after I get home. He's expected to be on the maintenance beat no later than eight in the morning. Unlike me, Abe is punctual.

I don't see either Butterball or the black-and-white stray. Cindy tells me they're sleeping.

"In the same room?" I ask.

She nods.

I look into the utility room, and there they are, snuggled up against each other like long-lost sibs. Who stole Butterball and replaced her with this love-kitty?

I return to the living room, sensing bad news.

"Did you go by the animal shelter?" I ask, hopefully, as I knock back a bourbon and water.

Cindy rises out of the Eames chair into the full upright position.

"Animal shelter? What are you talking about?" she says. "We can't send Rags to any animal shelter."

Well, that's it. I'm officially screwed. She's given the animal a name. Break out the Fancy Feast.

CHAPTER EIGHT

Friday, June 5

Cindy is feeding the cats, plural. I swear Butterball is playing nice with her new best friend just to piss me off.

I mention to Cindy that our landlady and my third ex-wife might not take kindly to having two cats in the unit, even if we are able to dance around the condo board's restrictions.

"Oh," she says, "I've already called Kate. She said she was cool with it, as long as Rags uses a litter box."

The whole world is conspiring against me.

Rags comes over and rubs his skinny body against my leg, marking me the way hobos were said to mark houses where the suckers lived back in the Great Depression.

Cindy is headed down to one of the YMCAs, where she's supposed to be home-schooling some East End kids who otherwise aren't going to get much book learnin' until COVID-19 is history.

"We're going to keep them six feet apart," she assures me.

The kids she's going to be teaching are fourth graders. Good luck, I tell her, keeping ten-year-olds socially distanced.

"Well," she says, "we've got to try. Don't worry, I'm not going to bring any mean old coronavirus home with me."

Like she can be sure of that.

I urge her to be careful. She's not in the death zone for the virus, age-wise. However, as she's so fond of reminding me, I have tottered past my sixtieth birthday.

"Always thinking of yourself," she says, shaking her head.

Cindy is hard not to love, even if she does drive me nuts on occasion. Whether it's stray cats or down-and-out kids or broke-dick old newspapermen, she tends to the needy.

GOOD NEWS and bad news for Adam. They're going to keep him in a private cell at the lockup, but there will not be any bail. He's locked up until something gets resolved.

When I talk with Marcus about the boy, he's somewhat incensed that the police don't seem to be motivated to check into the possibility that somebody other than Adam could have visited the Kellers on their last night alive. There are no cameras that could have caught any activity on the side of the building where we discovered that basement door.

I note that the cops aren't eager, even on a good day, to investigate crimes they think they've already solved, and they haven't had many good days lately.

I speak with Kate briefly, hoping she will see the wisdom in not doubling the amount of cat dander in a condominium she hopes to sell for a profit someday.

"You mean I should just tell Cindy to kick him out on the street or send him to a shelter?" she asks. "Is that what you'd do, Willie? Is that what you did with Custalow?"

Talk about apples and oranges. Abe Custalow is a human being, not a damn cat, and he had my back a thousand times when we were kids, growing up as the only blemishes on Oregon Hill's white population. When I found my Native American buddy homesteading in Monroe Park a few years ago, of course I was going to take him in.

There were times, I remind Kate, when she was on the verge of sending me to a shelter.

"Well," she says, "a tomcat like you deserved it on occasion, not like that poor, defenseless kitty."

I HAVE time, before work, to stop by and see how L.D. is faring in his exile.

He seems amazingly cheerful for a man who's a good five years from retirement and has no job. When I drive up, he's shooting hoops at one of those portable goals people litter the cul-de-sacs with. He is accompanied by a boy of about twelve who turns out to be his grandson.

"Oh," he says, when I inquire about his mental health, "my pension is pretty good, probably better than whatever you'll get when they kick your ass to the curb."

The boy giggles. L.D. tells him to pretend he didn't hear that.

"I only talk like that when I'm associating with bad people," he tells his grandson.

I try a couple of jump shots, if a ball delivered with one's feet less than two inches off the ground can truly be called a jump shot. Nothing in life disappears faster than hoops skills, and I realize I haven't played a pickup game in fifteen years.

"Man," the chief says, "I don't think you could jump over the morning paper, thin as that is. You got the vertical leap of a city bus."

I tell him that I could still beat his butt in a game of horse, which turns out not to be true. Playing basketball while wearing a mask, I discover, is like swimming with an anvil tied around your neck.

"Yeah," L.D. says afterward, as I catch my breath, take that damn mask off, and light a Camel, "don't worry about me. And don't bet the house that I won't be back in the saddle again sometime soon."

I ask him if he knows something I don't.

"I know plenty you don't know," he says, "and I'm going to keep it that way. But it ain't over yet, not by a damn sight, is all I'm sayin'."

I tell him about the unlocked door at the bookstore.

"And they hadn't checked?" he says, forgetting for a moment that he was actually the man in charge the night the Kellers were killed. "Well, it's probably nothing. Just you and that damn Marcus Green trying to stir up shit."

He warns his grandson again about cussing.

"Don't do as I do," he says. "Do as I say . . . aw, hell. You know what I mean. Don't get me in trouble with your momma."

Normally I wouldn't share with the chief, but since he's not in charge now, I feel a little more generous, so I tell him that I've gotten it on good authority that the Kellers might have left North Carolina five years ago under a cloud.

"So what? Everybody's got a skeleton or two in the closet. What's that got to do with somebody murdering them five years later?

"I don't care if that boy that's locked up is Jeanette's son, he couldn't look more guilty."

I note that I would like to make 100 percent sure before we send Adam to prison for the rest of his life.

"You're always looking for some crazy answer when the obvious one is right in front of you," L.D. says. "Sometimes, two plus two equals four, period."

I refrain from reminding him that my arithmetic has been better than his on occasion.

I COME in a little early, after picking up a Philly cheesesteak to go at the Bamboo Café. The newsroom, always fertile soil for rumors, is humming.

It isn't hard for us to socially distance these days, with about two-thirds of our once-formidable newsroom staff scattered to the wind. Even with Grimm Group, our corporate overlords, having sold the building to an investor who's renting out most of it to businesses that actually turn a profit, we are able to sit six feet apart.

That, however, doesn't keep what's left of the staff from gathering in mask-less herds to gossip.

The latest rumor making the rounds is that Grimm is going to outsource copy editing for all its papers to someplace in Wisconsin. This would have sounded like a sick joke a few years ago. Now it and pretty much anything else are in the realm of possibility.

Enos Jackson, who has been editing copy longer than half the reporters have been alive, seems particularly perturbed.

"What the hell," he's saying as I walk up. "Why don't they just let Spellcheck and Autocorrect do it? Why do you need humans at all?"

We all remember what happened a few years ago, when one of our more clueless reporters, an uninspired copy editor, and Autocorrect conspired to change "paramour" to "power mower" in a story about a state legislator resigning amid reports of multiple marital indiscretions.

"I always thought of him as more of a weed whacker," Sally Velez noted at the time.

I try to ease Enos's mind, but he and I both know he could be guest of honor at a farewell party sometime soon. Maybe someday I'll tell Enos about the coup I pulled with our then-publisher a decade ago when he was on the short list for very early retirement.

Sarah is in her office, so I stop by and bring her up to speed on what I know about the Keller murders.

She does not seem impressed with the fact that William Keller might have done something bad six years ago, but she's OK with me taking a little time to check into it.

"I mean," she says as I'm leaving, "I don't know what that's got to do with him and his wife getting murdered. And that piece you wrote about the unlocked door, does that mean anything?"

She asks me to hang back a minute.

"Willie," she says, "does all this digging have anything to do with the fact that you know this guy, Adam? I mean, if it does, maybe we ought to put somebody else on the story. God knows, between COVID-19 and all the rioting, you've got plenty to cover without getting mired in some wild-goose chase."

I remind Sarah that a few of my wild-goose chases have bagged some pretty impressive fowl.

She nods.

"All right, but just don't make it personal, OK?"

I ask her if she'd like a cat.

An old acquaintance works for the *News & Observer* down in Raleigh. I figure that's close enough to Durham that he might be able to give me some insight into the Kellers' pre-Richmond lives.

Rob Solomon must have turned into one of those people who checks his email every five minutes. He fires a message back to me by the time I've fetched a cup of newsroom coffee, which is not to be mistaken for actual coffee.

He sends me his number, and I call.

Rob and I are about the same age. We shoot the shit for a few minutes about some of our inappropriate behavior during the two years we worked together in our callow youth, before he moved south.

I remind him of the time one of the city editors caught him and one of the young women from advertising fraternizing in the men's room at six in the morning. Rob, who taught me what "chutzpah" meant and how to pronounce it, said he asked the editor what the hell he was doing in the men's room at that time of day, and the guy just quietly walked out.

He reminds me of an infamous mud-wrestling incident at one of the company picnics.

I catch Sally, who can hear half of the conversation from six feet away, rolling her eyes.

"Hey," I remind her, "let she who is without stain sling the first mud. I think one of the sports guys still has pictures."

Rob says to say hi to Sally, and I finally tell him what I'm calling about.

I brief him on the Keller murders and give him what information I have about them, including the approximate time frame of the incident in question and the fact that there was an auto accident that probably led to some people being dead. He says that it rings a faint bell with him, although he's covering politics and, unlike me, hasn't seen any dirt naps or highway fatalities in some time.

"So you think that might have something to do with their being killed?"

I tell him I don't know.

He says he'll call me back when he's had a chance to check their electronic files or quiz one of their other reporters.

"So you're still doing night cops? How long are they going to keep you in purgatory?"

Rob and I haven't talked in a few years, I guess. I explain that I've actually kind of bonded with the night police beat.

"Well," he says, "better you than me. No offense."

Most reporters, especially those covering the kind of statehouse beat Rob has and that I used to have, would not fancy being thrown out on the mean streets of urban crime. Hell, I considered quitting when it happened to me as punishment for refusing to do a hatchet job on a guy who was dying of AIDS.

But I needed the money, and I came to have an unexpected fondness for the people I ran across. The minor-league wise guys, grieving mommas, and earnest, clueless losers got to me in a way those slicksters down at the General Assembly never did.

After I've filled him in on my latest marital situation, he says he's late for a meeting.

Sally stops me when I head outside for a smoke.

"You were kidding, right? About that guy in sports still having pictures."

I tell Sally to embrace the memories.

MAYBE THE flames of BLM are flickering out. No windows get broken tonight. No gunfire is heard. The crowds I encounter along Monument and down at police headquarters remind me of the antiwar marches during Vietnam days. Most of that I've gotten secondhand, but I've seen the pictures. A lot of dope-smoking and face-painting. Love and peace.

Of course there's never a dull moment in the Holy City. Violence ebbs here and flows somewhere else. Chuck Apple, subbing again on night cops, has to cover a double homi on the South Side.

I file a lede on the nonaction on Monument Avenue and clock out. Cindy seems happy to see me home before midnight again. Custalow's over visiting his main squeeze, singing star-to-be Stella Stellar.

The cats appear to be in love. In light of this, I am pleased when Cindy informs me that Rags has been fixed.

"You didn't notice?"

I inform my beloved that I am not in the habit of examining the nether parts of cats, especially one that I had no earthly idea would be sharing my living quarters.

Knowing that he's been neutered gives me a little sympathy for our new addition. I offer this sentiment up to Cindy, who says she knows a lot of males whose lives would have been much less complicated if they'd been fixed.

"Less complicated," I concede, "but not nearly as much fun to play with."

Afterward, lying in bed, my mind turns to Adam Walker.

Maybe L.D. and Sarah and probably most other people are right. Maybe Adam is just an oddball with a screw loose who slipped from strange to homicidal for some reason.

But I've seen a few killers in my day, both before and after they were apprehended, and Adam just doesn't fit the profile. Most people who kill have a reason, and nobody can come up with a reason why a college freshman with no rap sheet would suddenly do something this awful.

Blameless kid kills kindly couple. Obviously my knowledge is not complete. Maybe Rob Solomon can fill in some of the blanks.

Or maybe I ought to just concentrate on what's definitely real. Between the pandemic and BLM, I don't need to be running up blind alleys.

Except sometimes I just can't help myself.

CHAPTER NINE

Saturday, June 6

There's a shitload of letters to the editor today calling for the statues to come down. Tomorrow, I'm sure Editorial will run another load bemoaning the Lost Cause's second surrender.

Maybe we should just let the readers fill the paper for us. Being a little shorthanded in paid journalists, we'll take all the help we can get.

A couple of unexpected consequences have given our beleaguered rag a nice financial boost of late, enough that Benson Stine, our publisher, has been known to occasionally smile. Maybe it'll be enough to save the copy desk.

Both boons spring from COVID-19.

First, our readers are dying. They're always dying, because newspaper readers are older than your average resident. But lately they seem to be passing away at an alarming rate. Last Sunday there were ten pages of obits, and I'm told tomorrow will be more of the same. People are starting to get the message that maybe coronavirus isn't just a bad cold or a mild case of the flu. But those paid obits are real money.

Not only are we getting more obits, but we're profiting from obit inflation.

If Deceased's Family A pays for seven hundred words to memorialize his life, Deceased's Family B feels they must go eight hundred at least if they're going to be able to hold their heads up at the funeral. And pictures add to the tab. The big trend now is to run a photo of the departed in his or her prime, like about thirty years ago.

"My goodness," I heard Clara Westbrook exclaim in the Prestwould lobby last week as she was perusing the paper while waiting for a ride and found one of her contemporaries had departed this vale of tears, "it looks like they've run Gladys McElroy's graduation picture with her obituary. She hasn't been that young since Reagan was president."

The second boost is from home improvement. Ad revenue from that sector is way up, I am told. Renovation seems to be the national sport now that we can't do anything else. A lot of people must be spending what was going to be their vacation money on putting in a new bathroom, upgrading the carpet, or otherwise fancying up the place where they're spending most of their lives now.

Even Cindy, who does not normally lust for the kind of digs journalists and teachers can't afford, was making noises last week about "doing something" about the kitchen cabinets, which look fine to me. They open. They close. We can store shit in them.

I reminded her that the kitchen cabinets are not ours to tear down and replace.

"Well," she said, "maybe Kate will kick in for part of the cost."

Maybe the damn cat population explosion will take her mind off cabinets for a while.

Things were pretty calm for most of the evening. Wheelie and Sarah felt that we had reached a point where I could go back to night cops again, leaving the young folks to mine what they could from the protests.

I'd been in the newsroom for an hour or so when Rob Solomon called.

"I found some stuff," he said.

What he found was a bit more than what Jumpin' Jimmy Deacon told me Thursday.

"It was a pretty big deal at the time. Pretty damn awful actually.

"Oh, yeah," he says, like it slipped his mind. "It might not matter, but the family he wiped out? They were African American."

According to the story Rob's paper ran, William Keller might have been a little more at fault than he led Jumpin' Jimmy to believe.

Rob says he's going to send me an email attachment with the gory details. It's in my basket by the time I get off the phone.

He's really knocked himself out. There are several stories attached—the one from the morning after the wreck and several follow-ups, the last one nine months later, at the conclusion of the trial.

William Keller was, according to the state police, well above the .08 level that defines "drunk" when they tested him later at the hospital. Amazingly he was treated and released with only minor injuries.

He was charged with three counts of vehicular manslaughter.

Later stories told of the widow's ordeal. She was burned over 50 percent of her body. There was nothing in any of the stories about her dying, but I'm sure she wanted to.

The story the next day had more details. Speeding was suspected but not proved. The victims' car seemed to have been going at a reasonable rate of speed, and the accident did not happen on a curve. It occurred on a long, straight piece of two-lane highway.

Another article a month later reported that the Keller family had hired a big-name lawyer who seemed, from what I was reading, to be Raleigh's version of Marcus Green: the guy you go to when you fucked up really bad and your daddy has lots of money. It also reported on the widow, who was still in the hospital with many more operations to go.

The ones he sent me on the trial, which didn't happen until nine months later, made for interesting reading.

It was heard before a judge, no jury. The Kellers' lawyer made a strong case for the victims' car having possibly pulled out from a convenience-store parking lot right in front of William, not giving him enough time to stop. The prosecutor pointed out that the collision occurred at least four hundred yards beyond that parking lot. The defense lawyer raised questions about the validity of the Breathalyzer test, claiming that William did not willingly take the test or that, sitting in a hospital emergency room and possibly being concussed, he was in no position to agree to it.

According to the story, there were plenty of character witnesses to attest to William's sterling reputation. The parents of the dead husband and father were there, but they weren't allowed to speak. The judge said they could have their say at the sentencing if Keller was convicted. They were, the story said, a tad upset. The widow was not able, physically or mentally, to make an appearance, her father-in-law told the reporter.

Late in the day, Keller and his lawyer met with the prosecutor and the judge in the judge's chambers. When they came out, Hizzoner said that William Keller had agreed to plead to lesser offenses: DUI and reckless driving. On the spot, he sentenced him to one year in jail, suspended, and three hundred hours of community service.

It was reported that the judge gave Keller a stern talking-to.

The dead guy's parents, as one might expect, did not react well. They never got a chance to testify at the sentencing. The father had to be restrained by a couple of sheriff's deputies.

Reading all this makes me cringe a little. I probably have driven several thousand miles drunk in my life. I once got arrested for driving the wrong way down Franklin Street outside the newspaper. By the grace of God, I never was unlucky enough to kill anybody. Careless, yes, but, reading this story, lucky as a son of a bitch.

I call Rob back to thank him for his help. He tells me that he thinks there was some kind of civil suit, and the poor woman who was burned and lost her entire family got something. Hell, everything wouldn't have been enough.

I set up a file on my computer with the names of everyone who might be helpful in finding out a little more about William and Susan Keller. The story says the dead man's parents are from Durham, and I have their names, so I should be able to track them down.

I've already gotten vital information on William's parents. They're at the top of my list. This is going to be a little tricky though. How do you approach a couple when you're trying to dig up dirt on their son who was just murdered?

Well, that's why they pay me the big bucks. Actually they don't pay me the big bucks, and I doubt that anyone above me in the newsroom would be that crazy about me continuing to flog this seemingly lifeless horse.

Still my curiosity is aroused.

Tomorrow might be a good time to try to connect with the Kellers.

THERE ISN'T much going on in the Holy City. The Gold Dust Twins, Callie Ann and Leighton, send in reports every half-hour or so. Things seem peaceful.

I have to run over to some place off Thirtieth Street where the cops have been summoned because of a body lying on someone's front porch. It turns out to be nothing though. Nothing, that is, unless you were the poor guy coming home from work who had a heart attack on his front steps and died there.

Peachy Love fed me a pretty good light 'n' bright, although I don't know how the hell we're going to use it until we get more details. A teller at one of the banks on West Broad set off the alarm sometime this afternoon because a Black guy with a mask came into the place. By now, you'd think everybody would be used to people wearing masks, whatever color they are, even in banks. The teller, who was white, said he "just looked suspicious." The gentleman was somewhat upset when the cops showed up and handcuffed him.

Peachy says she doesn't have his name yet, but the cops determined that he was a law-abiding citizen just trying to deposit a check.

"I'm sure he'll show up soon enough," Peachy says. "Just wait for the lawsuit. Or maybe he'll give you a call. Hell, if it was me, I'd be going to every TV station in town."

I tell her that I imagine Marcus Green is sitting by his phone. We apparently haven't achieved colorblind Nirvana just yet.

And then, sometime after ten, the peace is shattered.

Brave Wickham, gone these many years, suffers a second demise.

You could have watched it from our sixth-floor window at the Prestwould.

Down in Monroe Park, there stands—or stood—a statue to Confederate Cavalry General Williams Carter Wickham.

It isn't a big statue, only about seven feet tall set on a granite base. Like a lot of Richmonders, I've walked by it many times without really noticing it. We have so damn much Confederate statuary around here that it's easy to overlook the little stuff.

Maybe Wickham is the first to go because he was the easiest to pull down. Some kids tied a rope around the old soldier, and down he went. By the time I get there, he is lying on the ground, looking sad and confused. Some brave soul bothers to urinate on our fallen hero.

I see a trend. The governor says even Lee will fall just as soon as he can line somebody up to take him away. The mayor says July 1 is reckoning day for Lee's Monument Avenue counterparts. That's the first day he can legally do it. Some years ago, our decidedly un-woke state legislature prohibited localities from taking down monuments. This year, the Democrats got hold of the reins and reversed that edict. The change goes into effect July 1.

The way things are going, Hizzoner better hurry up, or events are going to overtake him.

The governor has started Phase Two of his plan to deliver us from the plague, although Richmond and Northern Virginia are still in detention. Maybe someday I'll get to have Sunday brunch at Joe's again.

The mayor delivered the news flash today that we are no longer the capital of the Confederacy, which no doubt is breaking news for many of the old guard.

And an asteroid the size of Monroe Park missed the planet by a mere 3.1 million miles.

"And they say there's no good news," I hear Enos Jackson mumble.

CHAPTER TEN

Sunday, June 7

The Prestwould's lobby is abuzz. Last night was about as exciting as it gets around here. I'm surprised they didn't have to break out the defibrillator.

Everybody on the south side of the building had a bird's-eye view of the hubbub that preceded and followed Wickham's demise.

A few of them seem determined to sell, although I'd bet my next paycheck that none of them will. The only thing most of our Prestwouldians dread worse than social upheaval is the idea of having to move again. There's a cemetery next to Oregon Hill, called Hollywood. Famous Virginians are buried there, including two presidents—three if you count Jefferson Davis, which many of those interred there would. It's also where present-day Richmonders of a certain class prefer to be planted. The joke around here is: From the Prestwould to Hollywood. No stops in between at smaller condos or rest homes.

Loudest bitcher of all, of course, is Feldman, aka McGrumpy. Feldman, who grew up in Brooklyn, is one of the leading proponents of saving Richmond's Confederate monuments from all "those people" who want to wipe the slate clean and start over.

"They even urinated on him," Feldman says, referring to the downed statue. "I saw it. What the hell do we have city cops for?"

As if, I think, some overworked Black city policeman is going to take on a mob to defend the Old South's honor.

"Well," Clara says, "at least nobody was hurt."

Other than someone spray-painting "BLM" on the front steps, our venerable building looks the same as we head out the front door. Across the street, Monroe Park also looks about the same as it did yesterday. They've already hauled Wickham off to wherever banished monuments go.

Custalow accompanies Cindy and me over to Peggy's, which is still our default brunch venue until the governor tells us it's safe to breathe on each other again.

Peggy and Awesome Dude are skipping the festivities today. Peggy says she's got a little cold and doesn't want to infect anybody.

R.P. and Andy get there shortly after we do. In the backyard, somewhat safely distanced, we break out the food, the beer, and the makings for many Bloody Marys.

"What the hell happened last night?" Andy asks. Cindy, who saw it all, gives him a blow-by-blow account.

"Good thing they didn't try that crap on the Hill," R.P. says. "There's houses over here that still have rebel flags hanging out front."

I remind R.P. that there aren't any monuments in Oregon Hill, Confederate or otherwise.

"Well, if there were," he says, "they'd play hell taking 'em down. Those old rednecks don't like outside intervention."

I wonder how much R.P. McGonnigal, who grew up on the Hill but hasn't lived there for at least twenty-five years, really knows about his old neighborhood. The best I can see, and from what Peggy tells me, it's pretty much been gentrified by the VCU crowd.

I go inside long enough to talk to Peggy, who keeps me at a distance and is hacking a little more than usual. She always has smoker's cough, for good reason. She doesn't understand why I'm not affected more, considering that I've kept R.J. Reynolds in business for the past forty years.

I ask the usual question anyone would ask of an aged parent who shows any signs of ill health in "these trouble times."

"Nah," she says, waving me off. "I ain't got it. Nobody around here's got it."

"Yeah," Awesome Dude contributes, "we don't even drink that shit."

It has to be explained to the Dude that Corona the beer and corona the virus are not even distantly related.

"Well, that might be so," he says, showing us a smile that is somewhat short on teeth, "but I'm sticking with PBRs, just in case."

"Just take care of your own self," my old mom tells me. "You're out there with all them rioters and all. No telling what they've got."

I push aside the possible ramifications of that "cold" and go back outside.

We dispense with the masks long enough to eat and drink our way through the provisions. Then, my cell phone begins playing a tune in my pocket.

Sarah Goodnight is calling, from the newsroom of course, to inform me that the Black guy who was manhandled by the police for wearing a mask into a bank has contacted the paper.

Thank you, Jesus, I think. The man did not go straight to the TV folks. Somebody is still loyal to print journalism.

"He says he wants to talk to you," she says. "I think you know him. In fact, we both do."

She seems amused, but she won't divulge anything else as to the identity of our mystery guest.

He lives on the North Side, she says, but he's sitting in the newsroom right now.

I thank Sarah for thinking of me.

"Who the hell else is going to come in on Sunday for something like this?" she asks.

"Says the woman who slept on the couch in the ladies' room last night."

"I did not. Well, maybe just a cat nap."

I excuse myself, leaving the six of them to argue over who makes the best Richmond potato salad, Sally Bell's or Mrs. Marshall.

We drove over because Cindy wanted to go to a winery down along the James this afternoon. It is possible, she is told, to sit outside there under a tree, drink wine, and listen to music. Because I need to get to the paper before this gold mine of a subject decides he's ready for television, I ask Andy to give Cindy and Abe a ride back to the Prestwould later, promising to pick up my beloved in no more than two hours for a ride down to Charles City County.

I park in front of the paper, in what used to be a perfectly good driving lane but is now given over to parking so that the former parking zone can be used by bicyclists, one of whom wheels past here every five minutes or so. The other day, one of the sports guys swears he saw a dog sleeping in the bike lane.

The mayor and city council, when they're not wrestling with minor irritations like mobs attacking the police station and monuments being torn down, are heavy into social engineering. If you make driving hard enough, everybody will just say "fuck it" and buy a bicycle.

THE AGGRIEVED citizen is sitting in Sarah's office when I come up. He looks familiar.

"Last time I was here," he says as he grins at me, "I was packin' heat."

Jesus Christ. Shorty Cole.

"How the hell did you get in the building?" I ask.

"No big thing. I just waited for somebody to walk in and went in after them."

Well, why not? Like the Prestwould, we don't have security guards anymore.

Of course, Shorty Cole probably is a good reason not to have security guards. That's what he was doing, for us, when he got it in his head to hold our publisher hostage a few years ago. Before our little excitement that day was over, I had managed to put myself between Shorty and the clueless Sarah, then a cub reporter. It was a wasted effort, because Shorty's gun wasn't loaded.

"What a reunion, huh?" Sarah asks.

We catch up. Shorty did six months with a whole bunch of years suspended for holding Rita Dominick at gunpoint for a while. The paper wasn't much interested in pressing charges. All involved figured he had a good reason to be upset.

Of course, if anyone knew what Shorty did later to avenge the death of the boy whose murder inspired him that day, he'd be a ward of the state for many years to come. Me, I'd have given him a medal for that particular act of retribution.

Shorty is, well, short. He's about five-two, and he seems to have lost weight since the last time we saw each other. He has a scar over his left eye. As a sometimes-employee of Big Boy Sunday, he occasionally has to fight above his weight class.

"So," I ask him, "what happened, at the bank?"

"Aw, hell," Shorty says, "I'm used to gettin' nabbed for driving while Black, or even walkin' while Black, but this is the first time I ever been caught bankin' while Black."

He gives me the long version of his brush with bankers and law enforcement.

"When the po-po got there," he says, "they checked and saw that I had a record. That got them real excited. And they wouldn't let me take the damn mask off. It was hard to breathe."

It took the cops about fifteen minutes, by Shorty's estimation, to sort everything out.

"They didn't even apologize," he says. "The bank lady, she was pretty upset. She apologized plenty, said she just thought I looked dangerous."

Hell, the teller was probably taller and weighed more than Shorty. What was it about his African American ass that made him seem like the only guy in a room full of people wearing masks who was aiming to pull a heist? Hmm. I'll have to think about that.

I ask Shorty if he's retained legal representation. I remind him that banks tend to have lots of money, and a lawyer can separate them from it easier than a guy with a gun can.

"Yeah, that's what Big Boy says. He said I ought to get that fella Green."

Just what I was going to suggest.

"You know I'd never do nothin' like trying to rob no bank," he says. "I'm a peaceful man, unless I get aggravated."

I wish Shorty the best.

After he leaves, Sarah and I revisit old times.

"It's going to be hard when I have to lay you off someday," she says, "after you saved my life and all."

I remind her that Shorty's gun wasn't loaded and hope she's kidding, but if it's me or her, who knows?

We do have some history, I remind her, and she says that some of that history is best left unrecorded.

A call to Peachy gets me a home number for Jimbo Stefanski, our acting police chief.

Jimbo sounds as if he's been liquid brunching a bit himself. He does not react well when I tell him what Shorty Cole told me. I don't mention that his own media gal tipped me off to the bank fiasco before Shorty showed up in the newsroom.

He denies that any undue force was applied, saying that "the subject" resisted arrest. I'm pretty sure banks have cameras, something I mention to Stefanski.

"Well," he says, after pausing for a moment to collect his thoughts, "I'm sure they'll back us up."

Probably not, I'm thinking. If the acting chief thinks this one will get swept under the table in these BLM times, he's dumber than L.D. Jones on his worst day.

I try to fill him in on the details of the car accident that led the Kellers to migrate to our fair city.

"And that's relevant why?"

"Well, the Kellers were not without enemies."

"Who the hell isn't? Stop being a goddamn pest, if that's possible."

With the chief's denial in hand, I find the name and number for a bank flack to speak to the issue, or at least get the name of the teller who started this kerfuffle. Of course no one's available to talk to me on a Sunday, but I can't wait a day to run this one. Who knows if Shorty isn't already paying a visit to one of our local TV stations? My only salvation if he does is that nobody will be there on Sunday either. We'll just have to say that bank officials were not available for comment.

I've written the story and filed it when my phone rings.

"Do you know what time it is?" Cindy asks.

It is, I see, about an hour after the time at which I had promised to pick her up and go to that damn winery.

I try to explain and tell her I'll be home in half an hour, tops.

"Never mind," she says. "I'm going for a walk. A long walk."

And she hangs up.

Surely she will understand my husbandly shortcomings when she hears what a pip of a story was dumped in my lap.

Surely.

It's too late to salvage this lovely afternoon. Anticipating an evening perhaps spent with the cats in the utility room, I might as well try to find out a little bit more about the late Kellers.

I am able, after a couple of wrong numbers, to get in touch with William's parents, whose names are Jacob and Mary. I discover that they seem to be in the general vicinity of rich.

It is no time for hard questions. They've just experienced the worst nightmare imaginable, losing their son and daughter-in-law in one seemingly senseless blow.

Mrs. Keller obviously doesn't want to talk to me at all, but after I relate that I did know their son and his wife, perhaps exaggerating the depth of our relationship, she softens a bit. I remind her that we did speak briefly at Adam's hearing.

"Do they know anything else about that . . . that thing that killed them?" she asks.

I tell her that Adam Walker resides in the city jail, without bail, and that it probably will be a few months at least before the trial. With COVID-19 shutting down the court system, God knows how long it will be before justice gets served.

"Well," she says, "we will be there, whenever it is."

She says Susan's mother has been in contact with them and will be in Richmond whenever the trial happens.

I eventually get to the point where she will either hang up on me or tell me something I don't know.

"Mrs. Keller," I begin, "you know, newspapermen are kind of nosy. I checked around and found a bunch of information about that accident William was involved in, back in 2014."

A brief silence.

"Oh."

Then:

"I don't see what that's got to do with anything. Just a second. Let me get my husband."

After a long couple of minutes in which I'm afraid the Kellers have hung up, I hear a man's voice.

He sounds as if I'm the last person in the world he wants to talk with.

"Who is this? Why are you bothering us? Haven't we suffered enough already?"

I try to explain that I'm only calling because, as awful as the double murder was, I'm not at all sure the right man's in jail.

"And who the hell are you to decide that?" he shouts. "Don't you all have police up there?"

They've been a little busy with other things lately, I explain. They might not have gotten it right.

"But what authority do you have to go snooping around about that damn car wreck? That's ancient history. And it didn't have a thing to do with him and Susan getting murdered. What the hell are you trying to do, besmirch my dead son's name? I ought to sue your ass."

I try to placate him, although that might not happen today.

"Something your wife said, when I met you and Mrs. Keller up here the day of the arraignment. I asked if you all knew of anyone who might have wanted to harm William and Susan, and she said something like, 'nobody up here.' Was there anybody down there that might have had a grudge?"

He doesn't say anything for several seconds.

"That's old business," Jacob Keller says. "Tempers were high at the time, but nobody's mentioned that since right after the trial."

He didn't say "since the trial." He said "right after the trial."

"Did something happen after the trial?"

"Just some phone calls. We changed our number. Listen, that was an unfortunate accident. Everybody felt horrible about it, but nobody meant any harm. Unlike what happened to William and Susan."

Might as well step in it with both feet.

"I did some checking up. Like I said to Mrs. Keller, I'm a snoop. You're pretty well off. It seems kind of odd that your son would be running a secondhand bookstore."

"He was his own man," Keller says. "He didn't want to be beholden to me. Now, if you'll excuse my French, fuck off."

And he hangs up.

I have the names of the victims of that accident. Maybe it's time to try to find the next of kin.

Sarah asks me what I'm doing, now that I've already filed the Shorty Cole story.

"Don't you have a home?" she says.

Maybe, I reply, and maybe not. I tell her the sad story about the winery trip that didn't happen.

"Damn, Willie," she says, "are you trying to go four for four? You'd better not fuck this marriage up."

I remind her that this whole mess could have been avoided if she had called someone else when Shorty showed up.

"Yeah, right. You never would have forgiven me if I'd let one of the Gold Dust Twins have this one."

Fair point.

She looks at her watch.

"Shit," she says, "we're supposed to be at a party at five. Jack's going to kill me."

Next time you feel the urge to give out marital advice, I tell her, talk to the mirror.

THE KROGER'S in Carytown is open on Sundays and praise the Lord, they have flowers.

When I come home with a dozen red roses and an order of tangerine chicken from Fat Dragon, along with a solemn promise to get to that winery the next time it is humanly possible, it puts my beloved in a somewhat forgiving mood. I'm glad she didn't change the locks.

When she hears the story of my unlikely reunion with Shorty Cole, she has to concede that only a fool would turn down a chance at a story like that.

I call L.D. Jones, because I think he might like to hear an amusing story. Since he was no longer in charge when Shorty got mistaken for a bank robber, this one bites somebody else's ass.

He already knows about it though.

"Yeah," he says, "I hear they're running around like their pants are on fire. The two knuckleheads who showed up probably will have to be suspended for a little while."

"With pay?"

"Hell, yes, with pay. They wouldn't have come there to start with if that damn bank teller had any sense at all. I hear she was white."

The chief sounds fairly chipper, for an old guy who might be losing his job.

I mention this.

"Yeah," he says, "you've got to take the good with the bad."

But then I hear him chuckle.

"You're off Mondays, right?"

Theoretically, I answer.

"Well, you might want to put in some overtime tomorrow. Could be an interesting day."

"They've all been interesting lately."

"Just stay tuned," he advises but won't say anything else before he disconnects.

After our Chinese dinner, I email my old buddy in Raleigh and ask him if he can get me whatever information there is to get on the survivors of that wreck that sent the Kellers to Richmond.

"You don't think Jeanette's kid did it?" Cindy asks me later while we're watching an episode of some bullshit true crime series.

"I don't know," I tell her honestly. "But there's a family down in North Carolina that has a pretty good reason to hold a grudge."

Maybe they're the forgiving type, or maybe not.

"So," Cindy asks, "what do you want to do tomorrow? You're off, right?"

It is with great trepidation that I tell her that L.D. Jones thinks tomorrow might be interesting.

I set the alarm for a reasonable hour and go to bed promising myself to check up on Peggy in the morning.

CHAPTER ELEVEN

Monday, June 8

The city got a breather last night. No smashed windows. No monument desecration. Richmond rested.

I made my one breakfast specialty this morning: pancakes. Still trying to soften Cindy's censure over that winery washout yesterday.

She seems to appreciate the effort, even if some of the end results were not exactly perfect.

"This one looks kinda like Feldman," she says as she examines one of them. "I like the ears."

"Don't let that spoil your appetite."

It doesn't seem to. By the time I've made enough for both of us, though, my phone starts talking to me.

Peachy Love is calling to tell me what L.D. was strongly hinting about yesterday.

"He's back?"

"That's why I'm calling you. The press conference is at nine thirty, down at city hall."

"How?"

"I've got a pretty good idea," Peachy says, "but you're going to have to get the whole story from the chief."

"Hey," Cindy says, holding up the syrup bottle as I'm heading out, "with all those monuments coming down, how long do think Aunt Jemima's gonna last?"

THE PRESSER starts right on time.

L.D. looks like he's trying very hard not to grin. The mayor looks like he just ate a lemon.

The mayor says that "after a thorough and vigorous examination of the police department's actions," L.D. Jones will resume his duties as chief of police. He thanks Jimbo Stefanski for his efforts in "these troubled times" and looks forward to much better relations between the cops and the citizenry. Jimbo isn't there, perhaps sulking over the end of his five-day reign as Richmond's chief of police.

L.D. doesn't say much, just that he is eager to get back in the saddle.

The whole thing lasts maybe five minutes. The TV stations and the local weekly that focuses on African American interests are there, and everyone wants to ask the reinstated chief a few questions, both about his surprising reversal of fortune and my story this morning on Shorty Cole's unkind treatment by the banking and law enforcement communities.

L.D. walks off and leaves them squawking.

Maybe I'm the only one who sees the mayor clench his fists for a second or so before he, too, takes his leave.

I call the chief's cell, and he surprises me by answering.

Before I can speak, he says, "Meet me over at the YMCA parking lot, the one behind the building."

L.D.'s car is there when I drive up. He has the engine running, for the air conditioning.

When I hop in, the first thing he says is, "All this is so off the record I might have you killed if it ever gets out."

As a fan of personal safety, I agree.

The chief has quite a story to tell.

"That son of a bitch didn't know who he was messing with," is the way he sums it up.

As it turns out, the chief takes notes. He even uses a tape recorder on occasion, illegal though that might be.

When all hell broke loose back on the twenty-ninth, it turns out that L.D. kind of saw it coming. According to his notes, he warned the mayor that trouble was brewing and suggested that a few preemptive arrests should be made. One of his lieutenant's informers spread the word that something less than spontaneous was planned for that Friday night.

What clinched the chief's redemption, though, wasn't the notes. It was his recorded conversation with our mayor early that evening in which he pleaded for permission to take firm action. He made the request a good two hours before the trouble started.

He has the tape with him. You can clearly hear Hizzoner say, "We don't want to act too hastily here. We have to let these people let off a little steam. They're angry and they have a right to be angry. No arrests. I repeat, no arrests."

"He said it twice," L.D. says, shaking his head and laughing. "The bastard said it twice."

L.D. could have brought all this up five days ago, "but I kept thinking they'd come to their senses. When I finally figured out that all they wanted was a sacrificial lamb and I was the one wearing the wool, that's when I played my trump card."

He said at first that he only told the mayor about the notes he'd taken, "but he said he had no recollection of saying anything like that, so I had to bring out the tape."

The mayor told him he had committed a crime, illegally recording their conversation.

"And I told him that I'd take my chances in court, but that I had a lot better chance of being found not guilty than he did of getting reelected.

"He cussed and fussed for a while, but he knew I had him by the short hairs. The mayor isn't really that dumb, and you could almost see him figuring the odds in that Phi Beta Kappa brain of his. What's worse, he was thinking, bringing the chief back after only five days of penance or being exposed as the guy who could maybe have nipped the whole thing in the bud?"

I note that the mayor seems to have made a wise decision.

"I've got to watch my ass, though," the chief says. "That son of a bitch will be doggin' me like a fuckin' bloodhound from now on."

I remind L.D. that he has outlasted three mayors so far.

"Five more years," the chief says. "That damn gold watch can't come soon enough."

I'm happy for the chief, but you have to wonder whether it's a blessing or a curse to be police chief in Richmond right now.

One, there's the pandemic. We've already had a couple of brawls that started when people refused to wear masks where they were obviously needed. Folks are getting cranky.

Two, there's BLM. Nobody believes the woke are going to stop at poor old Wickham. There is a lot of low-hanging fruit around here for those inclined to finally put the Civil War behind us. And in the wake of the woke are the looters, who use a little uproar to do some smash-and-grab.

Three, there's Shorty Cole. Shorty wasn't rousted on L.D.'s watch, but the chief is going to have to clean up the mess.

And, four, whether he knows it or not, he hasn't necessarily cleared the books on that double homicide by arresting Adam Walker. That's where I may have to, as I have so often done in the past, make L.D.'s job a little harder.

I BARELY have time to post something online about the chief's reinstatement when I get a call from Andi.

"She's got it," my daughter says.

"She" is Peggy, her grandmother and my mother.

"It" is COVID-19.

As is often the case, I have not risen to the occasion when the occasion called for it. I meant to call her first thing today about that cough, but then I got caught up in the L.D. Jones saga. Add this to the list of things I'll try to explain should I be called on to defend my sorry ass in the afterlife.

She started feeling sick yesterday, Andi says, and this morning she got Awesome Dude to drive both of them over to a clinic.

She hasn't officially been declared positive, but she's feeling pretty punk right now. She's coughing more than usual, and she can't taste anything.

Yeah, I agree, she's got it.

"What about Awesome?"

"Well, it'd be a damn miracle if he didn't have it. I mean, they're sharing joints, right? For all I know, she got it from him."

The two of them are self-quarantining now, Andi says, and waiting to see if they get sick enough to go to the hospital.

"You all were there yesterday, for that brunch thing, right?"

I admit that we were and explain that the rest of us were mostly outside while Peggy and Awesome stayed in the house.

"And she said it was a cold? And you believed her?"

Not much I can say to that.

"Well, I'm getting her some groceries and going by the drugstore. You might want to check in yourself."

Andi, who is well aware of my shortcomings as a parent, makes it known that she doesn't think much of my performance as a son either.

I drive over to Laurel Street. Peggy comes to the door, then tells me to stand back a little. The interior screen door is between us.

"Why didn't you tell me yesterday?" I ask.

She turns and coughs into the sleeve of the sweater she's wearing despite the fact that it's about ninety degrees outside.

"Hell, I didn't want you to worry," she says. My throat catches a little when I tell her worrying about people you love is kind of a basic requisite of being human.

She is more concerned about the brunch crew catching it than anything else. On the way over, it occurred to me that the rest of us probably should get tested, even though we were mostly separated from Peggy and Awesome.

Since Andi's on the case, there isn't much I can do other than stay and talk awhile. I can hear Awesome coughing in the background. At least Andi, like most of Richmond, is homebound at the moment, doing what work she can by computer. She says she's actually enjoying spending so much time with young William, my grandson, who is supposed to be experiencing kindergarten online. Like that's going to work.

I promise Peggy that I'll come by tomorrow. I tell her to be sure to wear a mask. She asks me what the hell for, and I have no good answer.

I call Cindy, who'll tell Abe, R.J., and her brother, Andy. I am hoping so many things at the same time. I hope to God my aged mother doesn't have this shit. I do not believe her lungs are up to a case of COVID-19. And I hope my wife and friends don't, plus who knows how many other people they've come in contact with today. And, selfish bastard that I am, I hope I don't have it.

Cindy arranges for us to get tested at a site they've set up in the parking lot outside our primary care doc's office.

"I feel awful about this. I should've known," she says. Welcome to the club, I say.

After taking Cindy home, I walk down to the newspaper.

Marcus Green's office is on the way. I stop in to see if he's been visited by one Shorty Cole and also to see if there's any news on Adam Walker. I make sure I'm at least six feet away from Marcus.

He says he visited the jail yesterday. Adam's not faring so well, and Marcus is still hoping to create enough doubt, sympathy, and trust to get some judge to let him post bond.

As for Shorty, I'm told he left an hour ago.

"I remember that shit about him holding somebody hostage at the newspaper," Marcus says. "Is he on the up-and-up? He seems like his head is screwed on right, but you never know."

Not knowing whether it's a plus or a minus, I mention that Shorty has close personal ties with Big Boy Sunday.

"I think they're kind of like brothers-in-law," I say, then try to explain what that means exactly, not mentioning the role Shorty played in avenging the death of Artesian Cole.

"Big Boy Sunday," Marcus says. "Good God. I thought I was through with that character."

Big Boy has given Marcus some business in the past, but I think he makes my favorite ambulance-chaser uneasy at times. Big Boy expects results, and he's a tough grader.

I try to reassure Marcus that Mr. Sunday will not be breathing down his neck on this one, and that I'm pretty sure Shorty is telling the truth about his bad day with Richmond's finest and our banking community.

"Huh. Well, we'll probably go after them then. Sounds like Mr. Cole is entitled to a six-figure apology."

Of which, I note, Green & Ellis will certainly rake in well into five figures.

"We're pro, not pro bono," Marcus reminds me.

I don't even know if I should step into the newsroom.

I call Sally Velez on my cell and have her meet me in the lobby.

After I assure her that I haven't been within six feet of my mother since she became noticeably infected, she says that she thinks she can set me up in one of the conference rooms if I'm careful to wash my hands and wipe down the keyboard when I'm through.

I'm not even being paid to work today, and things have quieted down enough BLM-wise that I probably can make this a quick in-and-out. Whatever I have to check up on can mostly be done from anywhere, including the old home place.

By two I'm out again. Before I leave, though, I do hear back from Rob Solomon down in Raleigh. He's left me an email that said to call him. He's showing a lot of interest in the story, which means he's probably looking to get a good byline out of it, too, for his own paper, assuming there's any story there.

"I looked," he says, "and we didn't do much on the Kellers when they were murdered. Just mentioned that they were from here, who his parents were, and so on.

"Whoever did the story didn't make the connection to that wreck back in 2014. Mostly we used what the AP gave us. We don't have a hell of a lot of institutional memory anymore, since most of the people who've been here long enough to be toilet-trained have either been shit-canned or jumped ship to shill for the people they used to cover."

I hear that. I ask him why he's still there.

"I work cheap," he says, "and I have pictures of the boss."

That'll save you, I tell him, until they change bosses.

"Yeah," he says. "I've thought of that. Well, retiring at sixty wouldn't be so bad. I can still swing a golf club. And Walmart's hiring."

He does have what I need, though: the names and some semblance of addresses for the survivors. The dead driver's mother and father live outside of Durham. The wife and mother, the only one to survive that night, is in an assisted-care place north of Raleigh.

What I want to know is whether there's anybody out there with the anger and the want-to to travel 170 miles and even that six-year-old score.

Solomon knows what I'm thinking, being a nosy-ass reporter himself.

"You're wondering if somebody other than the guy in jail killed the Kellers."

Something like that, I admit.

"Well," he says, "I hope you will be honorable enough to share whatever you find with an old friend."

I tell him that I have the same high hopes for him.

Is there honor among journalists? It depends on how big the story is.

BACK AT the Prestwould, Cindy has called off her tutoring lessons for the day at the Y to ensure that she doesn't pass the virus on to kids who don't need any more bad news.

Speaking of kids reminds her to ask me about Aurora.

"Aurora?"

A sigh emanates from my beloved.

"Aurora. Keller? The little girl whose parents were murdered?"

I tell her that I'm not sure. "Next time I talk to Peachy, I'll ask her if she knows anything."

"What a terrible thing, being left all alone like that," Cindy says, stroking the very compliant Rags as she says it. Butterball doesn't even appear to be jealous.

Using the names Solomon gave me, I start trying to track down the kin of that family wiped out in that 2014 wreck.

According to Google Maps, Booker and Carlotta Rose live in the northwestern part of Durham. Not all that far from Duke University.

I find a phone number, but nobody answers when I call, as if anybody ever answers a home phone anymore. I don't even have the option of leaving a message. Well, it isn't that far to Durham, although I'd like to know if I'm plague-free before making that trip, for my sake and everyone else's. But I'm starting to ask myself if I'm not reading too much into this. Then I try to imagine that clueless kid I saw in the city lockup tying two people up and then executing them. Jeanette said he doesn't even know how to shoot a gun.

Whoever killed William and Susan Keller, I can't convince myself that Adam did the deed.

Without much to do that won't potentially endanger the populace, Cindy and I go for a walk through the Fan. So far, I've been hit-or-miss about wearing a mask outdoors, but this morning's news convinces me to err, for once, on the side of caution.

It's hot and muggy, and the walk only succeeds in depressing me. We go past joints we loved that are closed, or the ones where you can stand outside the door like a beggar and have somebody pass food to you. And the ones that depend on bars to break even? Forget about it. We wonder how many of them will be able to survive weeks or months without some paying sit-down customers. We get as far as Joe's before turning around and walking back to our little quarantine love nest.

We see Fred and Louise Baron in the lobby as we return and make it for the elevator without them seeing us. Somehow we feel like we're untouchables. I've seen this before, in other people. You read the obituaries, and it's obvious from the details that the deceased was felled by COVID-19, but it's never mentioned. I find myself wondering what Peggy's obit will say, and then I stop myself from dwelling on worst possible scenarios.

Cindy chastises me for checking in at the office on a rare semi-off day, after I've already filed a story on the return of L.D. Jones, but I can't help myself.

I get Leighton Byrd, who tells me that some Confederate-loving citizens on Monument Avenue have gotten an injunction to save Robert E. Lee from the monument graveyard. I guess the governor should have had him taken down in the middle of the night. Asking forgiveness usually works better than seeking permission.

There's a move afoot to defund the police, which Leighton says isn't really as bad as it sounds. It sounds bad, I tell her. Can't they come up with a better verb than "defund"? Much of the white population will have visions of marauding gangs of Blacks raping and pillaging unfettered in their neighborhoods. The cops, meanwhile, have a great proposal. They're going to be more diligent about self-reviewing. "Your Honor, we find ourselves not guilty.

Again." I wonder if they cooked that up before L.D. got his office back.

Meanwhile city council votes tonight on whether to give emergency powers to the mayor, who probably wishes he had the emergency power to shoot L.D. Jones on sight.

The chief, facing demands to neuter his troops and a cynical citizenry somewhat leery of law enforcement self-reviewing, must wonder if it was worth it to save that recording.

CHAPTER TWELVE

Tuesday, June 8

To quarantine or not to quarantine.

We're pretty sure we don't have the virus, but who the hell knows? We have been told that we could know for sure as early as this afternoon whether we're positive. Abe, R.P., and Andy all assure me they've been swabbed as well.

Wheelie and Sarah are fine with me keeping my ass out of the office. Hell, they're more than fine.

"If you try to enter the building," Wheelie says, "I'll have the guard shoot you."

I'm pretty sure he is kidding, but just in case, I'll do what work I can at home. Maybe, I tell my bosses, I'll be able to come in for night cops.

It's not like I'm the only one working remotely. Word is that the powers that be soon will tell all the reporters to vacate the newsroom, either for safety's sake or to save electricity. It won't be much different than it is now, with everyone forced to take unpaid furlough for a couple of weeks (pick a week, any week) between now and the end of next month.

Two of the great pleasures of newspapering that made it easier to abide shitty hours and the knowledge that you were never going to get rich: newsroom camaraderie and after-work bar society. We are 0-for-2 these days.

I call Peachy to see if she has any word on how the little girl, Aurora, is doing. Might make a good story, I'm thinking.

"She's fine," Peachy says. "She was here yesterday."

It turns out that Peachy, who also is working from home part of the time, somehow arranged to keep Aurora for a while until the state figures out what to do with her.

"Do you know anything about, like, changing diapers? Do you know how to feed her?"

She calls me an asshole and reminds me that she is the oldest in a family of six kids.

"I was changing diapers when I was seven."

She says the baby might wonder about why she doesn't have a mommy and daddy anymore "but kids are resilient. At least, I hope so."

It's the second time she's been orphaned, Peachy says. Her birth mother let her go not long after she was born.

"Have they tried to get in touch with the mother?" I ask.

Peachy snorts.

"She gave her away once. Why the hell would they see if she wanted a second chance?"

I drive over to Peggy's. Andi is leaving as I park.

"How are they doing?"

"Not too good," my daughter says. "I wish I knew what to do. How do you know when they're sick enough to take them to the hospital?"

Nobody seems to know the answer to that one, although just about everybody appears to think that a hospital is about the worst damn place you could be if you've got the virus, to be avoided as long as you can breathe.

Andi says she's been tested, that she went as soon as she realized Peggy and Awesome were sick.

"I had to get William tested, too, because he was with me."

Peggy comes to the door. She seems about the same as yesterday. I tell her I'll get her whatever she needs, and to be sure to stay inside.

"Hell, I know that," she says. "Even Awesome knows that."

The Dude has spent the bulk of his adult life in a semi-homeless state, only rescued from camping out under the bridge by my mother's generosity. He likes to roam, but Peggy assures me she has him under control.

"Thank God," she says, "for cable."

She says she wishes she had made a will. Since Peggy's estate is probably in the low four figures, that isn't a major concern, although I keep that to myself.

I lie that Cindy and I already know we're negative. She looks doubtful, but then she starts hacking and wheezing and kind of forgets about it. She promises she'll tell me if it gets worse, although neither of us knows exactly how to define "worse."

L.D. Jones takes my call. He is already in midseason form, giving me hell for making Shorty Cole famous.

"That guy's a troublemaker," he says. "You ought to know that, after that hostage thing at the paper."

Even troublemakers don't deserve to be rousted for trying to make a deposit at the bank, I reply.

"Well, now that damn Marcus Green is all over us. Like we need any more bad news."

He does admit, off the record, that he doesn't know what the fuck the two officers who responded to the alleged robbery in progress were thinking, although he had plenty of spleen left to vent on the idiot bank teller.

Our readers have gotten quite a kick out of that story. The letters to the editor, even the ones from our redder outlying counties, seem to be able to see that Shorty Cole had reason to be a mite pissed, although some of them saw it as humorous as well as outrageous. Leighton tells me somebody had a sign last night that said, "Justice for Shorty," as if he'd been murdered by cops like that guy up in Minnesota.

I ask the chief if his minions are looking into any alternative theories about the Kellers' murders. He says they're exploring all the possibilities, whatever the hell that means. He doesn't seem too impressed when I tell him the latest I've learned about that six-year-old car wreck down in Carolina.

"Just leave the policing to us," L.D. says. "We've got enough problems without you stirring up more shit."

That's my job, I explain.

I CALL Rob Solomon in Raleigh and tell him that it looks like I'm going to have to drive down there if I want to find out any more about the star-crossed Rose family.

Rob, it turns out, has done some digging on his own, no doubt hoping to get a piece of this story.

He's found out, using sources from other reporters at his paper, the names of a couple of relatives he didn't know about yesterday.

"Here's the cool part," he says. "Booker Rose has a cousin who works in our pressroom. I'm going to interview the cousin today."

Would it be possible, I ask, with my fingers crossed, for me to speak with this gentleman?

"Well, actually, she's a lady. A lady pressman. Presswoman, I guess. I'll see what I can do."

I tell Solomon more than I have previously, including all the details about that door the cops never checked, plus what I know about the alleged killer.

"So he's your first wife's second son? Damn, Willie, you do get around."

I assure Rob that I'm not biased by this loose family connection, but that every instinct I have tells me the kid's no killer.

He says he'll be back in touch sometime after three.

In the interim, Big Boy Sunday calls because he wants to talk about Shorty's big adventure.

"I hear that fella Green is on it," Big Boy says. "I told Shorty to get him."

As usual, he sounds like he is in a car being chauffeured somewhere, no doubt by a future if not present felon youth. He is, also as usual, eating something as he talks.

"That wadn't right, what they did to Shorty," Big Boy says between bites. "I mean, if they'd been at the right place at the right time, they coulda hung him on this or that, know what I mean. But the man was just trying to do his business."

If it's any consolation, I tell my sometimes source, Shorty Cole is probably going to get a nice present from the bank and/or the police department.

"He could use a little green," Big Boy says. "Green from Green. Heh-heh."

I groan and tell Mr. Sunday to keep in touch.

CINDY GETS us a Philly cheesesteak with onion rings from the Bamboo. I'd prefer one Philly cheesesteak each, but one of the negatives of being married is having someone remind you that you aren't nineteen anymore and perhaps should eat accordingly.

Still she gives me the bigger half, rejecting my contention that halves are by definition the same size.

Around three thirty, Solomon calls again. He's already spoken with the pressroom relative of the Roses, who says that she would be willing to talk to me during her break, about seven. He gives me her number.

"What did you find out?" I ask.

"Well, she says she doesn't see her Uncle Booker and Aunt Carlotta that often, but she does know that they felt they were well and properly screwed by the legal system. Looking at what I dug up on the trial, I'm inclined to agree. There was suspicion on their part that race might have played some role in the judge's ruling."

"Or money."

"Yeah, there is that too. The lawyer the Kellers hired has been known to work wonders if he's paid well enough."

I know a guy like that, I tell Rob.

"It wouldn't surprise me," he says, "if the judge and Jacob Keller were members of the same club."

FIVE MINUTES after seven, I call the cell number Rob gave me. The woman who answers, Cilla Washington, says she'll tell me what she knows, as long as I don't use her name. I assure her that this is all off the record.

She tells me what she told Solomon, that Booker and Carlotta Rose are very bitter about the way things played out, justice-wise.

She also assures me that the Roses, who are their daughter-in-law's guardians, have gotten an undisclosed chunk of change from the Kellers' insurance company, "but most of that goes toward taking care of her." Poor

Marva, who lost her husband and children is, Cilla says, living "if you can call it that" in a nursing home that takes most of what the family got from the insurance settlement "plus her Social Security."

"Uncle Booker and Aunt Carlotta were named guardians because Marva's sorry-ass mother, who lives up in Maryland somewhere, acts like she doesn't even have a daughter, although now she's making noises about getting some of that lawsuit money."

The Roses try to visit their daughter-in-law "just about every day," Cilla says, but they already have a pretty full plate. They have six other offspring in various states of need, along with sixteen grandchildren "and some of them are always living with them."

Hairston Rose, their late son, was Cilla's first cousin. She says he was a hard-working family man who didn't drink "except once in a while" and was devoted to his wife and kids.

"Everybody was just tore up about it," she says, "but there wasn't nothin' anybody could do. We all thought that Keller guy got off pretty light though."

She says she didn't know about the Kellers' murders until Rob Solomon told her.

"It's not nice to say it," she says, "but maybe what goes around comes around, you know?"

I tell her about Adam Walker. I tell her why I think somebody else might have killed the Kellers, and I ask her if she thinks anybody in the Rose family was angry enough to have maybe tried to give justice a helping hand.

"You mean, like go up there to Richmond and kill 'em? Mister, we don't play that way. I'm not saying those people got what they deserved, especially the wife, who I understand wasn't even in the car when it happened, but maybe it all evens out in the end.

"We obey the law, even when we think it's given us a raw deal. We're used to raw deals."

I assure her that I'm not trying to besmirch the good name of the Rose family and ask her to please call me if she thinks or hears of anybody who might have gotten homicidally mad at the system.

Cilla has heard about the recent ruckuses in Richmond.

"I was up there one time, when my daddy visited an old cousin of ours. I was just a little girl, but I remember those big old statues of those rebel generals and all. I can see why some folks might want to see that stuff come down.

"No offense. I mean, maybe you want 'em to stay up."

I don't usually play the race card, which in my case is probably the two of clubs, but I make an exception.

"So your daddy was Black," Cilla says. "Well, then I reckon you know what I'm talking about."

She says she has to go, having used most of her thirty-minute dinner break talking to me.

I give her my number, and she promises that she'll give me a call if she thinks of anything.

I HAVE defied orders and good sense and come to the paper, promising that I will quarantine myself in one of the conference rooms.

You'd think Tuesday night would be an off night, riot-wise. Other than the happy revelation that the governor is letting Richmonders have indoor dining in restaurants again starting Friday, the night is pretty news-free, until it isn't.

Around eight thirty, Sally, who lives over near the Carillon and Byrd Park, gets a call from one of her neighbors, who says all hell is breaking loose.

She calls me in the conference room.

"My neighbor says they're tearing down one of the statues."

"What the hell kind of statues do they have around Byrd Park?"

I thought I knew where all the paeans to Dixie were.

"They tore down Columbus," Sally says.

I'm trying to remember which obscure Confederate she's referring to when it hits me.

"Christopher Columbus? How the fuck did he get mixed up in all this?"

I am advised to get off my butt and go find out. Chip Grooms in photo has the bad luck to still be in the building after dark, so he gets volunteered to come along with me. Aware of my current status as a pariah, he says he'll take his own car.

When we get there, we find that the mob that has been spreading through the city like a human coronavirus has landed at Byrd Park.

The statue stood, until about the time Sally got that call, at the south end of what has for the last couple of years been Arthur Ashe Boulevard, near some tennis courts where Arthur wasn't allowed to play in his youth, as he was not of the Caucasian persuasion. Even when Richmond does change, it is hard for us not to be ironic.

So there's old Chris, lying on the ground and looking as lost as Wickham did on Saturday. From what I can gather, it didn't take a Herculean effort. A few protesters used three ropes to bring the statue down.

One guy who admitted, or bragged, through his mask that he was involved in the take-down, said it wasn't planned. However, egged on by a crowd chanting "Tear it down," he and others obliged.

The cops, from what I can gather, were not in the mood to intervene. Perhaps feeling a bit sulky about all the shit they've been getting for overreacting, they underreacted.

"This land is Powhatan land," I hear one voice shout in the crowd. I wonder how Custalow, who is Mattaponi but also has a fair claim on a piece of the North American continent, feels about this.

The city changed Columbus Day to Indigenous Peoples Day last year, but I guess I'd never given much thought to how uninspired certain ethnic groups are when they hear about Columbus "discovering" their ancestors and telling everybody back in Europe about this neat place they could steal.

Grooms gets some pretty good shots of the vigilantes dragging poor Chris over to Byrd Lake, where they send him to a watery grave amid cheers and jeers. Lying amidst the goose crap there, he does look kind of sad.

The crowd is feeling pretty full of itself now, and some of the group seem to want to continue the rampage elsewhere, but the Columbus statue was pretty far from Monument Avenue. Most of the assembled multitude drifts off, feeling they've done their good deed for the night.

WHAT WITH our early deadlines, we're only able to get the bare bones of a story in tomorrow's paper, filed from my laptop in our study, along with a shot Grooms got of the drowned statue.

"What next?" Sally asks, when I call after I've filed. "Jefferson? Washington? How about Lincoln. They've got a nice statue of old Abe over by the Civil War museum."

I advise her to keep that thought to herself.

I write a longer version of Columbus's downfall for our online readers, because the freeloaders definitely deserve to get more thorough reporting than our dwindling faithful print subscribers. As I rant about this for about the millionth time, Sally reminds me that we do have a pay wall.

From what I'm seeing, I tell her, that wall works pretty well. Nobody much seems willing to kick in a few bucks to scale it.

I've already sent my story when my phone channels Marvin Gaye.

Cilla Washington, off her shift in the Raleigh paper's pressroom, has thought of something.

"I hope I didn't wake you up," she says. I assure her that she hasn't.

What Cilla thought of was Marva Rose's brother.

"This might not be nothing," she says. I wait for it. How many times have those words led me to something indeed?

Marva's brother has been something of a train wreck, according to Cilla. He's spent most of his adult life and much of his juvenile one before that as a ward of one state or another.

"He's about twenty-nine, I think, but I'm not sure. Anyhow, he got busted for breaking-and-entering several years ago, maybe a year before the accident, up there in Virginia. Martinsville, I think."

He got a fifteen-year sentence, which in Virginia is pretty much a fifteen-year sentence. We don't cotton to Commie liberal practices like early release in these parts.

"You asked me if anybody was mad enough about what happened to Marva and Hairston and the kids to do something about it. Well, Juwan, from what I know, he's kind of like that."

Juwan Chavis got in a bit of trouble shortly after William Keller's trial when he wrote a letter from the Southampton prison to the judge who gave Keller a slap on the wrist. It did not compliment the judge on his fairness.

"He said he was going to get even, although he didn't say how. Got him in some trouble, from what I hear. Might even have added some time to his sentence. I didn't think much about that when you asked me who'd be mad enough to, you know, do something. I mean, we only knew about it because one of my husband's brothers who lives in Petersburg read about it in the Richmond paper.

"But that was, what, six years ago? So I didn't pay it much mind. But after we talked, I remembered that Juwan isn't locked up anymore."

"Wait. He's still got some more time to serve, right?"

Not exactly. It turns out that the prosecutor who convicted Juwan had a habit of being a little too eager to see justice served. Some digging by the Southern Poverty Law Center revealed that he had withheld evidence that might have helped the defense in several cases.

"Including Juwan's," I guess.

"Right. So he's out awaiting a new trial. I know because he wrote a letter to Marva, telling her he was out, and her letters come to Uncle Booker. Aunt Carlotta had to read it to her, because Marva is more or less brain-dead, and Aunt Carlotta told me about it."

He's been out of prison for about a month, Cilla says.

"And nobody knows where he is?"

"Nobody wants to know," she says. "The guy's bad news. Other than Marva, that whole damn family's bad news. We haven't heard anything since that one letter."

Juwan Chavis is not supposed to leave the state of Virginia until his new trial.

"Did the letter say anything about settling old scores?"

"Not that I heard, and I think Carlotta would have said. Like I told you, it might be nothing. He wrote that letter to the judge six years ago. Time heals all wounds, isn't that the expression?"

Yeah, I say, but sometimes it just makes them fester.

I write the guy's name down so I can follow up tomorrow. Maybe Juwan Chavis is sitting fat and happy in Martinsville, awaiting his new trial.

Or not.

I'M HOME by midnight. Cindy and Abe are both still up, watching some flick on Turner Classic Movies that, from what I can see, I was lucky to miss.

I fill them in on the Columbus caper. They missed the eleven o'clock news, so it's news to them.

I ask Custalow what his thoughts are about Christopher Columbus.

"Man," says my lifetime friend, shaking his head, "I guess his time had come, but my folks have been pissed on by so many people in the last five hundred years that old Chris wasn't high on my list."

It's about as close as I've ever seen Abe come to airing a grievance.

"Who's next?" Cindy asks.

"Who knows?" I answer.

CHAPTER THIRTEEN

Wednesday, June 10

The story on Christopher Columbus's demise doesn't elicit that much outrage when I check out the comments online.

Most of those decrying last night's political statement or vandalism, choose one, seem to be of Italian descent. One of them points out, correctly, that Italian Americans weren't really considered white by the old guard here when the statue was erected. The donors wanted it to go on Monument Avenue, but it was determined by the Daughters of the Confederacy among others that old Chris wasn't quite Caucasian enough to merit that honor.

Those cheering Columbus's watery grave seem to have some Native American blood, not uncommon in a part of the state where two tribes, the Mattaponi and the Pamunkey, have reservations a short drive away.

The aging but sizable contingent that still mourns all the white unhappiness that followed Appomattox is strangely quiet on the subject, seeing Columbus as somebody else's ox getting gored, I guess.

Over breakfast, I tell Cindy what I've learned about Juwan Chavis.

"And all you've got is a letter he wrote some judge six years ago?"

I tell her that I'm going to dig a little deeper.

"Good luck," she says. From her tone, she thinks I'll need it.

She says she hopes we finally hear something today about our coronavirus status.

"Were you keeping six feet from everybody last night?" she asks.

"As much as I could."

"Was everybody there wearing a mask?"

I lie and say that almost everyone was. How is it possible to have a decent interview with young rioters when you both are mumbling through those damn masks that cut off much-needed oxygen to my addled brain?

I call Marcus Green. He's out, but Kate fills me in on what's going on at Green & Ellis, or at least the part that concerns me.

Marcus is pursuing the suit that hasn't been filed yet on behalf of Shorty Cole.

"Do you feel guilty for shaking down a cash-strapped city for a few million bucks that might be spent on, say, new schools or making sure roads don't have potholes deep enough to swallow my Honda?" I ask.

"In the first place," she says, "it'll probably be maybe a couple of hundred thousand instead of millions. Mr. Cole did not suffer serious injury, just emotional trauma. Thank God he didn't reach in his pocket for his keys or his wallet.

"In the second place, stupid deserves to be rewarded. And the bank is the one that's really going to take it up the butt. Your heart doesn't bleed for banks, does it, Willie?"

I'm just jerking her chain. When we were married, it was one of my favorite pastimes. Occasionally she did not find it amusing.

She's buried the lede, though, as we say in the newsroom. The real news is about Adam Walker.

"They did what?" I ask, raising my voice ever so slightly.

Marcus has managed to get a judge to set bail for Adam. Kate says her partner in life and law emphasized how dangerous it was for the kid to be locked up with other prisoners who might be inclined to think the murder of the Kellers was racially motivated, and that keeping him in a solitary cell was cruel and unusual.

"He also pointed out that the police didn't exactly cover all the bases there. You know, that unlocked door and all. And the question about twelve minutes being long enough to do the deed."

He is probably being released into his parents' custody about now, Kate says.

"I think they put up their home as collateral."

When I call the Walkers, Glenn Junior answers and says his parents are out. There's not a lot of Uber business in the midst of a plague, and it sounds like he's been drinking, although it's only a little after ten in the morning.

He doesn't volunteer any other information and seems a little dickish. I ask him if he knows about his brother's impending release.

"Yeah," he says. "I heard."

"So that's where your folks are?"

A pause.

"Yeah. The little nutcase is coming home, I guess."

I thank him for being so forthcoming. He hangs up.

I CONFIRM that Adam is out on bail and post something on the website.

Sarah Goodnight is in when I call to alert the newsroom.

"Well, that's a surprise," she says. "Any word yet on whether you're Typhoid Willie or not?"

I tell her maybe today, perhaps in time for me to do night cops.

"Well, don't push it," she says. "We'd just as soon you didn't infect the whole newsroom."

I tell her I'm much more worried about my seventy-eight-year-old mother and thank her for her concern.

"Oh, you know what I mean. Hell, even if you got it, you're too mean to die."

"I'm also sixty damn years old, and I've smoked about a million Camels over the past fifty years."

"Huh," she says. "Let me do the math. Two packs a day, 365 days a year . . ." She's quiet for a few seconds. "Nah, I figure you've smoked maybe 700,000 Camels, tops. You're good to go."

I thank her for clarifying that and tell her what I've learned so far about alternative theories regarding the Keller murders.

She, like Cindy, wishes me good luck.

L.D. Jones, when I contact him, doesn't seem energized about the facts surrounding Juwan Chavis.

"So he threatened some judge six years ago, and that's supposed to be his motive for killing two people?"

I reiterate that Chavis hasn't really had an opportunity to wreak revenge before now.

"Maybe," I add, "he's not a forgive-and-forget kind of guy."

The chief is not very happy that Adam Walker is out on bail now.

"If he'd been Black and done that," L.D. says, "you can bet your ass he'd not be breathing free air again."

If Adam had been Black, I suggest, he might not even have made it to the city jail after allegedly killing two white people.

"Meaning what?"

The chief knows exactly what I mean. Can you say "George Floyd"? But being one-and-a-half African Americans between us, we let it go at that.

"Call me when you've got some real information," L.D. says. I tell him not to worry about that "unless you read it in the paper first."

He does not wish me good luck. The chief has other things on his mind right now, like keeping Richmond from making the national news every night.

WHEN I stop by, Peggy and Awesome are both ailing, but my mother says they're not sick enough to go to the Virginia Commonwealth University Medical Center, which everyone over fifty in Richmond still calls Medical College of Virginia.

"People die in that place," she says. She's probably right, because most of them don't get to the big teaching hospital until everything else has failed. But with COVID-19 really starting to get everyone's attention, death tolls mounting and ventilators in short supply, people are being encouraged to ride it out until they can't.

I know Peggy's scared, because I can't even smell marijuana as I talk to her through the screen door. My mom probably hasn't been straight this long in decades. Do cold-turkey dope smokers have withdrawal symptoms? She says Andi is checking in on her every couple of hours "more than she ought to, if you ask me."

She asks me how I'm doing, and I tell her, again, that I've been declared virus-free, something I hope will be confirmed sometime soon.

THE LAST thing I need to be doing right now is driving across the state, potentially spreading disease and death.

Fortunately I know people. As a journalist of a certain age, in a business where people can live nomadic existences, I have my contacts, including one in Martinsville, where it is presumed Mr. Chavis resides.

Ella Minopee was one of the best columnists we've had at the paper in my tenure. She wasn't afraid to get her fingernails dirty. She found something to like about people nobody else wanted to touch with a ten-foot pole, and she made the readers see why she liked them. And she made you laugh. She said she got her sense of humor from her mother, who thought it would be funny to name her only daughter in such a way that, when you pronounced her name, it sounded like the twelfth through sixteenth letters of the alphabet. This sounded like child abuse to me, but Ella thought it was funny and never changed "Ella" to Susan or Rachel. Her column was called Alphabet Soup.

Ella drank a bit. She could out-guzzle any of the men who liked to hit the bars or go to one another's houses after work. She couldn't have weighed more than 120 pounds, but she drank above her weight.

I've tempted fate as much as Ella ever did, and I have paid the price for not always being as sober as an upstanding newspaperman should be, but demon alcohol never pulled me all the way down, the way it did Ella. Luck of the draw. When sober, Ella was much more disciplined than I ever was.

Back then management didn't do much intervening when it saw the trolley coming off the tracks. She disappeared for a week or more a couple of times, and whoever was managing editor always forgave her and told her to stop drinking, similar to telling a cancer patient to make the tumor go away.

Finally it came to a head one January fifteen years ago. They sent Ella to Florida for two weeks to do columns on what people did in the winter when they didn't need rock salt and snow shovels to survive. It was a sweet deal, but she screwed it up.

About the fifth day down there, she disappeared. By the time she resurfaced, she had lost the company car and wasn't sure exactly where the fuck she was.

They found the car, eventually, trashed outside Fort Lauderdale. She'd left the keys in it, gone into a beachside bar, and woken up in some guy's room three days later. Having "dated" Ella a time or three and shared many fifths of bourbon, I felt for her.

By the time she found her way back to Richmond, she discovered that managing editors didn't find black-out drunks amusing anymore. Ella was, at the tender age of forty-five and twice divorced, told to get some help and given plenty of time to do so, being rendered unemployed.

She disappeared for a while. To our shame, we didn't try hard enough to find her. Then, about a decade ago, she resurfaced in Martinsville, where an acquaintance who remembered her from better days hired her to write columns and also to mentor the young folks. At a paper that size, most of the folks were young. Most would either move to larger papers or take flack jobs before they turned thirty and had to think about mortgages.

And, against all odds, she thrived. I see her every year or so at Virginia Press Association awards banquets, where she inevitably is the biggest fish in her tiny pond of columnists at small dailies. It pains me a little to see her, remembering what a beauty she once was. On the other hand, my mirror asks who among us has aged well?

She claimed, last time I saw her, that she'd been sober for a decade, and I believed her.

So I put in a call to Ella Minopee.

She knows all about Juwan Chavis's unexpected release from prison.

"It was a pretty big deal around here," she says. "Some of the folks he burgled still live here. They're not too damn happy, as you can imagine."

I explain the possible link between Chavis and the Kellers.

"Yeah, I remember reading something about that double murder, but there's so much shit going on in Richmond that I kind of forgot about it."

She says it won't be that difficult to check on Chavis's whereabouts.

"It ain't that big a town."

She says she'll call me back later.

We talk a little about old times. She says that she has a boyfriend now.

"He's recovering too. We kind of keep an eye on each other."

She asks me if I'm staying on the straight and narrow.

I tell her that my path does not wind quite as much as it once did.

"You know," she says, "I still miss it. Every damn time I go to a wedding reception or pass a liquor store, I hear the devil calling my name."

Before we both hang up, she says, "Tell you the truth, Willie, I kind of wish I'd caught you between wives, if you know what I mean. Of course we might both be dead now if I had."

A LITTLE before three, Cindy gets a call. I hear her talking in the living room.

A couple of minutes later, she comes into the study.

"All clear," she says.

So I call the paper and give them the good news. I am at least temporarily virus-free. Chuck Apple probably is happy to be spared one more night on the police beat.

I let Andi know. She has just gotten back from her grandmother's and says neither Peggy nor Awesome is doing that great "but the doctor I talked to said she thought they probably were better staying where they are."

Jeanette calls to thank me for anything I might have done to get Adam temporarily out of jail. I let her know that I might have some more good news sometime soon, but not to get her hopes up just yet.

She says Adam's kind of nervous, even for him. She said he went for a walk in the woods back of their house an hour ago.

"Glenn's a little worried, about the house as collateral for the bail and all, but what are you going to do? He's our son."

I reach Marcus Green. We compare notes on what he knows and what I've found, most of which my ex has passed along to him already anyhow.

"The commonwealth's attorney ain't going to want to let this one drop unless there's rock-solid proof the boy didn't do it," he says. "The boy definitely seemed happy to be out from behind bars though."

Around eight thirty, Ella Minopee calls me back.

"He's gone," she says.

"Gone where?"

"Nobody knows, or nobody's willing to admit it if they do."

When Juwan Chavis was released from jail, he went to live with an uncle of his who lived outside Martinsville. Ella found the address and took a drive out there today. The uncle was there, but Juwan wasn't.

"His uncle said he wouldn't let Juwan use his car, so he called a taxi. Uber's not all that big down here. And then the uncle got a call from Juwan, who said he was taking off for a while to get his head on straight. Said he was going to visit his sister in that nursing home and then see a couple of other folks."

She says he left two weeks ago, on May 27.

Without a car, I asked Ella, how was he taking off?

"I'm getting to that," she said. "See, I know the guy that runs the only taxi service in town, and he was willing to put me in touch with the driver who picked up Juwan."

When Ella contacted the taxi driver, he told her where he deposited his fare—at the only car-rental place in town.

"I don't know how he even had the money to rent a car," she says. "Maybe he's broken into somebody else's house since he got out. Hell, it's the only life skill he seems to have mastered."

"So he rented a car."

"Yeah, and here's the good part. My boyfriend has a cousin who works the counter at the rental joint. They aren't supposed to give out information like this, but, you know, family being family, the cousin gave Harold the license number and make of the car Juwan rented. The cousin is a little worried that they might not see that Sonata again."

Ella gives me the information, which she says she's also passing on to law enforcement in her neck of the woods, without revealing her source.

"They're going to owe me big time for this," she says.

I tell her that I'm going to give that same information to the cops in Richmond.

"So you think he might actually have gone up there and killed those people?"

I'm not sure of anything, I tell her, but I'd like to find out.

Before we conclude our call, I think to ask her something else.

"The uncle he's staying with. Did you ask him if he ever mentioned his sister, and the accident and all?"

"Oh, yes," she says. "The uncle said he talks about it all the time. He said he's still pretty pissed about what happened."

Ella makes me promise to let her know what if anything I find out up here. It looks like I'm going to have to share the glory on this one, if it pans out, three ways.

When I try to reach L.D., he's out of the loop, probably trying to put out one of the metaphorical and sometimes actual dumpster fires that keep popping up. I leave a message about Juwan Chavis and the rental car on his cell phone, which is either turned off or he can't hear it or he sees my number and chooses to ignore me.

Working back, I know now that Chavis left his uncle's home in that rental car three days before the Kellers were found murdered. I know he was once pissed enough over William Keller's skating on manslaughter charges to threaten a judge, from prison. I know he's still pissed. What nobody knows is where Chavis was on the 29th, and where he is now.

I call Rob Solomon in Raleigh. He remembers Ella from his days at the paper here but didn't know she had landed sober in Martinsville.

"It'd be something if the three of us were able to break this," he says. "Kind of like a reunion, you know. We'll have to share a bottle of champagne. Well, maybe you could drink Ella's share."

He says he's found the judge who was threatened six years ago. The judge says he never got any more letters from Chavis "but he did seem a little shaken up when I told him that the guy was out awaiting a new trial and nobody knows where he is."

I ask him if it would be possible for him to check at the nursing home where Marva Rose is being warehoused, to see if she's had any visitors other than the Rose family.

I HAVE to get off the phone because Sally Velez has sent me an email:

"Adios, Jeff Davis."

The BLM crew has stepped up its game.

Where Davis Avenue crosses Monument, there stood the Jefferson Davis Memorial, honoring the Confederacy's one and only president. While some revere old Jeff, some of us think he was a lucky son of a bitch. Many folks who lead an armed rebellion against their country get invited to a necktie party. Davis died at eighty-one, twenty-four years after the war ended, but his monument ran out of luck tonight. Hell with the chief.

When I get to Davis and Monument, or as close as I can get in the aged Honda, there's a whiff of tear gas in the air, and Jefferson Davis's statue is lying on the ground, its feet higher than its head. The rest of the monument is still there, with Vindicatrix, goddess of payback, atop the pedestal. As with Columbus, it wasn't that hard to pull Jeff down. Vindicatrix, whose name Ray Long once said sounds like a particularly rough S&M madam, looks pissed.

There are the usual whoops from the newly empowered, the ones who aren't trying to rinse tear gas out of their eyes. I spy my old flatfoot buddy Gillespie standing at the base of what's left of the monument. Like most of the cops there, he seems to be equal parts irritated and perplexed.

"Jesus Christ," he says when he recognizes me in time to not Tase me. "What did we do to them?"

I mentioned the tear gas. He claims that was a defensive action, although the multiracial crowd here might disagree.

By midnight, a tow truck has come and hauled Jefferson Davis away. This late, most of what I can write is for online consumption.

It isn't hard to see where this is going. Little-known Confederate general. Italian explorer. President of the rebel nation. J.E.B. Stuart and Stonewall Jackson are within eyesight. Looking down the street, I can see a crowd already gathering around the Robert E. Lee Monument, which now sports all the colors of the graffiti rainbow and on which "fuck" is used as several different parts of speech.

How long, Marse Robert? How long?

CHAPTER FOURTEEN

Thursday, June 11

Maybe the most amazing thing that happened yesterday was that NASCAR got woke.

Well, the stock-car racing folks aren't fully up-and-at-'em, but they are wiping the sleep from their eyes and greeting a new morning.

NASCAR yesterday asked its fans to stop bringing Confederate flags to races. This probably will boost rebel flag sales, the stock-car fans being a rowdy lot that doesn't like to be told what to do, but it took some stones for the brass to make the effort. Next thing you know, they'll be banning beer coolers.

Sarah says Bootie Carmichael is writing a column for tomorrow's sports pages that will try to defend the Stars and Bars as a harmless part of "our Southern heritage."

"Maybe not everybody's Southern heritage," I reply.

"I know. I know. I'm trying to gently talk him out of it. I don't want to be censoring our columnists, even the ones who have their heads up their asses so far you can't see their necks anymore."

"At least he let you know ahead of time. Did I tell you about the time he wrote that column about lesbian golfers?"

"Oh, shit. Before my time, but we still get a letter now and then about it."

It is possible that Bootie, who predates even me at the paper, has not kept up with the times. His popularity among our readers slipped a little the last time we could afford a readership survey.

Maybe, I suggest, Bootie just wants somebody to talk him out of setting his ass on fire again.

Sarah says she'll do her best to fill that role.

THE CHIEF never got back to me last night, so I call him at nine.

Maybe because he knows he blew me off, he consents to talk.

"Can I come by?" I ask. "I'm COVID-free. I won't give you cooties."

He says he is expecting another busy day. I promise I won't suck away more than fifteen minutes of it.

His office is a mess, which is surprising. L.D., unlike me, is a neat freak. Usually everything on his desk seems to be at right angles. L.D. has done a stint as a marine.

Today there are three or four sticky notes stuck to the pad on his desk, several papers lie askew on its surface, and there's a coffee stain on the newspaper he was reading.

"You all are kicking us when we're down," he says, pointing to the photo on A1 of a cop who's dressed like he's expecting World War III spraying a young demonstrator.

"Did we doctor the photo?"

"Hell, I don't know. I wouldn't put it past you bastards. But you took it out of context."

"How so?"

He explains that the officer who got famous had just been called a "motherfucking pig" by the sprayee, who then spat on him.

"And you believe the guy?"

"I always trust my people," the chief says.

I mention that nobody I know can be trusted all the time, especially when it's not in the person's best interest to tell the truth.

"Hey," L.D. says, "I've heard what those assholes are calling us. Sometimes you've just had enough."

I tell him that I can't promise that our photographers will treat the police more kindly in the future, especially after one of them got his own face sprayed three nights ago.

The chief sighs. He picks up one of the Post-its, looks at it, and then wads it up and throws it into the trash.

"Maybe our fuckin' mayor did me a favor when he suspended me," he says. "When he took me back, I should have told him to shove it up his political ass."

I know L.D. doesn't mean it. Policing is all he's done since he got out of college and the marines, back in the day when we still played pickup basketball against each other.

"I need to let you know something," I say, hoping to change the subject.

"What?"

So I give him everything I learned yesterday about Juwan Chavis, how he went missing two days before the Kellers were murdered, how he's out there somewhere, presumably with a rental car, of which I have the make and license-plate info.

I've even gotten Ella Minopee to email me an attachment JPEG of Chavis's likeness, which I have sent to the chief.

He checks his email and finds it.

"That's all interesting," he says, "but what does it prove? I mean maybe the guy just decided to skip town.

From what you said, whatever retrial he gets probably won't keep his ass out of prison."

He says that Adam Walker still looks pretty good to him as the killer, even if the judge did set him free momentarily.

I suggest that it might still be a good idea if the cops were put on notice that a guy with a big-time grudge against the Kellers was loose for the first time since his sister's life and family were destroyed six years ago.

He grunts and says he guesses they could do that "if we can find any time between statue takedowns." When I informed him that Chavis's picture and license-plate number will be in tomorrow's paper whether he does anything or not, it seems to seal the deal.

When I ask him if it's possible to see any camera footage the cops might have taken or appropriated from the night of the twenty-ninth, he turns me down.

"We've got enough shit to deal with here without stopping to abet your wild-goose chase," he says.

As I leave, L.D. is looking at another of those sticky notes and tossing it into the trash.

THERE'S ENOUGH time before I clock in to take a stroll down Monument Avenue.

It's a mess, albeit a jolly one at present. All the monuments have been adorned with graffiti as high as our local artistes could climb, and people have gathered around them, especially the Lee statue and the one where Vindicatrix towers over the space once occupied by Jefferson Davis.

People of all races and ages are wandering along the wide median that usually is only frequented by joggers and the occasional sunbather. Whole families are out here. I wonder if the ones with grade-school children are concerned about the new words their kiddies are picking up. Hell, what am I thinking? They probably know them already.

At the Lee Monument, one scribe has written "HERE'S UR CONTEXT," no doubt commenting on the many years that cooler heads lobbied to put some wording on the statues suggesting that perhaps Lee *et al.* did not walk on water. Apparently some of our residents decided the best way to put Confederate hero-worship into context was with ropes, chains, and spray paint.

A couple of vendors have set up shop on the grass around the despoiled memorial, selling hot dogs and tacos, sweating behind their masks. A couple of people are handing out bottles of water.

Walking around to the north side of the circle, I run into Andi and young William, who turns six next week and will start first grade in the fall, plague willing.

He seems fascinated by all the colorful and profane utterings on the side of the monument. He's a smart boy. He's been able to read for a year now.

"Can I say that word?" he asks his mother, who tells him that, no, he cannot, that it's a grownup word and can only be used in special circumstances.

"But they say it on TV all the time," he says, making me wonder about parental supervision at Chez McGinnis. Of course Granddad isn't much help there either. I've been known to use the fuck word a time or two, although I'm trying to watch my potty mouth around William.

After I let out a rather colorful observation about the umpire when he and I went to a Flying Squirrels game last August, I had to convince him that you could only use language like that at ball games.

Andi told me that Walter took him to a high school basketball game last winter. When some kid threw an errant pass into the stands, young William apparently turned to

Walter and said, very solemnly, "He fucked up, didn't he, Dad?"

As Walter picked up his jaw off the floor, William told him it was OK, that Granddad said it was all right to talk like that at ball games.

Andi says she's just been by to see her grandmother. No change.

My offspring thought it would be an educational experience for her son to get a little alfresco history and civics lesson on Monument Avenue.

William, though, seems more interested in hot dogs than social justice. I oblige him.

I HAVE enough info on Juwan Chavis to write something. Wheelie and Sarah agree. A lot of it will be conjecture, but we're telling our readers that while Adam Walker is free on bail, a career criminal who had every reason in the world to hate the Kellers is out of prison and unaccounted for.

This is the first time I've linked all the pieces together in print: that terrible accident that wiped out the Roses, the judge's amazingly merciful disposition of the case a year before the Kellers moved here, and now the fact that Juwan Chavis is on the loose.

This is not my favorite kind of story, because it's going to have a lot of question marks in it. However, it's probably not libelous and it'll sell papers. The bar's not all that high for print journalism these days.

AND, BEFORE I can really get into that story, it changes on me.

Jeanette calls. She's in tears.

"He's gone."

I am sure I know who "he" is. And I'm right.

Adam borrowed one of the family cars last night, and he hasn't returned.

"Have you called the cops?"

"I don't want to, not just yet," she says. "Maybe he'll come back."

Or maybe he won't.

I can hear Glenn yelling at her in the background and figure that he's not on board with her telling her former husband that Adam's on the lam.

I advise my ex not to wait too long. Once the authorities find out he's missing, there's going to be hell to pay. They might even hold her and Glenn responsible if they keep his disappearance a secret for a couple of days.

"He doesn't know what he's doing," Jeanette says. "He's like a child in some ways."

It won't be easy to convince whoever finds him to handle him with kid gloves, I think, but don't say. I tell her that if he isn't back by tomorrow morning, they really have to let the cops know.

"We're going to lose our home!" she says. Jeanette is a sensible woman, even-keeled enough to put up with me for a time, but I can tell she's close to losing it. I try to reassure her that they won't forfeit their house, that Adam will turn up somewhere, sometime soon. My only concern is that he won't turn up on his own, and that whatever sheriff's deputy or state cop finds him won't have a lot of patience.

And then there's another possibility, which neither of us wants to talk about.

"Does he have a gun?"

Jeanette told me before that he doesn't, and she tells me again. She knows where this is going. Maybe Adam has just decided he's enjoyed about as much of life as he can stand.

She promises me that she and Glenn won't wait any longer than tomorrow morning before calling the cops. I promise her that I won't write anything about it in the paper for the time being.

I FINISH the story, file it, and check on the mayhem front. The mischief in our city tonight is mostly of the mundane, drug-deal-gone-bad variety.

I've already explained to Sarah and Wheelie that I'm duty-bound to share this information about Juwan Chavis with our two alumni at their papers in Raleigh and Martinsville. They're not thrilled with that arrangement, but they know I promised.

I don't tell them about Adam's disappearance. Not yet.

On a hunch, I pay a visit to Chip Grooms in photo.

He's been there for most of the demonstrations, including the rioting the first night. He looks tired. Our photo department is, like the rest of the operation, somewhat decimated.

I know that he took a lot of shots along Broad Street, near Remainders of the Day, and that he was there, shooting and posting what he shot, into the wee hours.

I ask him if I can look at what didn't make it into the paper. He wants to know why, and I show him the photo of Juwan Chavis.

"Do you think you'd be able to tell if you saw this guy in the crowd?" I ask.

"Might not be that easy," he says. "I mean, most of those idiots were wearing masks, which kind of makes them look alike."

But he indulges me.

Between us, we are able to look at most of what Grooms shot that night. He's right. Most of the crowd is masked and virtually unidentifiable.

We go back as far as one A.M. before we find what I'm looking for.

I don't see it, but Grooms says, "Wait a minute. Take a look at that one, over there in the corner of the frame."

He enlarges the photo on the screen. If it isn't Juwan Chavis, it's his damn twin brother.

The shot was taken about a block from the bookstore. A crowd is cheering as a trash dumpster blazes away.

Without a mask, and with the same rather spectacular dreadlocks he wore in the photo Ella sent me, it definitely looks like our guy. He's just standing there with his arms folded, taking it all in.

"When was this shot?"

He checks and tells me 1:12 A.M.

"And you think this is the guy you're writing about?"

"I'm about as sure as I can be."

Grooms sends me a JPEG. I copy it to L.D. Jones, who won't see it until tomorrow.

There's no way to prove that the guy in the photo is Chavis, but it has me convinced.

SOMETIME AFTER ten, while I'm trying to get the particulars from Peachy on a shooting on Catherine Street over near Abner Clay Park so I don't actually have to go to the scene, Rob Solomon calls.

"Chavis was in Raleigh," he says.

He went to the long-term care place where Marva Rose is housed. They wouldn't let him in, of course. They're not supposed to let anyone in those places these days, since they seem to be Ground Zero for the virus. At one facility out in Henrico, they've lost about three dozen from it so far. The unlucky folks who work there are not good life-insurance risks either.

But Rob, bless him, waited until one of the workers was leaving at the end of her shift. Using all the charm at his disposal, he was able to get her to talk about Marva.

"I told her that I'd never mention her name, and she said she didn't care whether I mentioned her name or not. It was her last day there. She said twelve dollars an hour wasn't nearly enough to risk dealing with 'that corona shit.' She said they were having to use the same protective gear several times."

At any rate, she was familiar with Marva Rose. Rob said it wasn't that big a place, maybe thirty patients.

And she remembered the day her brother came to visit. Apparently he made quite a scene.

"She said he wouldn't take no for an answer," Rob said. "He said he wanted to see his sister, and he wasn't going to leave until he did. She said he was, and I quote, 'a scary-looking motherfucker.' "

They finally reached an accommodation. They wheeled Marva over to one of the windows and let Juwan stand outside, separated by a pane of glass, but at least he could see her.

"She said that seemed to satisfy him," Rob tells me. He stayed for maybe ten minutes, and then he was gone.

I had shared Ella's photo of Chavis with Rob, and when he showed it to the recently former employee of the assisted-care place, she said it was definitely him.

I ask the sixty-four-dollar question.

"Did she remember when he was there? Like what time?"

"As a matter of fact, she did. She says that they had a little socially distanced party for the residents that Thursday at three thirty, and they were just getting everything set up when Chavis, if it was Chavis, showed up. She said it was two weeks ago."

May 28. I thank Rob and promise to treat him to all the four-buck Bloody Marys he can drink at Joe's next time he's in town and life is back to normal.

"You always were a big spender," he says. I tell him that I'm sending him and Ella both the crowd shot from the early hours of the thirtieth with the guy I'm sure is Chavis in the background.

"So this is going somewhere?"

"Looks like it. You got the story we're running tomorrow, right?"

"Yeah. We're doing something on it here but emphasizing the Roses more."

Ella emails to thank me for sending the story in time to get it in Friday's paper. She is the copy desk for the paper tonight, after filing her column. Not *on* the copy desk, she types. *The* copy desk.

"Which means I get to edit my own copy," she adds. "A dream come true." Ella, like me, knows that everybody's copy needs a second eye.

By THE time I get home, it's almost midnight. Custalow's gone to bed, but Cindy has waited up for me, more or less. She's lying on the couch, snoring adorably with a little drool running down her chin. Butterball and Rags are on the floor at her feet.

"I wasn't sleeping," the guilty dog barks, wiping her chin.

I give her a kiss and tell her about my night.

"He visited his sister in Raleigh the day after he left, and then you've got his picture in a crowd on Broad Street the next night, the night that couple was killed?"

"Sure looks like him."

She can't believe that Adam has disappeared.

"You've practically got him off the hook," she says.

"But he didn't know that."

"So when can you run something about that in the paper?"

I tell her what I've filed for tomorrow. If Adam doesn't turn up, I tell her, I'll be writing that too.

"Man," she says, shaking her head, "you really know how to stir shit up."

I don't stir it, I correct her. I just tell our readers what it looks like.

CHAPTER FIFTEEN

Friday, June 12

I get a call from L.D. at eight thirty, while I'm on my second cup of coffee. Cindy's already gone to her nonpaying temporary tutoring job.

"What the hell is this?" the chief asks.

He is referring to the crowd shot I sent him, along with a note asking that he check the guy in the left corner, the one with dreads and no mask.

"Is it just me," I ask, "or is that character a dead ringer for the man in the photo I sent you yesterday? The one I was telling you about."

"So what? So the guy was in town. We haven't found that Sonata you gave me the info on, by the way."

L.D. is a little testy this morning, partly because of this morning's story and partly because more shit happened last night, after I left the building. That's the way it goes. If I'd waited until one A.M., I'd have heard about it and been there.

Some bubbas in trucks crashed the BLM party at the Lee Monument. One of them ran into a bicyclist. The guy wasn't hurt bad enough to go to the hospital, but all hell broke loose.

Sarah sent me an email, sometime after two, giving me a heads-up. The message said that she would have called me, but Leighton Byrd was on the scene and was able to post a story on the website. I found the email forty minutes ago. As always, I'm pissed that I wasn't there. If I were forty years old instead of sixty, would Sarah have woken me up rather than sending me an email?

At any rate, Leighton did a fine job. The cops managed to apprehend several guys in pickups, who seemed to be packing for Armageddon. They were relieved of everything from assault-style rifles to body armor. The whole thing inflamed the crowd, as if the fire needs more damn gasoline.

"Now we've got people out there with guns on both sides," the chief says.

"Not to mention the cops."

"We're supposed to have guns, goddammit."

In our gun-worshipping commonwealth, it seems to be OK to bring a bazooka with you when something pisses you off, which makes civil discourse tricky. L.D., like most of the cops, would like to see the citizenry a little less well-armed, even if the goons who showed up last night were allegedly on the side of law and order. Well, law and order and maybe the Confederacy.

The antifa folks and the boogaloo boys aren't wearing uniforms, so the cops aren't even sure who's raising hell. And with all the shit they've been catching for liberal use of tear gas and stun guns, they're showing a hesitancy to step into the fray.

"We're damned if we do and damned if we don't," is the way the chief puts it.

This crap is getting serious. On Wednesday night in Portsmouth, some poor guy who was in the wrong place at the wrong time was seriously injured when a Confederate statue landed on him on its way to the ground.

Enos Jackson's suggested headline, "Dead soldier fights back," was rejected.

At least there is some effort being made to find Juwan Chavis. Hell, he's probably not even around here anymore, but he's got to be somewhere, and the state police and other localities' cops are in on the hunt now.

L.D. concedes that the guy Chip Grooms captured in that photo two weeks ago does look a lot like Chavis.

"But we don't even know if he's done anything. Maybe he has relatives here. Maybe it's not even him. All you've got is a man who is waiting for a retrial and went on a road trip."

I feel bad about not telling the chief about Adam Walker's disappearance. When he finally does learn about it, he's going to firmly believe that I knew Adam was gone long before the authorities did. I'll lie like a dog, of course, and swear that I rang the alarm as soon as I knew he'd split. I've got to give Jeanette and Glenn first dibs on this one.

I wait until ten for Jeanette to call me, and then I call her.

She's in worse shape than she was yesterday, if that's possible. They still haven't heard from Adam.

"You know what we talked about last time we talked," I remind her.

I further point out that Adam might need help, might be holed up somewhere not knowing what to do next.

But I don't feel that good about my advice. A couple of years ago, the city cops shot and killed a naked deranged man out by I-95. It was pretty difficult to claim that he was packing unless he had a pistol up his ass. Sending guys like Gillespie out there to deal with the mentally or psychologically impaired sometimes doesn't turn out so good. Still the Walkers letting the cops find out on their own that their son disappeared while he was out on bail and living in their house isn't going to play well.

"You need to let them know something. This is going to be on you and Glenn if you don't do something right now."

Basically I tell Jeanette that if she doesn't call them, I will, and it will go a lot better if she makes the call.

She promises she will.

Just in case she changes her mind, or Glenn changes it for her, I wait fifteen minutes and call the chief.

"Jeanette just told me," I lie. L.D. is not exactly believing it, but nothing my ex told him gives me away.

"What do you think about your goddamn alternative theory about the Kellers' murders now?" he asks, not quietly. "Sometimes you've got to accept what's staring you in the face and stop with the Sherlock Holmes shit."

He goes on to rant about the judge who set bail and Marcus, who talked him into it.

I am not in a position to argue with the chief right now, although Adam Walker as a murderer still doesn't make sense to me. It is obvious, though, that any enthusiasm on the part of the constabulary to find Juwan Chavis is gone.

There's nothing to do now except write something for the website about the prime suspect in a double murder going on the lam. Sarah doesn't seem too pleased, since my story in this morning's paper more or less portrayed Adam as an innocent victim of police gun-jumping.

"This isn't the last word," I tell Sarah. She suggests that maybe it ought to be.

I tell her that I stand on my record when it comes to instinct, but my former protégé and present boss doesn't seem inclined to back me. Hell, I can't blame her. Like she says, innocent people don't run.

"Usually," I concede, but point out to her that Adam had every reason, when he took off, to believe that the world in general thought he was guilty as hell.

"And he's not tuned in to the same station as the rest of us," I add.

"Just write what you know about the guy disappearing and stop with the sleuthing."

"Did you really say 'sleuthing'?"

She tells me to shut up and get to work.

"We still don't know what really happened this morning at the Lee Monument," she says, "and Leighton's sleeping late today. She had a long night."

Unspoken: Because I left too soon. Ouch.

"Willie," Sarah says, "you didn't know about this ahead of time, did you? I mean, I know he's your first wife's kid."

I assure her that I would never stoop so low. She says "huh" and hangs up.

Then Cindy calls. She wants to meet me at Joe's Inn for lunch, since it is now possible to dine inside again, if we're very, very careful.

Nothing I'd like better, I tell her, but I've got some sleuthing to do first. She says that's OK, that there's a guy who's also helping with the tutoring, and she's sure he'd like to join her.

"He's quite the hunk," she adds.

"You can't blackmail me like that," I tell her, but she knows she can.

I'm at Joe's at noon. She already has a table. They're only seating at every other one. This seems a little sketchy to me. Everybody who's already seated has removed their masks, like the coronavirus can't climb over those partitions between booths. Plus, how the hell is the place going to pay the bills only using half, at most, of its capacity?

"What the hell, Willie," Cindy says when I express my concerns. "Of course we have to take them off to eat. Are we supposed to eat through the masks? Maybe we can order soup and then strain it through the cloth."

So we live dangerously, and the spaghetti Albert was damn good.

I'm interrupted halfway through our first on-site restaurant meal in months by a call from Marcus.

"So when were you going to tell me he split?" my favorite lawyer asks. "Just gonna let me read about my client's disappearance on your damn website?"

He is no more inclined than L.D. or Sarah to believe that I knew nothing of Adam Walker's disappearance until this morning.

"Spare me, Willie," he says. "The important thing now is to find the little bastard, fast."

I ask him how convinced he is now of Adam's innocence.

"Innocent or guilty, he's my client, but he's sure as hell not making it easy for himself, or me."

He's read what I've written about Juwan Chavis, but I can tell that he doesn't have the time or inclination to get fired up about Chavis right now.

"When they find this not-suspect of yours, whoever he is and wherever he is, and he breaks down and tells the cops he did it, then we might have something," he says. "Right now, all I'm thinking about is a client who was lucky as hell to get bail and has skipped town."

I ask him about Shorty. He says he's filed the lawsuit, so I'm free to write about that.

"He wants the money right damn now," Marcus says. "I have to keep telling him that it's going to take some time. He's probably not going to be happy, either, when he finds out how much the government will take of whatever he gets."

"The government and you," I remind him.

"Yeah," Marcus, "I should work for free. Maybe I'll give away all my worldly goods and spend the rest of my life doing good deeds, tryin' to get to heaven."

After lunch, Cindy and I put our masks back on and head our separate ways.

First thing on my agenda is checking on Peggy.

She and her permanent houseguest look pretty awful, but Peggy says she isn't having any breathing problems, "not really," and neither is Awesome.

"Maybe this was just a false alarm," she says, but we both know better.

She says she's not smoking weed in the interim, which is a big deal for a lifetime enthusiast like Peggy.

"That's got to be weird," I tell her. "It would be interesting to see if you smoked a joint now, if you'd still have the munchies, with no taste buds and all."

"Good thing this isn't happening to you," she replies. "If you got the bug and had to stop smoking them damn Camels, you'd probably fall over dead."

Well, that's another good reason not to catch the virus. Stop smoking or stop breathing. Hard choice.

I've never been what you'd call a fearful person. If you looked up the phrase, "Fools rush in," you'd probably find my picture beside it. But this has me kind of spooked. Maybe I'm getting old.

"You know what today is?" my old mom asks.

"June 12," I reply.

"It's Loving Day."

"Like Valentine's? Isn't that in February?"

I'm just jerking Peggy's chain. Loving Day, in our great state, commemorates the day that the United States Supreme Court took the commonwealth of Virginia to the woodshed and told it that mixed-race marriages would forevermore be legal. The Lovings grew up just up the road in Bowling Green, and there's noise now about putting one or both of those brave people on one of those pedestals on Monument Avenue. Not the worst idea in the world.

Since my father was the now long-deceased African American Artie Lee, who died six years before he and my white mom could have legally gotten married in their home state, this has some significance to Peggy and me.

I tell her that I wish I could give her a hug, and that I owe her quite a few when this whole mess is over.

"Don't worry," she says. "I'll wait. I'm not going anywhere."

I hope to God not.

I'M IN no hurry to get to the newsroom. They don't officially start paying me for another hour and a half. So I park the car in the company lot and walk over to Broad Street.

Remainders of the Day sits there, boarded up and abandoned. At least it hasn't been torched yet. Some stores on Broad have reopened, but there are still a lot of vacancies, and I wonder how many of them will stay vacant.

When I peek inside through the gap between the plywood slats, I see that the books are still sitting there, abandoned and unwanted.

I'm guessing that the owner hasn't been able to find anyone yet to lease this albatross.

I'm startled when the door suddenly opens.

"What the fuck do you want?"

That seems to be the fat man's stock greeting. He's probably come around to see if there's anything he can salvage before he lights a match.

He recognizes me.

"Oh, yeah. Willie Black. You still snooping around? Hey, I can sell you some books, real cheap."

I tell him not to let my wife know, or we'll have to hire a U-Haul to tote them away.

He says he can't get rid of anything out of the Kellers' apartment yet.

"Ongoing investigation, or some such shit. They better hurry up though. This place looks like it could catch fire most any minute."

The fat man takes his cigarette out of his mouth and waves it around, in case I miss the implication.

I tell him about Adam Walker's disappearance.

"Damn," he says, "you don't think he'll come back here, do you?"

I tell him that I think this is about the last place we could expect Adam to show up.

"I been reading some of that crap you've been writing, about that Black fella that might have had a hard-on for the Kellers. Well, I don't suppose you're going to be barking up that tree anymore now."

Maybe not, I concede. I ask him if I can go upstairs again and see whatever there is to see up there "in case I missed something the first time."

"Knock yourself out," he says. "Hell, I don't know if the cops have even gone up there since the first night or two."

He goes up with me. It's just the way it was when I saw it nine days ago. Those prints leading away from the scene of the crime just end, like somebody stopped and took their shoes off. It does occur to me, though, that, unless Adam got rid of those shoes before he left the building, something's not right. In the video that led the cops to him, he's not carrying anything, certainly not a pair of what appear, from the prints, to be work shoes. He didn't look like he was barefoot either. And there weren't any bloody shoe prints downstairs.

"Well, the police must of looked for them," the fat man says. "Course if he'd thrown them in one of the dumpsters out back, they'd be in the landfill by now. City picks up once a week."

This is making less and less sense to me.

We go back down to the first floor. The owner lets me explore the basement by myself.

It doesn't appear that the cops looked down here very carefully, if at all. Hell, why would they? They had no reason to think the basement had anything to do with this.

That one light overhead doesn't give me much illumination, but I do finally spy a wastebasket next to the door that was unlocked. I drag it over into the light and see that it hasn't been emptied in maybe the last fifty years. There might be nineteenth-century artifacts in there for all I know.

It's half full, mostly paper and cardboard, along with the remnants of something that might once have been food. And the remains of a dead mouse.

But a flash of color, sitting on top of the pile, catches my eye. I reach down and pull up an empty cigarette pack. Marlboros.

I'm pretty sure that the Kellers weren't smokers, something the owner of the place confirms when I show him the pack upstairs.

"I'd've kicked their asses out if they were smoking in here," he says, taking a puff. He also says he's pretty damn sure that nobody else has been in that basement recently.

I'm equally certain that Adam didn't smoke. Why? Because he didn't ask for a cigarette when we visited him in jail. I can confirm that with Jeanette.

The pack looks to be of recent vintage, unlike the rest of the flotsam on the floor.

I wrap the cigarette pack in a discarded paper towel and thank the fat man for his time.

He's muttering to himself as I leave, something about books.

FOR A Friday night, things are pretty quiet on the cop beat. The demonstrations have been relatively peaceful. Yeah, there was a fatal shooting over at one of the housing projects that might be worth five inches on A2.

The whole front page is COVID-R-US. There's a piece on the first day of indoor dining. There was a brawl at one of my favorite joints, a place over in the Devil's Triangle more renowned for its libations than its cuisine. For some reason, the rules say we can't sit at the bar, only at tables or booths. A couple of the regulars took exception to this. Fisticuffs ensued when the bartender and the only waiter tried to get them to give up their stools. A couple of cops had to peel off from BLM duty to restore order and issue citations.

And, of course, neither of the regulars was wearing a mask.

The bartender pretty much nailed it:

"This is why we can't have nice things."

I am able to reach the Walkers about nine thirty. Glenn answers the phone and passes it on to Jeanette without speaking. I don't think he likes me.

"No," she says, "Adam doesn't smoke. He never did."

I explain why I asked. She says they still haven't heard from their youngest son. I tell her I'm sure they'll find him soon. I doubt that she believes me. I'm not sure I believe myself.

Why, I ask myself, was there an empty pack of Marlboros in that bookstore basement, when neither the Kellers nor Adam smoked? And who was wearing the amazing disappearing shoes?

The chief has his hands full right now. He doesn't want to hear any more discouraging words about a double murder he wants to believe is already solved. He wants a solved case to stay solved.

Nobody gets what he wants all the time.

CHAPTER SIXTEEN

Saturday, June 13

The plague marches on. This morning, we're up to about 1,540 dead and 54,000 positives in Virginia. Last week, I heard Jack Clatterbuck, the weekend sports desk guy, say it was just another case of the flu, nothing to get your balls in an uproar over.

"And it's mostly minorities," he said, then, looking over at me, said, "No offense."

Last night I noticed Clatterbuck sitting a good ten feet away from anyone else on the sports desk and wearing a mask.

Today I have to have a serious talk with the chief.

Peachy says he's taking Saturday morning off. There'll be plenty to occupy him after that. Something called the 5,000 Man March is planned for the afternoon, starting at the Lee Monument at one.

"Does that mean only men can march?" Cindy asks over breakfast. I agree that the wording is unfortunate but is unlikely to deter folks of all genders, races, sexual orientation, and ages from showing up. The city is Red Bull woke.

I explain that first I have to go see L.D.

He's home when I get there, mowing the grass.

"Don't you have a couple of grown kids still living at home?" I ask when he shuts the thing off and wipes his sweaty brow.

"Yeah. They're not afraid of work either. They'll lie down right beside it and take a nap, no problem."

I take the plastic baggie out of my pocket, the one with the Marlboro pack inside.

"Not your brand," the chief says.

I explain.

"So you found an empty cigarette pack, and you don't think Walker smoked, or that the victims did."

"I'm sure of it, L.D."

He does seem intrigued by my insight concerning the shoes.

"He could have put them back on when he got downstairs," the chief says, trying to figure some way that my theory won't make sense.

"But then there'd be tracks, and some blood, on the floor by the front door, and I'm sure your boys checked for that."

We walk over to the sycamore that shades the Davises' yard and most of the house.

"OK," L.D. says. He doesn't have to say anything more. It's as close as he'll ever come to conceding that he might have jumped to conclusions.

I try to make it easy.

"I can see why everybody thought the boy did it," I tell him. "Everything pointed to him. But you didn't know then what you know now."

He lifts his sweat-soaked T-shirt that's stuck to his overdeveloped belly and fans his midriff with it.

"But that still doesn't explain why he ran."

"He'd spent twelve days in the lockup by then, and he wasn't that stable to begin with. Plus, when he got out on bail, everybody from the commonwealth's attorney on down made it clear that he was guilty as hell and that the eventual trial was going to be just a formality."

"And Jeanette and her husband, they haven't heard anything else from him?"

"If she had," I tell the chief, "she'd have told me, and I would have told you."

He gives me the fish-eye and says, "Eventually."

Nobody's sighted Adam or the car yet, although I'm not sure anybody's been looking all that hard.

"How about the other car?"

No sign, either, of that Sonata or Juwan Chavis.

"Probably long gone from here," L.D. says. "But we're going to send out a BOLO to every law enforcement organization in this part of the world."

Which tells me that the search so far has been somewhat, to use one of Cindy's words, desultory. Last time she used it, I think she was referring to my enthusiasm over the still-unfulfilled promise to take her to that winery.

I leave L.D. to his lawn. As I'm going, one of his sons, the twenty-year-old, I think, comes around the corner of the house, sees his dad and the lawn mower, and does a quick one-eighty.

MY DAILY visit to Peggy starts badly.

"The dumb bastard just took off and left," she says. Since only one dumb bastard lives at my mom's rental house, Awesome Dude is on the loose.

She's coughing as she explains it to me. She woke up at eight, late for her. Awesome, who thank God sleeps in the other bedroom, was gone.

She asks me if I can find him.

"How?" I ask. "Where?"

"I don't know," she says, "but he ought not to be out loose."

That's probably true of Awesome on a good day. Somehow he was able to look out for his ass all those years before Peggy took him in, but it's hard to figure how. I've known him since he was an alleged student at VCU, thirty-some years ago, and he never has been what folks around here call "quite right."

I'm expected to help cover the 5,000-human march in an hour or so, but I need to at least make an effort to find the guy, if for no other reason than to keep him from possibly contaminating others.

It doesn't take long to locate him. I go down Laurel Street to the river overlook and there, on the park bench above the James, is the Dude.

He doesn't try to get away when he sees me, just slides over. I decline a seat and ask him if maybe he ought to be back at Peggy's until he's feeling better.

He does look awful.

"Aw, Willie," he says, "I needed me some fresh air. I got tired of being florentined."

Nevertheless he lets me take him back to Peggy's.

She welcomes him with a hug.

"Hey," she says, "we're gonna beat this crap together."

THE RALLY does come close to achieving its promised 5,000 bodies. It's a nice, sunny afternoon and the crowd is in a peaceful mood.

Lately I've wondered more than once if these smiling, peaceable folks I see in the sunshine are the same ones burning city buses and throwing shit at cops after dark.

The mayor tries mightily to put the onus on outsiders, "outside agitators" as our older mossback readers like to call them in their screeds to the editor. The lefties say it's neo-Nazis from Indiana or Alabama or some damn where else. The right-wingers put it all on antifa, a group that can be so annoying as to almost make one sympathetic to fascism.

Maybe buses roll into Monroe Park at dusk and deposit bad guys in our midst. That would be the comfortable answer, although I'm far from sure it's the right one. My belief is that we have enough homegrown meatheads here in RVA to keep the flames of anarchy burning.

Nothing's burning this afternoon though. It's all sweetness and light, if a bit on the loud side, as they march from the Lee Monument down to Arthur Ashe Boulevard and then over to West Broad. The biggest deal is that a cousin of George Floyd, the guy who was choked to death by the Minneapolis cop, is here.

Besides that, the only thing kind of extraordinary is the motorcycle gang. Talk about playing against stereotype. They're here to show support for the Black Lives Matter folks. And the lamb shall lie down next to the lion.

I get a few quotes from some of the motorcycle people and pass them on to young Leighton. I don't even bother to write anything myself for the paper. Leighton has it covered anyhow. And I have a full night on the police beat ahead of me.

As I'm walking over to where I parked my car on Rowland, I feel a tug at my elbow. Jumpin' Jimmy Deacon.

"Hey, hoss," the world's biggest sports nut says. "How's it hangin'?"

I haven't seen Jimmy since he told me what he knew about the Kellers. It occurs to me that I should have bought him a drink or something. Jimmy, though, never takes offense at snubs, if he even notices them.

"Jimmy's been followin' all the stuff you've been writing about the Kellers," he says. "So you don't think that whack-job kid did it?"

I tell him that I don't know, but I'm starting to doubt it.

"And he skipped town?"

I nod.

Jimmy is shifting from one foot to the other.

"Well, that don't sound good."

I'm starting to tell him that I have to be at work in fifteen minutes and promise, again, to have that beer sometime soon, when he says something that stops me.

"You know, I think I might of saw that car. Not sure, but it's kind of suspicious."

"What car?"

"The one that fella from Danville was driving. The one you wrote about."

He means Martinsville, I'm guessing.

"When? When did you see it?"

Jimmy seems happy to be of use.

"I can't be sure," he says, "but I'm pretty good with cars, and Jimmy walks around a lot. Burns off energy, you know."

One of the places Jimmy walks is over in Scott's Addition, a mixture of hip bars and restaurants and hard-core industrial.

The place is bisected with alleyways, some more navigable than others. It has a special place in my gut, since one of the aforementioned neo-Nazis almost made Willie postmortem there last year.

In one of those alleys, close to a place that sells Texas-style barbecue, as if we need more damn barbecue in Virginia, and a cidery, Jimmy saw a Sonata without any tags parked in a place where apparently nobody ever drives, dead in the middle of the block.

I ask him why he hasn't mentioned this to the cops yet.

"Hell, I called 'em yesterday and they said they'd get back to me, but I don't think they took me serious."

I get Jimmy to hop in the venerable Honda, and we go over to Scott's Addition.

"Man," Jumpin' Jimmy says as he takes in the grandeur of the Honda, "how old is this thing? They don't pay you enough. And it smells like cigarettes."

I park on the street next to the alley entrance. The alley bends a little, so you can't see all the way through to the next street. There ahead of me, in that bend, is the Sonata. It's some shade of blue and, as Jimmy said, the plates are missing. The right-front tire is flat.

A quick look informs me that it is the property of a rental-car agency down in Martinsville.

This time, I really and truly do intend to buy Jimmy a beer or three. I take a couple of pictures of the car and send them to the chief, along with instructions as to where to find it.

L.D. might want to light a fire under the ass of whichever one of his subordinates didn't take Jumpin' Jimmy Deacon seriously.

So I have something to write about. It would be unfair to my source if I didn't mention that he tried to tip off the police and nobody got back to him.

"YOU FOUND it yourself?"

Sarah seems impressed. I have to disabuse her.

I tell her that, actually, the man who found it was one James H. Deacon, known to his friends as Jumpin' Jimmy.

"And you put your faith in a guy named Jumpin' Jimmy?"

He found the car, I point out, which is better than Richmond's finest did.

There's still the matter of confirming what I know already, that the car Jimmy found is the one Juwan Chavis rented in Martinsville. A call to Ella Minopee, a quick check by her, and a call back to me nail that down.

"The story's getting quite a bit of attention down here," she says. "We have a lot of slow news days. The rental agency was pretty happy when I gave them the good news. They're going to send somebody up there to pick it up."

I remind her that it won't be that easy. If the local cops don't have their heads completely up their asses, they've already got somebody over there to impound it as evidence. The combination of the car and that discarded Marlboro pack ought to be enough to ramp up the search for Chavis.

"Yeah, I'm sure you're right. Well, I'll tell them to get in touch with the police first before they make that long trip."

She says nobody will admit to having seen the man anywhere in the Martinsville area since he took off.

I make a call to Rob Solomon in Raleigh and fill him in on the latest. He says he's checked with the police, and there has been no sign of Chavis down there since he visited his sister.

L.D. isn't too happy when I call.

"How long did you know that car was there?" he demands.

Why, I ask, would I keep something like that a secret?

"Force of habit," he says.

He is not pleased when I tell him the hard truth: It's going to be essential that I tell our readers how Jumpin' Jimmy Deacon called the city cops yesterday and got nothing better than a promise to "look into it."

"That's his story," the chief huffs.

"Well, it's a pretty good one. I don't have any reason to doubt that it's true."

"This is going to make us look bad," he says.

"I'm sorry about that," I tell him, "but maybe you ought to hold off on shooting the messenger and find out which one of your dumbass people didn't think a tip about Juwan Chavis's car was worth following up."

"We've been a little busy, as you might have goddamn noticed."

He hangs up.

There wasn't much left to say anyhow. Any good will that existed between L.D. and me this morning has disappeared faster than the last donut at a cop confab. Sometimes I wonder if my old basketball buddy and I can ever be friends again, after he's stopped chasing criminals and I've stopped reporting on his fuckups. Nowhere in the book of journalistic ethics, a very short volume, is there anything about it being OK to pull punches for your friends. Oh, I've pulled punches before, but it was usually so I could get some of that quid pro quo later.

I'll admit that it's a tough time to be a police chief. The way things are going, L.D. might wind up being the only one in history to get suspended twice in ten days.

THINGS DON'T get any easier after sundown. Either those smiling, happy idiots who were marching this afternoon have gotten much more cranky or they've brought in reinforcements.

The everyday crime scene is quiet, so when Leighton calls in and says the shit has hit the fan again around the Lee Monument, I'm out the door.

When I get there, people are pissed off. According to whom you believe, a patrol car drove into a group of peaceful protesters around the monument circle or a couple of cops, trying to avoid being besieged by an angry mob, slowly extricated themselves by driving off.

I find Gillespie, hidden beneath half a ton of riot gear, standing nearby. He swears that there's no way anybody was injured.

"The guys were going like two miles an hour," he says. "The protesters had the car surrounded. They're just making shit up to make us look bad."

They don't need much help, I want to tell him. When you show up like Rambo, you can expect a little pushback.

Still I don't see any signs of human carnage. Leighton catches up to me and says she's going to just write what each side said and let it go at that.

"There are some scary fuckers out here," she says.

"Cops or civilians."

"Both. And some of the civilians, I don't even know if you could call them civilians. A lot of them are armed, and a lot of them don't like each other. I don't know antifa from antacids, but I know a skinhead when I see one. There's too many guns out here."

"Welcome to the twenty-first century."

She brushes back a strand of hair.

"Well, it's the first century I've had much experience with, but I gotta tell you: So far, you can have it."

CHAPTER SEVENTEEN

Sunday, June 14

Cindy, Abe, Andy, and I get the big back table at Joe's. Social distancing is no problem, because there seems to be only one other table in use this fine Sunday morning.

The governor has said we can eat indoors, with restrictions, but R.P. McGonnigal, a man who has had a couple of health issues, says he thinks he'll wait a bit before rejoining the gang.

"Come on," Andy says when he calls him to give him a ration about staying home. "That's bullshit. You only have to worry if you're like over sixty or . . . yeah? Oh, yeah. OK. Never mind."

He shuts the cell phone.

"What'd he say?" Cindy asks.

"He said for me and Abe and Willie to look at our driver's licenses."

"Man," Cindy says, "that's cold. Looks like I'm the only one in here who's legal."

We ask our server if they're checking driver's licenses to make sure no senior citizens are in attendance.

She snorts.

"Don't need any driver's license to figure that one out."

I'm still getting used to being sixty. Cindy doesn't make it any better when she says I'm now in my seventh decade. Those folks who gifted me with Ensure and Depends at the big blowout Cindy threw for me in March didn't help either.

There was more action after I left the Lee Monument last night. The woke apparently didn't want the party to end. It was too late to make the Sunday paper, of course, but I've posted what I missed on our website. Leighton Byrd had a busy night.

Everybody at the table has an opinion about what's happening in our fair city. Andy says he's upset with how Monument Avenue "looks like a trash dump." Cindy tells her older brother that none of this would've happened if somebody had done something about those monuments other than talk about context for the last few decades.

Maybe Abe has the best take on it.

"I was watching this documentary the other night, about Germany. And it showed all those cities that got pretty much leveled in World War II. And you know what? You look at them now, and you can't even tell there was a war.

"If Hamburg and all those places can come back from that, we can handle a few monuments getting trashed."

I weigh in by noting that there are some people who might even see a few less Confederate monuments as an incentive to move here.

"If you want that type," Andy mumbles. Cindy kicks him.

My beloved is still working with kids who otherwise wouldn't be getting much education at all. As she has pointed out to me, Internet is not a given in the parts of our fair city where outsiders come only to kick out delinquent renters or buy drugs.

She says she had an interesting encounter on Friday.

"I looked up," she says, "and there was your old pal, Big Boy what's-his-name."

"Sunday."

"Yeah. He came by and brought the kids each a lunch, which probably was the best meal they had that day."

"Was a barbecue sandwich part of it?"

"How the hell did you know that?"

Big Boy, hardened criminal that he is, likes to give back to the community, even if a healthy diet isn't atop his priority list. And I'll bet the kids liked it better than an apple and a container of yogurt.

One time, when I became aware from a third party that he'd given a five-figure sum to keep some sad little East End church's lights on, I was feeling brave and asked Big Boy about this duality in his character.

He didn't answer at first, mainly because he was digesting a large portion of pork.

"Willie," he finally said, "I read something awhile back, about them so-called robber barons, like Carnegie and Vanderbilt and Rockefeller and all. Man, they did shit to folks that I'd never be able to do today, worked 'em like dogs for nothing and stole everybody else blind. Didn't pay taxes if they could get away with it. And then they give a little bit of it back, to museums and colleges and such, with their names on everything, so folks would know how kind and generous they were."

We were sitting in the back seat of his car. He let go with a belch that surely registered on the Richter scale. Then he continued.

"So just think of me as one of them robber barons, just tryin' to do a little good, maybe get my ass into heaven one day."

He laughed hard enough to shake the car. The teenage thug driver looked back to make sure Big Boy wasn't choking on anything.

"Yeah," I tell Cindy, "Big Boy has his good side."

"Well," she says, "those kids acted like he was God or something."

One or two of them, I don't want to tell Cindy, probably will be working for him before too many more years.

AFTER WE get back to the Prestwould, I call Jeanette. She's a wreck. No word yet from Adam. When I make a call to Peachy Love, she says nobody in Virginia or any of the neighboring states has found him or the car, but she hasn't checked yet today.

But she calls back five minutes later.

"They found it."

The Walkers' car was located in a Walmart parking lot in Bluefield, over on the West Virginia line. The vehicle seemed to have been parked there for at least a couple of days. Adam's been gone since Thursday.

"But no sign of the boy."

"Damn. If he'd just show up, somebody could tell him that he's practically off the hook for the Kellers' murders."

"Yeah," Peachy says. "That'd be nice."

I hear a child babbling in the background.

"Oh, that's Aurora."

"The Kellers' little girl?"

Peachy says she's keeping her for the weekend, to give her some kind of normal life, short-term.

"She's just starting to walk, so I have to watch her like a hawk."

Peachy says she's sure somebody will want to adopt the little girl. None of the late Kellers' parents are interested "and they're kind of old anyhow."

She says she has to take the girl back to human services soon because she's needed downtown.

"Shit's blowing up down at headquarters," she says, then adds that she doesn't mean a real explosion, just an angry mob. Apparently last night's unpleasantness has leached over into the daylight. People seem to be pissed off 7/24.

When I call Jeanette back, she is less than happy to learn that they've found the car but not her son.

Something occurs to me that for some reason didn't before. Every human over five years old in the United States has a cell phone.

"He left it right here, on his dresser," Jeanette says.

Neither of us verbalizes what we know. This is not good news.

Sunday would normally be a day of Bloody Marys and rest for me, but normally everybody wouldn't be wearing masks and trying to take over the police station.

I tell Cindy that I'm going to the paper to check something out.

"Are you going to be able to make it to Andi and Walter's in time?" she asks. I am supposed to drive over to my daughter's place in the Fan for dinner tonight. Cindy had to beg off because of a previous promise to spend some quality time with her sister.

"It's only two thirty," I inform my beloved.

"Yeah," she says, "but time has a habit of slipping away when you step inside that newspaper building."

I promise to be back in plenty of time to keep Andi happy.

Actually I'm not going to the newsroom. Police headquarters are a fairly short walk. I alternate between wearing a mask and taking drags on a Camel. My half-ass approach to pandemic safety is met with disapproving glances as I walk along Grace Street.

"Dude," some toothless guy at the homeless shelter yells as I walk past, "put on the mask."

The barricades on the block around headquarters aren't enough of a deterrent. City and state cops, and maybe some feds, are surrounding the building. I see L.D. Jones standing back of the barrier, trying to reason with the unreasonable.

Pacification isn't one of L.D.'s stronger traits. After being shouted down by protesters with bullhorns of their own, he says something that I lip-read as "Fuck it" and goes back inside.

Callie Ann Boatright is on the scene. I guess Leighton finally decided to take a day off.

Callie Ann, who is twenty-four and was hired pretty much the same day as Leighton, seems a little out of her element here. She doesn't seem to have quite the killer instinct of her reporter buddy. I point her toward some people who might be able to help, like Peachy and Gillespie.

A helicopter is hovering, adding to the general sense of paranoia on the part of some of the crowd. It's a little early in the day for tear gas, but the cops, maybe with the chief's approval, are giving the multitude a matinee spraying. I estimate that there are about three hundred protesters, although I get in trouble every time I try to guess the size of crowds. One side will say it was too small; the other will say it's too big.

Some of them disperse. Others start picking up the canisters and throwing them back at the cops. It's as close to a pitched battle as I've seen this BLM season. I see a handful of participants wrestled to the ground, so maybe we'll find out if the rabble-rousers are "outside agitators" or homegrown. Probably, I'm guessing, some of both.

I can't get anywhere near the building. One cop, a tough-looking character at first glance who looks like a scared kid inside all that gear, threatens me with bodily harm if I don't back off. I don't think my status as a print journalist is going to open any doors today.

But I do have L.D.'s cell number. He must rue the day he gave it to me.

He answers.

"Where the hell are you?" he asks.

I tell him I'm right outside.

"You're going to make it look like this is all our fault," he says. "We didn't do a damn thing. Those guys in the squad car last night were afraid for their lives."

"We gave you a fair shake."

I'm right about that. Leighton didn't take sides in her story, just reported what the cops said and what the protesters said.

"Well, they were lying and we weren't."

It would do no good to mention to the chief how many times I've been lied to by cops over the years.

He doesn't have much to add to what I already know about Adam Walker's missing car turning up.

He says that the other found car, the one rented by Juwan Chavis, is being gone over for God knows what, and that there's still no sign of the man himself.

When I ask him if it's fair to say that Chavis is at least a person of interest in the Kellers' murders, he says, "Yeah, fuck it. Go ahead."

That's about all I'm able to get out of L.D. today.

"When we know something," he says. "we'll tell you. Now if you'll excuse me, I'm up to my ass in alligators."

I WALK over to the paper and stay long enough to write something for the website and tomorrow's paper on Juwan

Chavis being elevated to the status of person of interest in the double homicide. I call the Bluefield police, who confirm Peachy's info about Adam Walker's car. Apparently there was no sign of foul play, and nobody admits to having seen Adam anywhere around the Walmart.

Since it's still only four o'clock, I hike back to the Prestwould, and then drive over to the general vicinity of the Lee Monument, just to see what if anything is going on there.

The small crowd around the statue isn't nearly as surly as the one down at L.D.'s domain, although the paint along the base is now about three coats deep in messages. It's actually kind of pretty, if you look at it the right way. Cindy, who knows more about art than I do (and who doesn't?) says it has kind of a Jackson Pollock feel, if Pollock had used the word "fuck" a lot in his work.

I talk to a couple of folks, who seem more joyful than angry.

"I never thought I'd see this day," an older Black woman close to Big Boy Sunday's weight class says. Me either, I concede.

Nothing really to write about here, and it's time for me to head back and then go to my daughter and son-in-law's place for an early dinner. Flying in the face of her genetics, Andi is a healthy eater. Maybe her years of waitressing dampened her zeal for greasy comfort food. I'm still sated from the artery-clogging brunch at Joe's, though, so it's all good.

The car is parked over on Allen, a block and a half from the monument. I get in, take off the damn mask, and reach for a Camel. By the time I get to Andi and Walter's, I've sucked it down to the nub.

The evening goes as well as an evening can go that includes a vegetable tart as the entrée. Young William is his usual charming self, eager to show me how well he can read and asking when we can go to a Flying Squirrels game again. God only knows, I want to say. Andi's been doing more hands-on parenting than usual, compliments of the pandemic shutting down day care.

She wants to grill me about what's going on with her half-brother, Adam.

At thirty-one, she's twelve years older than he is, and I know she felt sometimes used as a teenager when she had to act as unpaid babysitter for Adam and Buddy, but he is family. Sometimes it's hard for me to get my mind around the fact that Andi had a whole other life after I abandoned her and her mother, complete with a stepdad and a couple of baby brothers.

"Mom's out of her mind about it," Andi says. She spent the afternoon with the Walkers, trying to calm Jeanette down, while Walter took care of William. "Buddy's kind of useless, and Glenn just kind of wants to go off and mow the yard or do anything but talk about it."

I tell her that I wish I could have more encouraging news. I tell her I'm pretty sure, at this point, that Adam didn't kill the Kellers, but I'm not sure he knows he's not at the top of the suspect list. Plus he has to know he's a fugitive.

"I wish he'd call or something," my daughter says, and I tell her that he didn't take his cell phone when he left.

"Aw, shit," she says. William echoes her sentiment, to her dismay.

I'm out of there before ten. Walter McGinnis, a very serious accountant who does have to work tomorrow, looks as if he's fading fast. It's funny. All those years on night cops plus a natural circadian clock that favors the wee hours mean I'm more awake than my daughter and son-in-law are.

"Let me know when you hear something," Andi tells me when she kisses me goodbye.

I'm back at the Prestwould in five minutes.

Cindy gets the good parking space, the one inside the fence that allegedly keeps bad guys from stealing her Prius. Other than the recent BLM unpleasantness, there isn't much crime around here, unless you think panhandling is illegal, but the Prestwouldians always feel better knowing there's some kind of barrier between them and the great unwashed.

My space is back of the building. There are lights there, sort of. It's fair to say you couldn't read a book by the ones closest to the Honda's designated space.

Some jackass has parallel-parked his boat of a vehicle so that it's about a foot into my space, which isn't all that big to start with. To make it worse, I don't think the offending party even lives in the Prestwould.

I'm about to write the individual an unpleasant message about parking etiquette and leave it on his windshield when my night takes a decided turn for the worse.

I never even see the guy until I open the car door and there's a big-ass gun a couple of inches from my face.

"We need to talk," he says.

He looks like his picture, except maybe smaller than I expected.

"Juwan Chavis?" I ask.

He doesn't say anything, just smacks me upside the head with the gun butt.

CHAPTER EIGHTEEN

My head hurts like a bitch. My mouth is filling up with the coppery taste of my own blood. I'm pretty sure dental work is in my near future, if I have a near future. The gag plus the blood is making it hard to breathe.

It's pitch-black in here. It takes me a few seconds, once I come to, to realize that I must be in the trunk of the ancient Honda. My head is jammed against either the Fix-a-Flat or the stuff you spray on the car windows to de-ice them. I can smell the wool from the old army blanket that's been in here since I bought it cheap at a secondhand store ten years ago.

Juwan Chavis, assuming he's driving, must be trying to hit every pothole in the city. With my wrists and ankles apparently tied, I keep bouncing around like a spare tire. There isn't much to do except go along for the ride. Despite my obviously dire circumstances, I keep wanting to take a nap.

Finally, and it might have been five minutes or an hour, because I do kind of drift off, the car stops. I am the least bit claustrophobic, and so it is a relief when I hear the lock pop on the trunk. The fresh air of Richmond has never smelled so sweet.

Chavis is looking down at me. Good citizen that he is, he's wearing a mask. I can only see his eyes, but he doesn't appear to be smiling.

I'm still afraid he's going to just close the trunk again and walk away, or maybe set the damn thing on fire and let me burn to death.

"Hell," he says, "I reckon we'd better get you out of there."

He then amazes me. Juwan Chavis is stocky, but he's no more than five-foot-eight. However, he somehow pulls me halfway out of the trunk, throws me over his shoulder, and then I'm being carried up a set of steps, then through a doorway.

He throws me down on a bare floor, none too gently.

"Damn, man," my captor says, "you're a heavy motherfucker."

He drags me over to one of the walls and props me up against it. When he moves to take off the gag, I start to ask the first of many questions I have. He holds his hand up, with the index finger extended in my direction.

"If you make a fuss," he says, "I will seriously fuck you up."

I got a brief, upside-down view of my surroundings as Chavis was doing the fireman-carry up those stairs. My vista was of a parking lot and the back of buildings that look better from the front than they do from the rear.

When I get a whiff of hamburgers grilling, I know where we are—within smelling distance of Citizen Burger, whose burgers my prominent nose would recognize anywhere.

We are in Carytown, either just north or just south of Cary Street itself. On a Sunday night, Citizen would be one of the few joints open and serving food after ten o'clock. After the vegetarian fare at Andi's, a Citizen burger with some onion rings should have my mouth watering, but I'm a little uneasy and queasy at the moment.

From the sound of the occasional passing car and the laughter of a few alfresco diners and drinkers at Citizen and the Daily just down the street from it, I deduce that we are on the second floor, probably one of those apartments just above the myriad retail establishments in Carytown, an eight-block patch of Richmond that usually delights me, with its dearth of chain stores and wealth of funky local joints. However, dying here would definitely color my feelings for the place.

I assure my captor, in as calm a voice as I can manage, that I have no desire to "make a fuss."

"What do you want?" I ask as I spit some blood onto the floor.

He answers a question with a question.

"You're the one that been stirring up all that shit about me, ain't you?"

He asks it with the gun poking the right side of my aching head.

"I'm just trying to get the truth," I say, knowing how lame it sounds, but at least I stop myself from asking him not to shoot the messenger. Juwan Chavis doesn't seem like the type to appreciate dark humor.

He laughs, sort of.

"Well, like that dude said in the movie, I ain't sure you can handle the truth."

"Try me," is all I can think to say. I'm not Tom Cruise.

CHAVIS SAYS he more or less lucked into finding me after he'd decided I was the bane of his existence.

"My luck, not yours," he says and laughs.

"I got a meal at one of them places over at the park where they feed the homeless, like that's gonna save the world, and I heard one of the bums say your name.

"I asked him who you were, and he told me you gave him a dollar or two sometimes, what a great guy you were and all, and that you lived right next to the park. The bum even knew what kind of car you drove, said he made it a point to be close by when he thought you might be coming out."

Yeah, I think I know that guy. Some toothless friend of Awesome Dude's who hits me up now and then. No good deed, etcetera.

So Juwan Chavis made it a point to hang around the parking lot where my car was parked, always after dark.

"Took two nights to catch you comin' in. By then, I had a plan."

We are, I soon learn, uninvited guests. Chavis, who has had some experience breaking into places, slipped in here three days ago, after crashing at two other places.

Looking around, I can see that the landlord apparently hasn't been able to rent this dump for a while. There are cobwebs in the corners of the room, and one of the panes is broken in one of the windows, maybe by some of our woke rabble-rousers. Obviously the electricity has been turned off. It feels like it's at least eighty degrees in here.

Chavis gives me a brief primer on breaking and entering.

"You can tell which ones ain't been lived in for a while," he says. "Wasn't any lights on for a couple of nights, and there ain't no name on the mail slots outside for this dump."

We're definitely on the north side of Cary, probably near the Byrd Theater, which, like almost everything else, is closed until Mr. COVID goes away.

Chavis has been in Richmond since the twenty-eighth, the day before the Kellers breathed their last.

"Didn't plan on staying long," he says, "but then, you know, shit happened."

He already knew where the Kellers lived.

"Wasn't that hard, with Facebook and all. Why do folks put all this stuff out there anyhow? Ain't no secrets anymore."

He took off in the rental car, after visiting his sister one last time.

"She was an angel," Chavis says. "I was the bad seed, you know, and she was the good one. She deserved better. Hell, I don't even know if she knew who I was when I saw her in that place she's at now."

He wipes a tear away with the back of his right hand, the one with the gun in it.

"I wanted some justice."

I don't even bother to ask how a convicted felon awaiting a retrial and probably a resumption of his time in stir managed to get his hands on a weapon. Hell, it's Virginia.

I told him what I knew about the note he wrote to that judge six years ago.

"Yeah? Then I expect you know how pissed off I was. That just wasn't right. I wanted to make it right."

He says he was able to break into the Kellers' rental through that door leading to the basement. No surprise there.

"Got there the night before all that shit went down," he says.

He left the door unlocked and slipped back in the night of the twenty-ninth. They were still upstairs in the store "so I went down the street, had me a few beers, and then some white dude give me a toke or two. I was just taking in all the ruckus. Black folks was pissed off, but the white ones acted like they was the ones that was done wrong."

He came back after midnight, then said he waited in the basement until two A.M.

"I thought they'd go to bed and I'd catch them sleeping, you know, but finally I couldn't wait no longer. They was watching TV and all, didn't hear a thing until I was right there in their living room. It was the middle of the night, but with all that shit going on outside, I guess they couldn't sleep."

He says they both went right along with it "like sheep to the slaughter." He tied up William first, and then Susan.

"She even put her damn hands behind her back, like she was trying to help. She begged me not to hurt the baby, and then I heard the kid crying in the other room."

He didn't have a solid plan. He says he thought maybe he'd just let them know what sorry-ass people they were to wipe out a whole family and then let Daddy's lawyer get them off the hook.

"But then I'd leave, and they'd know who I was, and they'd call the cops. They swore they wouldn't, if I'd just let them go, but I knew I couldn't do that."

He shakes his head.

"Once they knew who I was, that Marva was my sister, I didn't really have no choice."

He goes over to the window and looks out.

"You know what really got me? When I told them I was Marva Rose's brother, they looked at each other like, 'Who the fuck is that?' They didn't even remember her name.

"That's when I knew I had to do 'em both."

When the Kellers were reminded of who Marva Rose is, Chavis says they got a little frantic.

He laughs.

"She even tried to put it all on him. She said she wasn't there, didn't have anything to do with it, like maybe I'd just kill him and leave her alone."

He says he shot her first so that William Keller could suffer a little more.

"And then he begs me to let him live, on account of the baby."

He shakes his head.

"You know the crazy thing? Hell, you know this already. But the baby, she was black as I am. What was up with that anyhow? Did they feel guilty or something?"

William didn't have a chance.

Afterward, Chavis says he left with the baby crying in the other room.

"I felt bad about that," he says, like abandoning a crying nine-month-old was his worst deed of the evening. "At least I shut the door to the bedroom before I did it."

He says he wasn't quite sure what to do next. He'd considered just driving back to Martinsville "which would have been the smart thing, I'll grant you."

But then he says he got caught up in the moment.

"All that shit going down, people pissin' on old Robert E. Lee's statue and all, and I thought I'd hang out for a while."

Then, by Sunday, he sees that the cops are looking for a white kid after seeing Adam on the camera leaving an hour later.

"They didn't even think about looking anywhere else," he says. "That back door, hell, I just slipped out into the night."

I ask about the shoes.

"Dumped 'em in a dumpster a block away. I had an extra pair in the car."

He turns the gun back toward me.

"And then you had to stick your big nose in it and fuck things up."

He looks closer at me.

"You passin'."

I explain that passing for white hasn't been necessary for quite some time in Richmond.

His laugh is colder than a witch's tit.

"Yeah, but it sure don't hurt, does it?"

He lights up a Marlboro and starts pacing. He wonders if I don't feel some sympathy for him, "considering how this was just one more case of Whitey getting it over on the Black man."

I don't bother to tell him how much I dislike murderers, whatever their color or that of their victims. What can you say to somebody who's waving a gun in your face, a gun that's been used a few times recently?

I try to change the subject by asking the $64,000 question.

"Why did you leave that cigarette pack in the trash?"

He stops pacing.

"What?"

I explain about the empty pack of Marlboros in the basement trash, and how neither the Kellers nor Adam Walker smoked.

"Well, ain't you the clever one?" he says. "How was I supposed to figure somebody'd look through the trash? I reckon you passed that on to the cops."

I lie and say they found it on their own.

"Just one more nail in the coffin," he mutters. "Well, they ain't got me yet."

I ask the question I've been dying, excuse the pun, to ask.

"What do you want from me?"

Chavis smiles.

"I was comin' to that," he says.

Then he asks me if I'm hungry.

"I see there's a Mickey D's down the street," he says.

My appetite isn't that great. It is possible I'm concussed. And there are better burgers than a Big Mac in about four places between here and the McDonald's he saw, including the aforementioned Citizen Burger. But what the fuck. I tell him to bring me a Quarter Pounder and some fries.

Maybe the fact that he's treating me to a late dinner is a positive sign. I could use one.

He takes out a cell phone, and I see that it's mine. I wondered why I wasn't getting any calls. Surely, I was thinking, Cindy was missing my warm body by now.

He's turned it off, of course.

When he turns it back on, he notes that I've gotten "a few" calls. I tell him that'd be my wife, who might be wondering where I am.

"Well, she's just going to have to wonder," Chavis says. "Huh. What's your bank?"

I tell him Wells Fargo.

"What's your pin number?"

And then I know who's paying for dinner.

I give it to him. He gags me again and promises he'll be back before long. He takes the phone, which I'm sure will reside in a trash bin very soon.

He's back in half an hour. Even in my current straits, the burger and fries taste good once he ties my hands in front of me so I can eat. Not the worst last meal you could get, I guess.

Then we're both sitting on the floor, him facing me and playing with the gun. The streetlights through the busted window only allow me to barely make him out.

I remind him that he was going to tell me what the hell I'm doing here. I'm not sure I'll like the answer, but anything to keep him talking and maybe try not to look like another sheep to the slaughter.

He puts his hand to his mouth and extracts a bit of hamburger from between his teeth.

"You caused me a lot of trouble," he says finally. "I figured I'd stick around here a few days, raise a little hell. It's pretty easy to steal shit when everybody's busting out the windows for you."

He laughs.

"But then you go gettin' in my business, and I felt like I had to lay low. And then there was that goddamn piece-of-shit rental car."

He says he'd parked it on one of the streets in what I know to be Scott's Addition and mostly was getting around on foot or bus.

"And then I come back on, I think it was Thursday, and the fucker has a flat tire. So I look in the back, where they keep them crappy little spares, and there wasn't no spare. The motherfuckers sent me out without a spare tire!"

He waves the gun around for emphasis. I hope the safety is on. He seems like he'd welcome the opportunity to discuss the missing spare with the rental-car company, if he wasn't in hiding.

He says the car was parked right next to an alley, so he drove it in there on three good tires and left it as far off either of the two connecting streets as he could and removed the license plates.

"What else was I gonna do?" he asks. "By then I was pretty sure they was looking for me. I sure as hell didn't want to shine no spotlight on me."

I commiserate with him over the sorry quality of car-rental companies in this day and age, but he still hasn't answered my question: Where do I fit into all of this, other than dead?

"What I want from you," Juwan Chavis says, "is a ride."

It turns out he has a cousin up in Maryland "that might be able to help me out, but I need to get up there, and I ain't feeling safe on no train or bus."

He grins. I can see a gold tooth glinting in the meager light.

"You're gonna drive me to Bel Air, Maryland."

I don't know where that is, but I readily, even eagerly, agree. Driving to Bel Air, Maryland, doesn't sound like the worst thing that could happen to me in the near future.

He waves the gun around. I can see him and it better now that my eyes have adjusted to the dark.

"After all, I think you owe me, motherfucker, after all the grief you've done caused me."

I ask him if we're going to start now. If so, I'm going to need a massive injection of Red Bull. Even my night-owl circadian rhythms are starting to do a slow dance.

He waves the gun dismissively.

"Nah, man. We can wait until the sun comes up. You look like you could use some sleep."

He says it with something close to compassion. He even finds a raggedy-ass blanket from somewhere for me to rest my weary head on.

Outside it's gone quiet. The last of the Sunday night drinkers have called it quits.

I lie there in the dark, wondering if anybody out there is missing an aged, slightly beat-up night cops reporter with a splitting headache.

Once in a while, I look across at Chavis, who has thrown a sheet over himself and lies with his back against the wall opposite me.

Once, when it's been quiet for a while, I wonder if he's asleep. As I wonder, though, I see his bloodshot eyes pop wide open.

"Don't even think about it," he advises.

I could use a smoke.

CHAPTER NINETEEN

Monday, June 15

No need for an alarm clock this morning. The bullhorn does the job just fine.

"Juwan Chavis," the voice from below booms out, "this is the police. We know you're in there. Release the hostage and we can talk."

I look at my watch. It's not quite seven. I'm reminded of the big-ass 10K race Richmond holds every year—well, every year we're not in the middle of a plague. They hold it on a Saturday in November, and it starts right underneath our damn bedroom window in the Prestwould. We always forget until some asshole with a major outdoor voice welcomes all the runners and wakes our asses up.

This is kind of like that, except the big noise is about something more important than a foot race. And the voice is that of our beloved chief of police.

Chavis is on his feet and crawling over to the broken window. I can see blue lights reflecting off the wall behind me.

"What the fuck?" my captor says. What he sees down below can't be making him very happy.

He slides back from the window.

"How'd they fuckin' find us?" he asks, looking at me accusingly. "Goddammit, you fucked me, didn't you? You must of let them know."

It seems trite to congratulate Chavis on using the fuck-word as three different parts of speech in ten seconds.

I thought about my future, assuming I have one, last night for some time before I drifted into a sleep interrupted by dreams I do not ever want to have again.

It occurred to me that, unless Juwan Chavis was smart enough to take the license plates from the rental car and put them on mine, that the aged Honda was sitting in a parking lot in the alleyway behind Carytown's shops with the original plates. It might as well have had a neon sign attached with my name on it.

Even Richmond's finest, I felt hopeful, could figure this one out after Cindy called and reported a missing husband.

This morning my optimism has been rewarded.

Maybe the cops, once they found my car, did a little searching. Maybe somebody saw a glimmer of light from Chavis's cell phone, or maybe they found some evidence of my abduction on the stairs leading up here. Maybe a pack of Camels fell out of my shirt pocket.

They obviously waited for sunup to make their big play.

I swear to Chavis that I have not done anything to alert the authorities.

"How could I?" I ask, since I'm tied up and don't have my cell phone with me.

He seems to be considering shooting me anyhow, just for the hell of it, but then decides to go in another direction.

He grabs me by the shirt collar and pulls me over to the window.

"Look out there," Chavis says. "Let your cop buddies see you."

I do as I'm told, peeking over the sill at the street below. They've blocked off Cary Street, and about half the police force seems to be standing in the middle of it, looking in my direction. For good measure, there's a rescue squad vehicle there, and a couple of fire trucks. Ready for any eventuality apparently. On the sidewalk across the street, I see my beloved.

As soon as my head pops up, a couple of L.D. Jones's quick-draw artists have their weapons pointed at me, trigger fingers itching for action. The chief quells their eagerness. Much as he'd like to shoot me, it wouldn't do much for his bid to avoid being suspended twice in two weeks. Accidentally shooting a mixed-race reporter is definitely bad PR.

"If you want to see this fucker alive again," Chavis yells, "you'll back the fuck off."

I'm wondering whether the "fuck" in "back the fuck off" is an adjective or an adverb.

L.D. wants to keep the guy talking. He asks him if he has a cell phone, but Chavis yells back that they can hear each other just fine without any help.

"If you all aren't off the street and out of here in two minutes," he says, "this asshole's going down. I'll shoot him right in front of you."

The chief urges him not to do that, to give him some time to get everybody packed up and gone. He continues to try to engage Chavis in conversation, with less-than-sensational results.

"We know you didn't mean to kill those folks," he says. "We know it must have been some kind of accident, some kind of misunderstanding . . ."

The window disappears in front of my eyes. I think at first that the cops are firing in, but it's Chavis firing out. He's obliterated that broken window so there's nothing but daylight now. I clean shards of glass off my lap as best I can.

"Don't try to bullshit me," he advises L.D. and his minions. "I know what you all goin' to do to me, but I ain't goin' down easy, I tell you that."

The gunshot has only served to further animate the police below. Finally, though, L.D. calms Chavis, assuring him that his troops will be moving out shortly.

Indeed several of the squad cars, plus the fire truck, do trundle off. For some goddamn reason, the guy driving the truck feels it necessary to sound that ear-splitting siren that I think they must use every time they take the truck out for a spin.

"They're going," I tell Chavis, who's in the shadows.

"All of them?"

I admit that there still is a police presence out there, including one of those converted Humvees cops seem so fond of. But things do seem to be quieting down.

"We just want to make sure Mr. Black is safe," the chief says, maybe the first time he's made that a priority. "When you come out with him and we see that he's OK, we'll let you go on your way."

Chavis laughs quietly and humorously.

"They must think I'm an idiot," he says. "Yeah. Minute they got you, they're gonna shoot my ass. Ain't gonna be any arrest and trial, no sir. They gonna give me the George Floyd treatment."

I try to assure him that Richmond cops aren't like that, but I have my fingers crossed. I've seen our local boys do some crazy shit when the adrenaline and testosterone kicked in at the same time.

We wait maybe fifteen minutes. I am heartened that Chavis hasn't shot me yet. For a man with two notches on his .380 caliber pistol already and a small army of cops surrounding him, he does not seem that bloodthirsty at the moment. "Nothing to lose," does not seem to be his mantra, at least for now.

Finally he decides to take matters into his own hands, at least as much as that's possible.

He yells down to the chief, who has dispersed most of his cavalry, although God knows how many are hiding in the weeds, waiting for Chavis to give them a decent shot.

I peek out the window again, and I can see a glint atop the building opposite us. A few seconds later, I detect a little movement.

"Snipers," I say. I don't know why I would tell Chavis that. Maybe there's something to that Stockholm syndrome shit, or maybe I just don't want to get caught in the crossfire.

My captor looks at me. It might be surprise I see in his eyes or even a touch of gratitude.

"Yeah," he says, "I figured on that."

He grabs me and hauls me back away from the window.

"Come on," he says. "It's time to go."

He pulls me back into the dark room and then to my feet.

I ask him where exactly we're going.

His grin seems a tad maniacal.

"Freedom," Chavis says. "We're going to freedom."

Since I have no doubt there are quite a few cops guarding the stairs I was carried up last night, it's hard to see how this is going to end well.

"You're my ticket out of here," he says.

He frees my hands, and then my feet, advising me not to try anything dumb. The gun pointed at my head reinforces his dictum against stupidity.

When he opens the door, he makes sure my body is in front of his, and he frog-marches me down the stairs like that. The car is right next to the stairs, and I can't see any cops closer to us than maybe one hundred feet. I'd have planted somebody a little nearer to the only exit out of the apartment, but that's just me.

He unlocks the passenger-side door with the remote key, then shoves me inside with him right behind me. He pushes me over the hump and emergency brake in the middle, then commands me to drive.

I can see at least four cops, all loaded for bear, standing a safe distance from what Chavis hopes is his getaway vehicle. With that gun resting firmly against my head, nobody in blue seems eager to stop us.

As I back out and then head down the alleyway, I am reminded of a story from years ago in which state police in North Carolina set up a roadblock at the Virginia border on Interstate 85 and then opened fire on a kidnapper and his victim. Unfortunately they somehow got the idea that the kidnapper would be driving, which was bad news for the abductee, who was shot to death several times over.

Please, I pray, make the Richmond cops smart enough to know the abductee is always the driver.

As we turn on to Colonial and head away from Carytown, with a slow-motion parade of cop cars behind us, I ask Chavis if he'd mind taking that gun away from my noggin before he accidentally shoots me.

He takes the weapon away and is about to answer when his head explodes.

As it turns out, there was another sniper perched in the bushes alongside Sheppard, waiting for my head and Juwan Chavis's gun to achieve a little separation.

Brain matter and blood have splattered all over my face and made a mess of my shirt. I don't even remember stopping the car. Maybe we just coasted onto the curb, miraculously not hitting anything. Did I scream like a little girl? No comment.

In seconds, a big cop in the requisite World War III gear drags me out and hauls me across the street. For some reason, he searches me, as if I might have been Chavis's accomplice instead of his victim.

A lieutenant comes up and tells the idiot to stop treating me like a goddamn accomplice. I'm about half-blind from the parts of Juwan Chavis's head that are now stuck to my face. Somebody hands me a rag, and I wipe it off as best I can.

The chief gets there probably half a minute after Chavis's demise.

"Goddamn, L.D.," I say as he peers down at me and takes in the mess his sharpshooter has made of my clothes and exposed skin, "what the fuck? What if he'd missed? What if the guy had pulled the trigger before you shot him?"

"Well," he says, "if you do it right, that doesn't happen. And believe it or not, we usually don't fuck up. Anyhow close doesn't count, right?"

Maybe it's my imagination that there is a twinkle in the chief's eye.

They let Cindy through, and she's semi-hysterical when she sees me, before I assure her that all that mess on my shirt was someone else's remnants.

Against the advice of the paramedics, I stand up, confident that I'm suffering no ill effects from my brush with eternity that a shower and a trip to the cleaners won't fix.

Cindy ensures that she, too, will be sending out some laundry soon by hugging me with both arms.

"You fucking idiot," she whispers through her corona mask. "When are you going to stop trying to get your ass killed?"

Later I'll point out that I truly did not wish to be kidnapped and used as a hostage by a crazy man.

Right now, though, I'm happy just to embrace the embrace.

THE MAIN paramedic advised me to take it easy the rest of the day. He said something about PTSD, but I told him I didn't think you could catch that in just twelve hours. Talk to me later.

Screw rest. If I don't get into the office and write this, Wheelie or Sarah will send Leighton Byrd or some other lean and hungry youngster over to write about me. If I'm going to be subjected to cops playing William Tell with my noggin, I'll be the one to write the story.

After a good, long shower, after which the stall surely will need a thorough cleaning, Cindy does force me to take a little nap. Even without Chavis residue, my face is no prize. The area around my eyes is a mixture of purple and green, compliments of that pistol-whipping. I've lost a tooth. I think I'm down to twenty-six now.

It is a little hard to sleep after you've cleaned brain matter off yourself, though, and an hour later, I'm headed out the door, with Cindy on my heels, threatening domestic violence if I leave.

There is some surprise in the newsroom when I walk in. It's almost eleven A.M., and there are only nine people in sight, but they all descend on me like horseflies on a dead deer. Any news outlet with an online presence has already given the public the basics: Murder suspect assaults and hijacks police reporter and is blown away by cops.

Sarah is the adult supervision, so she gets first crack.

"What the hell are you doing here?" she asks.

I have a story to write, I explain.

Leighton, who seems to live in the newsroom, touches me carefully on my battered face and asks me if I'm concussed. Her concern would be touching if I didn't know that she probably would sign away her future first-born for the chance to write this one herself.

I assure her, and the rest, that I'm fine, other than a bit of a headache and a sore back from sleeping on the floor in an abandoned apartment last night.

"Well, take it easy," Sarah says, frowning. When I sit down, she peers at the top of my chrome dome.

"You've got something . . ." she starts to reach down and brush it away, then jumps back.

"Oh, shit!"

So I make a quick trip to the washroom and then get to work.

Before I proceed to tell our readers about my most recent brush with the Reaper, I do have to make some calls.

Jeanette has already heard about this morning's excitement. She sounds happy that I'm alive, which is generous of her, considering my track record as a husband.

"But they still haven't found Adam," she says.

I tell her not to worry, that, wherever he is, surely he'll learn very soon that he definitely is not the prime suspect in a double homicide. I only hope that's true.

I'm also duty-bound to call Rob Solomon in Raleigh and Ella Minopee in Martinsville. They'll get the story I wrote, before it gets sent to the Associated Press, and they can use anything I give them to do their own, localized versions of the recent weirdness.

"Damn," Ella says when I catch her at lunch, "you're gonna need a major bourbon transfusion, Willie. And maybe some new underwear too."

It's also essential that I call my old mom, who might or might not have heard the news.

She has.

"What the hell, Willie?" she says, stopping to cough. "How much do they pay you to do this shit anyhow?"

She and Awesome Dude are, she says, feeling a little better today.

"Not good enough to break out a joint, I hope."

She tells me to mind my own business.

I do agree to let Leighton interview the chief, who no doubt will take the opportunity to point out that, against all evidence to the contrary, the police can do something right once in a while. There might be a smidgeon of concern among the woke readership over a Black man being deprived of the opportunity for a fair trial, or even an arrest, but anybody who reads my piece won't have that much sympathy for Juwan Chavis, who took a grudge about as far as you could take it.

Bootie Carmichael trundles over from the sports department and has the last word before I start writing.

"Brother," he says, putting his meaty paw on my shoulder, "if that ain't entertainment, I'll kiss your ass."

CHAPTER TWENTY

Tuesday, June 16

For some time, the rumor around the paper has been that we'll stop being a seven-day operation sometime soon. Hell, bigger cities than Richmond don't get a print paper delivered to readers' doorsteps every morning.

The smart money, among the newsroom cognoscenti, was on Tuesday. You don't have any weekend sports news to impart (unless you count Sunday night stuff that ends too late for Monday's paper), and the new week hasn't really gotten up and running yet.

Today's edition might make the bean counters at Grimm Group headquarters, who are Satan's handmaidens, think twice.

Even Tuesday can be a big news day.

The stem-winder on the Kellers and Juwan Chavis runs ninety inches, which would have caused wailing and gnashing of teeth in the past, before we barely had enough reporters to fill our shrinking news hole. Sky's the limit these days.

I tell the tale from the Keller murders on May 30 through Adam Walker's arrest and then the mounting and finally overwhelming evidence of Juwan Chavis's guilt and his confession to an ink-stained wretch he'd kidnapped.

Adam is exonerated, but nobody knows where he is. My epic meandered through the sad story of the Rose family that put Chavis on the road to vendettaville. A lot of this had been dribbled out in bits and pieces already, but a good reporter knows that you have to tie it all together at some point. That's what wins those three-dollar Virginia Press Association awards.

The first-person bit, on the joys of being kidnapped, hearing Chavis's confession, and having a human head explode inches away from my own, pretty much told itself and ate up another sixty inches. Chip Grooms somehow got there in time to get a nice photo of me cleaning myself up in the shooting's aftermath.

Leighton's interview with the chief added another thirty inches to the package. Poor L.D. Everything that happens in the city of Richmond seems to land on his head. He and the police department are still catching heat for real and imagined misdeeds. There were more protests last night, and the section of Grace Street around headquarters will not be open to traffic again for some time.

And, of course, the knee-jerk reaction to Chavis's killing is to trot out the BLM flag again.

"If he'd been white," one of the self-appointed woke leaders said in the story Leighton filed, "they wouldn't have been so quick to shoot to kill."

As the guy whose head was in close proximity to that .380 caliber pistol, I have to disagree. If Chavis had been allowed to leave the city, there would have been a torturous procession along I-95 that would have ended badly at some point, maybe for me and Chavis both. Plus, doesn't the chief get a little credit for saving the life of a man who can claim some African American heritage?

The protesters have branched out. Some of them went to the mayor's home last night and created quite a ruckus.

This no doubt will make L.D. even more popular with the guy who would fire him in a heartbeat if he could.

Already Hizzoner seems to have the chief lined up on the sidewalk, with his hands on L.D.'s back, as one of those fancy new Pulse buses approaches.

"We are appalled at some of the actions of our police department," the mayor said when he held an impromptu press conference this morning. "We want to make sure that the excessive force that seems to be endemic in our police department is brought under control."

In other words, please don't picket my house anymore. It's not my fault. The police did it.

I talked with L.D. this morning myself, mostly to thank him for saving my ass yesterday.

"Can I send you my laundry bill?" I asked.

I couldn't resist adding: "Were you really sure your guy would be able to pick off Chavis and miss me?"

"Willie," the chief said, "if he had missed Chavis and killed you, I'd be out of a job right now, tape or no tape."

I told the chief I was glad he had his priorities in order. Priority No. 1: Don't get fired. Priority No. 2: Don't kill reporter.

"Hey," he said, "you can't live forever."

As I haven't had a nonworking day in a while, I am taking a little comp time. Cindy takes care of that gap in my scheduling by reminding me that I still haven't made good on my promise to take her to that winery down on the James River off Route 5.

Busted. My complaint that my face hurts and might scare small children if I go out in public doesn't get me an ounce of sympathy.

She advises me that I've got to "get right back on that horse." I point out that this particular horse threw me pretty badly yesterday.

"I don't see any of the other reporters getting kidnapped and almost shot," she says.

That's because they aren't trying hard enough, I reply.

"To get shot?" she asks.

I tell my beloved that we'll hit the road as soon as I make a couple of calls. She rolls her eyes, no doubt remembering how a couple of calls can turn into another "off" day shot to hell.

But it can't be helped.

A call to Peachy confirms that they still haven't been able to find Adam Walker. However a trucker says he picked up a guy hitchhiking on a stretch of highway between Hillsville and Galax. When he saw a story and picture concerning the search for Adam in a *Roanoke Times* he picked up at a Sheets station afterward, he was pretty sure it was the guy to whom he gave a ride.

The trucker let Adam, if it was Adam, off in Laurel Cove, near where the Appalachian Trail crosses a US highway. That was yesterday afternoon.

"The driver told the cops out there that the kid talked about hiking the AT, although he didn't seem to have any hiking equipment with him. He said he just wanted to get away for a while."

Peachy says the trucker told the police that the kid seemed "a little squirrelly."

Yeah, that sounds like our boy.

So the cops down there are looking for him. They have been told and retold that Adam is not a threat, that he is probably unarmed, and that he is not a suspect of anything more serious than jumping bail over a crime he did not commit.

Peachy promises she'll keep me informed, and that somebody will be in touch with Jeanette and Glenn.

Just in case the cops aren't giving top priority to notifying the Walkers, I call.

Churlish Buddy answers the phone and then passes it on to his mother. I can hear him say, "I think it's Andi's asshole father."

I tell Jeanette the latest, which doesn't thrill her. The idea of Adam on the Appalachian Trail fills me with dread, and my concerns are one degree of separation from Ground Zero. She says that she is going to take off work the rest of the week and drive to Laurel Cove.

I try to discourage this, noting that he's had a whole day to go somewhere else. Laurel Cove must be three hundred damn miles away from here. It's like driving to New York City. Before our conversation is over, she's promised to at least think about it. Glenn apparently can't afford to take off work, so she'd be on her own.

"How about Buddy?" I ask.

"Oh," Jeanette says, "he's got other things going on. I don't think he'd care much for making that trip."

Other than Andi's very early years, I was never heavily involved in nurturing the young. All the survivors say it's worth all the sweat and tears you put into it. Thinking about Jeanette and Glenn's offspring, one of them lost and addled somewhere out there in the big world and the other one apparently as worthless as a broke-dick dog, I do wonder if I've missed all that much.

There isn't a lot for me to write about for tomorrow's paper. I leave a message for Sarah in case anyone wants to do the latest update of Where's Adam?

Then it's off to the winery we go.

Wineries aren't a bad option in "these difficult times." As long as the weather's good, and it usually is in Virginia this time of year, there are plenty of places to sit outside and nurse a bottle of vino while you nosh on overpriced sandwiches. Cindy seems to like it. The James is just across the big field out back of the place she's chosen.

Virginia wineries aren't bad. I'm sure wine snobs from California turn up their noses at our cabernet francs and viogniers, but my simple-ass taste buds can't really tell the difference between a twelve-dollar bottle and a hundred-dollar bottle, so I'm good.

I get some strange looks. I feel like I should have a mask that covers my whole face instead of just my mouth and nose. The purple and green have intensified if anything.

"Got in a fight with a guy who wouldn't wear his mask," I explain to a woman at a table ten feet away when I catch her staring. Cindy has to assure her that I'm kidding.

Hell, nobody's wearing a mask out here. Unless you punch a hole in the thing and drink wine through a straw, it isn't going to happen. They do not, however, allow you to smoke outdoors, lest you give the cardinals cancer.

We talk about Adam. Cindy knows him less well than I do, but she's worried too. She tends to worry about the needy, which is why I'm sharing my living space with two worthless cats who only see us as food dispensers.

"Maybe you should ride down there with her, maybe drive her down," Cindy says.

"You trust me to take a long road trip with my ex-wife?"

She laughs.

"You're harmless," she says. I'm hurt.

She latches on to the idea and, as is her wont, will not let it go.

"The cops aren't going to knock themselves out looking for him," she says, "and if they do, they need somebody down there making sure they know the boy's harmless."

"I don't have any more vacation days," I protest.

"You worked the last three Sundays and Mondays," Cindy points out. "That's six days they owe you. Plus you've got your damn unpaid furlough."

We leave the winery by three thirty. On the way out, a guy in a business suit at one of the tables we pass looks at me and says, "Nice job, Willie."

Reporters do not often get recognized, which might be a good thing. It does kind of make my day, though, hard as I try not to show it.

"You are ridiculous," Cindy says.

I explain that I really need to check in briefly at the office, just to see if anything's happened regarding Adam.

It's after seven, and I spend the built-up points I earned by finally making good on our grape expedition.

"Don't get caught up in all that crap at the monuments," she says as I'm leaving.

In the lobby, where he seems to live, Feldman gets a look at my face and shakes his head.

"I wish you wouldn't get involved with so many criminals," he says. "It gives the Prestwould a bad name."

I congratulate McGrumpy on reading the paper and advise him to mind his own fucking business.

Leighton has cooked up something from the information I left with Sarah plus her own digging. Adam was allegedly seen on the streets of Laurel Cove, but nobody knows where he is right now.

She also informs me that he is officially not a suspect in the Keller murders. No shit. Now somebody's got to let Adam know.

The woke apparently are aiming low tonight. We get word that some of them are in the process of taking down a small monument in the Fan near the VCU campus commemorating some forgettable Civil War escapade.

I get there after the deed has been done. J.E.B. Stuart, Stonewall Jackson, and Marse Robert are still standing, probably because their removal might require more than a few drunk millennials and Gen Z kids with a rope and pulley. It's worth a few words though. The newsroom has a pool going on which monument will go next, and I don't think this one even made the list.

I feed a few grafs to Leighton, who seems grateful, then head home.

When I tell Cindy that Adam was spotted in Laurel Cove today, she redoubles her efforts to have me drive my first ex-wife out there.

Finally I succumb. I would rather pull out my own fingernails, but I owe Jeanette for not killing me in my sleep during our storm-tossed marriage, in which all the waves were created by Willie.

I call her. She is still hell-bent on going tomorrow morning, with no volunteer codriver. I offer my services, silently hoping she will decline.

She doesn't.

"I'd like to leave as early as possible," she says after thanking me. "How about seven?"

"In the morning?"

She does agree to drive here and pick me up.

Cindy kisses me and thanks me for being a rock.

A rock would be allowed to remain stationary, I reply.

"Still, it's a nice thing."

"Do you mind if we share a room?" I ask.

"Not as long as you keep one foot on the floor."

CHAPTER TWENTY-ONE

Wednesday, June 17

We reach Laurel Cove at twelve thirty after dodging eighteen-wheelers on I-81 much of the way. My butt has gone to sleep, and the rest of me would like to.

The ride down was not unpleasant, despite the fact that Jeanette chose not to let me befoul her minivan with cigarette smoke. We do have a lot in common, especially a daughter and our much-beloved grandson.

I compliment her, not for the first time, on raising Andi after I left. She says it was a pleasure.

"You don't know what you missed," she says, giving me a hint of a smile.

Yes, I tell her. I do.

"You aren't such bad company these days," my ex says as we breeze past Roanoke. The unspoken addendum to that sentence is: "compared with what an asshole you were back then."

She says Glenn wanted to come, but blah-blah-blah. He's going to drive down after he gets off work. I wonder what kind of father and husband would send his wife out alone on a mission like this, but he might wonder what kind of father and husband would abandon his family for a little pussy.

If you screw up as much as I have, you don't have the luxury of being judgmental.

THE LAUREL Cove cops are less than helpful until Jeanette makes it clear that, as Adam's mother, she'd damn well better get some information, otherwise the media—here, she points to me—is going to have some unkind things to say about Southwest Virginia law enforcement.

They finally tell us that they think they have him cornered. In just the past three hours, somebody in a vacation cottage not far from the AT reported what appeared to be a break-in at the place next door. The cops, including a couple of state police, responded and saw what appeared to be a young white male intruder inside.

"Please be careful," Jeanette pleads after she fills the cops in on what they should already know: The guy they have cornered is innocent.

"He's has Asperger's. Sometimes he acts out."

"Ass what?" one of the deputies says. This seems to pass for high humor, to judge by the chuckles that follow. Jeanette patiently explains.

"Well," the older of the two troopers says, "we'll be OK as long as he doesn't do something threatening."

Jeanette starts to say something else but then doesn't.

I put out my Camel and point out that Adam almost certainly isn't armed.

"Sir," the guy says, in a tone that makes "sir" sound like "shithead," "you'd be amazed by how many law-enforcement personnel have been killed by so-called unarmed individuals."

A skinny local cop asks just what my connection is to "the suspect."

I explain that I am the ex-husband.

"So he's your son?"

"No. We've been divorced a long time."

"So the suspect is no kin to you?"

I explain as patiently as I can that he is not a suspect.

"You can call the police chief in Richmond," I say. "He'll tell you. The commonwealth's attorney has dropped all charges."

Barney Fife says he doesn't think that will be necessary, that Laurel Cove is capable of taking care of its own damn law enforcement.

We are driven a couple miles west by one of the state cops. He takes a right off a winding stretch of road that in no way resembles a US highway, and then we climb for what seems like a mile, passing two other dwellings. People come out to watch as the state car goes by. It seems they don't get much excitement around here.

"There it is," the cop says, pointing to an A-frame on top of a little rise. When we get close enough to park, the view is spectacular. You can see about four layers of mountains off to the west.

"Bet you don't have anything like this in Richmond," our driver says. I have to concede that this is true.

There are a couple of county cars here already, in addition to a state police vehicle and an EMT presence.

"Oh, my God," Jeanette says. "Do they really need all this?"

"Got to be ready for anything," the state cop says.

There are half a dozen state and local uniforms behind a big-ass rock that sits in front of and twenty feet below the front door to the A-frame, which is maybe one hundred feet away.

They've apparently been waiting for word from on high before trying to coax Adam out, although these guys don't appear to be the type who would be good at saying "Please."

Half an hour after Jeanette and I get there, on some unseen signal, the show begins.

"Adam Walker," booms the bullhorn-enhanced voice from the state cop five feet away. "We know you're in there. Come out and no one will be hurt. You need to step outside, with your hands in the air."

"God," Jeanette says to me "It's so loud. It's going to freak him out."

No response from Adam, if it's Adam in there.

Another entreaty gets the same nonresponse.

Jeanette has been begging the guy with the bullhorn to let her talk to her son.

Finally the bullhorn guy shrugs and hands it to her.

"Adam," she says, her voice hoarse and frantic, amplified by the bullhorn. "It's your mother. Honey, please come out. You didn't do anything wrong. They got the guy who did it. We know you're innocent. Please just do what they say. Everything's OK. Just come out."

Nothing happens for another thirty seconds. One of the state cops starts talking about charging the A-frame.

Then we see the front door open slightly. I hear metallic clicking. Locked and loaded.

The state cop grabs the bullhorn.

"Just step out with your hands in the air," he says. Jeanette is screaming, trying to make herself heard.

Adam comes out onto a covered front porch, seemingly an inch at a time.

"Put your hands in the air!" the cop screams. "Hands in the air! Hands in the air!"

Adam has grown a scraggly little beard and looks like he hasn't combed his hair since he took off. He looks confused, but he does put his hands up.

He moves a couple of steps forward, toward four wooden steps. Two of the cops scramble up the hill toward him, guns at the ready.

"Get on your knees!" one of them commands. "On your knees, right damn now!"

He stops at the edge of the steps, hands still above his head. If he gets on his knees, he'll topple forward. Instead he starts to walk down the steps.

The cops are all screaming now, and Adam looks like he's losing it a little.

He looks past the cops to Jeanette. He smiles at her. Then he reaches down like he's going to put his hand in his pocket.

Aw, shit. I've seen this movie before.

There isn't time to do anything except scream "No! No!"

Adam is blown back by the first shotgun blast. More small-arms fire finishes him off, and he rolls down the steps and onto that pretty front yard with the view of four ridges in the distance. Maybe that was the last thing he saw.

CHAPTER TWENTY-TWO

The rest of the day is kind of a blur.

I am able to get in touch with Glenn after Jeanette gives me his work number.

I have to tell him three times before he believes it, then says he's going to get in his truck and drive down, which he already was planning to do in a couple of hours.

I urge him to have somebody else drive, but I'm not sure he's even listening.

"Gotta find Buddy," he says. Then he hangs up.

The EMT people, after determining that Adam is gone, turn their attention to Jeanette, who is sitting on the ground, looking off at those faraway mountains.

"She's in shock," one of them confides to me, as if even a damn liberal arts major couldn't figure that one out.

I look at my watch. It's not yet three in the afternoon. Good God. It seems like we've been up here for days.

The cops are all in a huddle, no doubt trying to figure out how to cover their asses. Must be their worst fucking nightmare, shooting an unarmed kid to death while a reporter and the kid's mother look on.

Yeah, when they search his blood-soaked pockets, all they find are the keys to that car he abandoned in

Bluefield, plus eighty-seven cents in change. They're so discombobulated by it all that they don't even seem aware that I am looking over their shoulders.

I didn't get the iPhone out in time to record the shooting, but I do get a lot of shots of the body and the cops standing around looking guilty and freaked-out.

Finally the huddle breaks up. The oldest state cop comes over to talk to Jeanette, who is being attended to by the paramedics. She is adamantly resisting a trip to the local hospital. I finally assure everyone that I will take care of Jeanette until her present husband shows up.

"We were told he was armed," the state guy says.

"By who?"

He can't say. The answer probably is nobody.

He starts telling me about some drunk five years ago who shot a deputy when the deputy thought the drunk was just reaching for his car keys.

"You can't just shoot him in the leg, or Tase him or something?" I ask, knowing already what the answer is. When cops shoot, they're aiming to neutralize you. Nothing neutralizes you like being dead.

"She told you he had Asperger's," I remind the cop.

He shakes his head and looks at me.

"You're going to make this sound like we shot him for no reason," he says.

I tell him I'm just going to report what I saw, and if he tries to stop me, it isn't going to go so well.

He moves in a little closer than I would have liked.

"These local guys," he says, "they don't mean any harm, but they get all jacked up when they think there's going to be some action."

I assume from what he's telling me that it was the local cops who did the shooting. Well, he'll have plenty of time to tell that to the investigators.

"Coulda been worse," I hear the skinny deputy say. "He coulda been Black."

At my age, maybe I couldn't have taken him, but rage can be a great asset in a fistfight. The state trooper grabs me halfway there, and an older deputy pulls Barney Fife away.

In the meantime, everybody within earshot of a one-way gun battle has ascended or descended on the place to gawk. This high up, it's already starting to get a little chilly. It feels like April instead of June.

I ask the trooper if he can get me and Jeanette the hell out of there.

The state police give us a ride back into town, where we are offered the hospitality of some kind of town hall. I try to help Jeanette, who's bouncing from one thought to another. Funeral. Got to let the rest of the family know. Can I call Andi? Where's Buddy? How do we get the body back to Richmond?

I find that there's a motel a block away. I call and make a reservation.

"Come on," I tell Jeanette. "We're getting you out of here."

We get checked in. I call Glenn to tell him where we are. He's already to Charlottesville, with Buddy in tow, but still four good hours from here.

"You need to sleep," I tell my ex, who says she might never sleep again.

The EMT folks did give her something to help her chill, and I convince her to take it. By four thirty, she's out cold.

Even on the worst day I've had in quite a while, the reporter in me kicks in.

I sit on the other bed and make some calls, first to Andi and then to Cindy. Neither of them is willing to believe what I'm telling them. I have to persuade Andi not to come here, that we're headed back to Richmond as soon as humanly possible. Cindy wants to come get me. I tell her I'll catch a ride with Jeanette and Glenn.

And then I do the thing you'd expect a good reporter to do. We go to the battlefield afterward and shoot the wounded.

The enormity of it is such that nobody believes what I'm telling them first time around.

"Sarah," I say, trying to speak slowly and not yell, "just get somebody on the phone who can take dictation. I'll fill in the details later, and, no, I don't have a goddamn laptop with me."

"They really killed him?" Sarah asks.

"Don't make me say it again."

"Email it," she says. Of course. I'm struck again with how twentieth century my addled brain is.

I go into the bathroom so I won't wake Jeanette. I sit on the toilet and start writing on my iPhone, which takes forever, since the iPhone's keyboard was made for elves. I'm hoping there is at least one decent copy editor left in the building, because this one is going to need some work.

I keep my own self out of it, other than to note that the events were observed by a reporter from our esteemed rag.

There's plenty to relate from the scene of the crime though: the mother coming down from Richmond with a reporter to try to reach her son the last place he'd been seen, the local cops taking mother and reporter to the scene of the standoff, although I change "standoff" to "cabin where Walker allegedly had been seen" because standoff implies that two equally well-armed parties are at an impasse.

This was more like carpet-bombing an ant.

When I start writing about the shooting itself, I find that the details are particularly well-ingrained in my brain. There is little doubt that law-enforcement personnel and their fucking lawyers will dispute some of the details. All the more reason to get it all down now, while it's fresh.

They can't get away with saying that he was armed, unless they kill me first. Too bad that I, like apparently almost everybody else in this damn country, doesn't immediately go for the iPhone camera when anything even potentially interesting happens. I do send some post-mortem shots from the scene though.

They can say Adam wasn't follow orders fast enough, that he was moving toward them in a threatening manner, but they will have to overcome the eyewitness accounts of both me and Jeanette if they want to make that stick.

I even get in the line from that graceless deputy, about being thankful the guy they killed wasn't Black. Yeah, it'll cost him his job. Fuck him.

I get a little purple in the lede:

"Adam Walker looked confused and unsure about what to do next. Finally he took that fatal step forward, and a chain reaction began, one shot following a hail of others. Adam flew backward and then tumbled down the steps, landing in the front yard, his body occasionally jerking when another bullet hit him. He probably was already dead. The distant mountains across the valley beside the A-frame might have been the last thing he saw. The last thing he heard probably was his mother's screams."

I silently apologize to the sleeping Jeanette, for sharing her grief with thousands of strangers. It's what I do.

GLENN GETS there sometime after eight. Buddy's with him, looking like he wants to hit somebody.

By then, Jeanette's been awake for a couple of hours, and I've helped her get the wheels in motion to have Adam's body sent back to Richmond after they've done an autopsy, although what the hell they'll find, I don't know. Maybe they'll find traces of some drug in his system so the cops can claim he was so strung out that they had to shoot him.

I want to leave the Walkers alone with their grief. It's easy enough. Somebody has to drive Jeanette's car back to Richmond, and the three of them intend to stay here overnight and drive back in the morning in order to take care of "the details."

Jeanette thanks me, as does Glenn, who wants me to tell him, blow by blow, how his younger son was shot to death.

"I reckon you're going to put this in your damn paper," he says.

I tell him the world needs to know, if there's going to be any kind of justice.

"Justice," he repeats the word like it's a curse. "There ain't enough justice in the world to make up for this."

Glenn Walker might not think he has a lot in common with George Floyd's family right now, but he'd be wrong.

CINDY SAYS I'm an idiot. She says that a lot. She thinks I ought to just get a hotel room.

"Even if you want to drive partway, stop at the Hotel Roanoke or somewhere. You're too old for this shit, Willie."

I tell her that I'll drive until I get tired.

With a can of Red Bull inside me and another one on the seat, I get into a groove. The interstate at night can be kind of soothing, in a twisted sort of way. After a while, the miles just go by unnoticed.

I stop and call Sarah again before ten to see if she was able to salvage the iPhone epistle I sent earlier.

"It was fine," she says. "Just had to run it through spell-check."

Yeah, who needs editors when you've got spell-check?

She was able to find out that no one from state or local law enforcement in Southwest Virginia had checked to confirm that Adam had been cleared.

"You did tell them, right?"

I confirm that I did and note that they'll probably deny it, but that Jeanette was by my side when I informed them of his innocence.

She says it's been a typical night in Richmond, typical for mid-June 2020 anyhow. They've put a concrete barrier around the Lee Monument, where the crowds are large and loud but mostly peaceful. You can still add your work to the graffiti adorning it, but you can't drive a truck into it anymore.

"It hasn't been that quiet a night in the newsroom either," she adds.

More layoffs are coming. Just when we think we've hit rock-bottom, Grimm Group comes in and digs another subbasement for us.

"Any police reporters on the hit list?" I ask as I take a gulp of the second Red Bull.

"I don't think so," she says. "We'll know for sure tomorrow. But they'd sure as hell have a hard time firing your ass after what happened today."

Another day like this, I tell her, and they won't have to fire me.

CHAPTER TWENTY-THREE

Thursday, June 18

I kept driving. Roanoke became Lexington became the exit to I-64 outside Staunton. Somewhere in there, Cindy called, and I promised her I would stop and find a motel soon. I don't even remember going over Afton Mountain and more or less came to as I passed the Short Pump Mall abomination on the edge of the suburbs.

Cindy didn't even wake up when I stumbled in the front door sometime after three.

NEXT THING I know, she's waking me up. The clock reads 7:14.

"How did you get here?" she asks.

Red Bull, I explain, then roll back over.

When I wake up again at nine thirty, sleep is pretty damn impossible. Cindy is waiting for me in the living room. Apparently there are no young minds to mold today.

I give her the sad details, although she's read many of them in the morning paper already.

"I can't even imagine what that must be like," she says, then cuts herself off short. Custalow, enjoying a rare morning away from his thankless duties as the Prestwould's maintenance manager, is in the kitchen, making coffee. The big Indian knows how it feels to lose a child. The son he barely knew has been gone four years now after an episode we'd all like to forget. I hope he has at least forgiven me. Yeah, it was him or his son, but I didn't ask Abe to choose. I did that for him.

Our condo-mate acts as if he didn't overhear Cindy and asks me to repeat some of what I've said already. Then he claims he has to check on a leak up on the twelfth floor.

Marcus Green calls me sometime after eleven. I know his ambulance-chasing ass wants to be the Walkers' attorney in their inevitable lawsuit against the trigger-happy idiots who killed their son. I guess he has first dibs, having been Adam's lawyer.

I urge him to show a little restraint.

"They won't even be back in town until this afternoon at the earliest."

"You're not talking to some guy that's just hung out his shingle," he replies, all huffy. "I know how to deal with the bereaved."

I am sure Marcus will ensure that Jeanette and Glenn eventually get compensated greatly for something money can't replace. I know that Kate will ensure that he treats the family with dignity and respect.

"You might be one of my witnesses in this one," he says.

I tell him that's fine, that I took very good notes.

"Yeah," Marcus says. "I read the paper. Good job."

He's quiet for a couple of seconds.

"You know, Willie," he says when he speaks again, "don't take this the wrong way, but I'm not the only one out there cashing in on somebody's grief. At least they'll get a check from me when it's all over."

I tell him to go fuck himself, and then I hang up.

The bastard's right, of course. Watching Adam Walker get shot to death and then telling the world about it might save my sorry-ass job and earn me some cheap press-association hardware. I can claim that I did it all in the pursuit of truth and justice. When I go into the bathroom to shave, that's what I tell myself.

I'm in the newsroom by two. Most of the staff is now working from home until the plague passes. What few staffers who are there have more to think about than my recent adventures. A lot of them were called in for bad news.

The layoffs were indeed announced today. I am still among the living, although my relief is mixed with guilt.

The whole damn copy desk is going, going, gone. The Grimm Group has decided that those anonymous toilers at some Midwestern location can do all our copy editing for us from now on, because they have so much institutional and geographical knowledge about the greater Richmond area.

My old drinking buddy Ray Long has, I learn, come and gone after cursing the paper that was until today his employer for most of his adult life.

Enos Jackson, lean, balding, and wearing the same kind of white shirt and black pants he's worn for forty years of newspapering, is in the process of cleaning out his desk. Actually there isn't much cleaning to do. He has a smallish cardboard box in which I see a chipped coffee mug, a few notepads, a bottle of aspirin, and a Cal Ripken Jr. bobblehead doll.

We chat for a few minutes. Enos is already sixty-five, so I'm less sympathetic toward him than I might be, but I know he doesn't have much in the way of outside interests other than the Orioles. This probably is the first year he hasn't gone up to Baltimore for a few games. I wonder what he's going to do with himself.

He takes down his COVID mask for a few seconds and says he'll be fine.

I don't know why I do it, but I tell him something that's been inside my head for a decade now. I tell him about the time I secretly (or so I thought) blackmailed our then-publisher, the redoubtable and now late Grubby Grubbs, into leaving him off that year's death list.

He nods his head.

"Yeah," he says, "I knew about that."

"How?"

The usual newsroom way. Nobody can keep a secret. Grubby mentioned it to Wheelie, who probably blabbed it to somebody on the copy desk while swearing that person to secrecy, and eventually Enos knew.

"You've been a good friend," he says. Enos is not one for grand emotions, or even small ones. When he reaches out to shake my hand, it means something.

Something suddenly clicks in my brain. Every Christmas for the last decade, some Secret Santa has left me a fifth of Knob Creek at my desk. In my vanity, I often pondered whether it was some female staffer silently smitten by my charm and good looks. I never knew who Santa was, until now.

I promise him that he and I will go up and see the Birds again next spring, when this pandemic shit is past.

He nods and says that'd be fine.

We leave it at that. I wonder if I'll ever see him again.

Sarah and Wheelie are in Wheelie's office. At least they had the good grace to deliver the bad news themselves. Benson Stine, our most recent publisher, has taken a powder, as publishers often do in trying times.

They congratulate me on doing such a fine job of exposing the Walkers' wounds to our dwindling readership.

"That must have been awful," Sarah says. "I mean, she was right there . . ."

Wheelie asks me if I'm planning to write anything else for tomorrow's paper. I tell him I don't think there's much left to say. I know they'll want some kind of wrap-up for the Sunday edition, where I'll probably write the same thing I wrote today, with maybe a little more postmortem. Might have something about a lawsuit, although Marcus has plenty of time to file.

"You look like shit, by the way," Wheelie says. "Why don't you take the rest of the day off?"

They tell me that Chuck Apple had his hands full subbing for me on night cops last night.

The hell-raising at the Lee Monument and around police headquarters was minimal, but there was some considerable unpleasantness at one of the more popular joints over in Shockoe Bottom.

A group of assholes went in without masks and refused to put on the ones they were offered by the poor son of a bitch who was tasked with guarding the door. They had him outnumbered four to one, but then the regular clientele took over.

"They had to take two of them to the hospital, along with one of the patrons who threw the guys out," Sarah says, "and the place apparently is a wreck. Chuck said they were still brawling out on the street when he got there."

In the paper this morning, which I'm finally reading, one of the wounded warriors said, "Why should I wear that [bleeping] mask? The [bleeping] president doesn't wear one."

Those damn COVID masks have everybody a little cranky. They make it hard to breathe. They fog up your glasses so you can't see.

I've seen corona rage rear its head at the Prestwould. People who didn't wear masks themselves until they saw people getting sick and dying put them on, and then, when they see other people deciding the mask just isn't their style, they get a case of the red-ass.

Marcia the manager was reduced to tears on one occasion, Custalow told me, because of a resident who refused to cover up and was rude about it. Abe said he had a talk with the offending party, who then saw the error of his ways.

I'M PONDERING taking Wheelie's advice. It is hard for me to believe all that's happened in the last thirty or so hours. Between the 300-plus-mile drives to and from Southwest Virginia and the shitstorm in between, not mentioning a kidnapping, I do feel a little tired.

But then, news happens.

Sarah answers the phone, and it's the attorney general's office.

"They've got an injunction," she says.

A circuit court judge has saved the Lee Monument, to the frustration of the governor and the attorney general, who no doubt already had the trucks lined up to haul Marse Robert away.

Sarah says she can call Leighton Byrd, who's working from home on a big Sunday piece about the city's efforts to educate its students if this mess isn't over by late August.

"I've got it," I tell her and Wheelie. They tell me to go home, that Callie Ann Boatwright or one of the other kids can handle it.

They don't really argue that strenuously though.

The judge, it turns out, lives near enough to the monument to have concerns about property values. The plaintiffs are also mostly Monument Avenue residents. One of them claims his great-granddaddy had the original deed that says Lee stays where he is until hell freezes over. The attorney general's office says there soon will be a cold snap in Hades.

God knows how long this crap will be tied up in the courts.

I go over to the Lee Monument to get what Mark Baer used to call the zeitgeist before somebody on our now-late copy desk pointed out that nobody knew what the fuck zeitgeist was, and that he'd spelled it wrong anyhow.

The crowd around the statue is larger than usual. Apparently word of the stay of execution has gotten out. I walk down Monument Avenue a block or so to check out the damage and see damn little of it. There is some graffiti here and there on people's front steps, but nothing like what I've seen on the evening news from other, more woke burgs.

A Black man even older than me is sitting at the base of the monument.

I ask him how he feels about the injunction.

He looks up at me with bloodshot eyes.

"How the fuck you think I feel?" he says. "How you feel?"

Right.

The old guy lifts himself to a standing position.

"Don't worry," he says, looking up at Lee. "He's coming down. Uh-huh. Change is comin.'"

CHAPTER TWENTY-FOUR

Sunday, July 12

"What a fuckin' week," R.P. McGonnigal says.

That pretty much sums it up.

Actually it's more like a week and a half. On July 1, the first day it could have been done legally, the mayor had a crew remove Stonewall Jackson's statue as a crowd lined the traffic circle and cheered. The next day, down came Matthew Fontaine Maury, Pathfinder of the Seas.

The mayor's workers waited until last Tuesday, the seventh, to remove J.E.B. Stuart from Stuart Circle.

Only Lee remains. He's kind of lonely looking, sitting there on Traveller with all his war buddies gone and his base a rainbow of graffiti. Cindy suggests that maybe we could take Lee down and leave the horse.

"We could say it's Secretariat," she says, referencing another famous Virginian. "All horses look alike, right?"

"Kind of feel sorry for him," Andy Peroni says.

"He's had a good run," R.P. says. "Hell, he's lucky they didn't string his ass up. Isn't that what they usually do to traitors?"

This draws an angry scowl from one of Joe's regulars at a table ten feet away, which is as close as you're allowed to sit until the plague abates.

"Don't worry," Abe says. "We've got him outnumbered."

The Oregon Hill gang's all here, with the exception of Francis Xavier Johnson. Goat's quarantined at the president's house of the college he runs up in Ohio, but we've got him on Zoom.

The back table is rocking: There are Cindy and me; Abe and Stella Stellar, whose hair is streaked red, white, and blue, patriot that she is; R.P. and his latest boyfriend; and Andy.

"Did you see my picture?" Stella asks. Of course we did. There she was on A1 of the July 2 paper, standing next to the prone Stonewall, with one foot on his head, which gave our readers more than a glimpse of Stella's patriotic panties.

"Good thing I dressed up that day," Abe's girlfriend and aspiring musical sensation says. The only assumption one could make from that was that Stella thought wearing underwear was "dressing up."

"So what about Lee?" Goat asks over R.P.'s iPhone. "When's he going down?"

We tell our old buddy that the courts will have to decide that one.

He wants us to catch him up on everything that's happened.

I tell him that will take a while.

Our server keeps bringing Bloody Marys and finally suggests strongly that we order some food. In between, we bring Goat up to speed.

"Tell him about Shorty Cole," R.P. says.

So I tell that story.

Shorty is in the money, as much as he ever has been, although all the details haven't been ironed out. Marcus Green has been working the city like a rented mule, until finally he and the mayor and city council came to an agreement, in which Shorty Cole is to be amply compensated for the distress and humiliation he suffered at the hands of Richmond's finest.

"They arrested him for wearing a mask?" Goat says before he laughs so hard that he has to wipe spittle off his computer screen.

"You ought to try it," I advise.

"Hey," my old buddy says, "I'm not gonna give you friggin' cooties from two states away."

Goat says he hopes the Walkers get a damn good payday too. He knew Jeanette back when she and I were married.

My first ex has been taking it hard. I've been out there twice, once with Marcus and once with Cindy, who gets along with Jeanette better than you'd expect from two women who have been, at different times, married to the same man. Yes, Marcus is representing them, just as he did their son before Adam's untimely and unnecessary death.

Marcus has gotten a lot of free publicity expressing his outrage over that incident.

"She's having a hard time," Cindy says. "They both are. Well, all three."

Yeah, even Buddy seems to be showing signs of not being a complete asshole. Both times I was there, he was sitting by his mother, even holding her hand. Glenn was there, too, but he doesn't seem to want to talk about any of it.

"Well," Goat says, "you ought to get a damn Pulitzer Prize or something for this. Damn, you've been abducted by a murderer, wound up wiping his brains off your shirt, and witnessed a death by cop. Hope they're paying you well."

I'm just happy to have a job, I tell Goat and the rest. If I could have had that disaster down in Laurel Cove turn out differently and not have a story that got picked up by the national AP, of course I'd have done it in a New York minute.

I tell him about Ella Minopee and Rob Solomon too. They got the story from me as soon as I'd filed it to my own paper, and both of them were able to put their own local spins on it. Maybe they'll be able to bank that for when their own rags start laying people off again.

"Could be worse," Ella said when we talked a week later. "There's one weekly just up the road that's down to one staffer now. She's the reporter, editor, photographer, everything. I think she even has to sell ads."

Rob said the Rose family, when he contacted them, was glad that an innocent man hadn't gone to prison for murder, although he said they would have liked to have seen Juwan Chavis get a fair trial. I tell Rob that the Roses and I will have to agree to disagree about that.

I even heard from William Keller's father, who called out of the blue one day to thank me for helping them get some kind of closure.

"Violence begets violence," Jacob Keller said, sounding biblical and very tired.

He's right about that. A drunk and careless but otherwise harmless man wipes out a family in a car accident. He gets off light thanks to his daddy's money. The brother of the wreck's only survivor decides justice needs a helping hand and kills the man and his wife, leaving their adopted girl an orphan again. A weird kid gets arrested for the crime, and by the time the authorities realize he didn't do it, he's on the lam. The aforementioned brother, also on the lam, kidnaps a reporter and gets his ass shot to death. The weird kid reaches in his pocket at the wrong time and suffers a similar fate.

Counting the Roses, the Kellers, Juwan Chavis, and Adam Walker, that's seven dead and nobody living left to blame except some overeager cops down in Southwest Virginia.

Oh, L.D. Jones's boys had to do a little fancy dancing over Chavis's shooting, but not even the BLM folks had much enthusiasm for taking up the cause of a kidnapper who got blasted to eternity while holding a gun to a reporter's head. For the time being, the chief's job is safe.

Goat keeps interrupting me because he can't keep it straight.

Finally I tell him I'll email him a copy of the story I did the Sunday after Adam was killed. Handley Pace in design even came up with a very helpful diagram to go with it.

"Isn't there any good news down there?" Goat asks. "I'm thinking about slashing my wrists."

Well, I tell him, other than the fact that I'm alive, there are a few things.

First, the fat man didn't have to burn down his building. Some fool is leasing it and opening another bookstore, God help him. He's going to call it The Day After. The fat man says he let the guy have all the books inside for nothing.

"What the fuck else am I gonna do with books?" he inquired.

Second, and much more importantly, Peggy and Awesome Dude have somehow survived the coronavirus.

"I told you we'd be OK," my old mom said when I stopped by two days after Adam was shot. "I'm too tough to die."

Maybe, I suggested, marijuana cures COVID.

"Bullshit," Peggy said. "I didn't touch the stuff after we tested positive."

They are still testing negative and feeling better. The close encounter with the Grim Reaper will not, she assures me, stop her from self-medicating now that's she's on the mend.

"You ought to try it," she told me. "Might help you kick the Camel habit."

And there's another bit of good news.

Aurora has a home.

After we finish brunch and finally, to the great relief of our server, leave, Cindy and I have another stop to make.

Pechera Love is renting a house in the West End. I haven't been inside since she moved. Ronald, her long-time boyfriend, has migrated down here from DC and has gotten a job doing something for Capitol One, something with computers, so I don't understand, but it pays well.

There are pink balloons on the mailbox outside.

Cindy has picked out a plush toy bunny rabbit about the size of Aurora herself, which I'm toting up to the front door.

Ronald answers. I've never actually met him. He's a handsome man, maybe three inches taller than me with a complexion somewhere between mine and Peachy's. Cindy will tell me later that he's café au lait on the color chart. I think he's a little past fifty, if I remember what Peachy told me.

He seems pleased enough to see us. Maybe, hopefully, he doesn't know that Peachy and I experienced some horizontal happiness many years ago.

We go into the living room, where Peachy is sitting on the couch and watching Aurora walk. This is fairly new stuff for the girl, and Peachy looks ready to dive and catch her first time she falls.

"Don't hover," Ronald says.

Peachy and Ronald have become foster parents, with every intention of making Aurora theirs permanently. Apparently not being married is not a deal breaker these days. Peachy says they're planning to take care of that anyhow.

"Gonna make me an honest woman," Peachy says.

Aurora seems enchanted by the monster pink rabbit we've brought. She and it go tumbling to the floor, and the little girl squeals in delight.

"Nothing I ever gave you made you that happy," I mention to my bride.

"Keep trying," she advises.

ON THE way back, Cindy wants to stop and see what Monument Avenue looks like in its new, post-Confederate incarnation.

We walk from Arthur Ashe Boulevard down to Stuart Circle, admiring the colorful ruins of Jackson, Davis, and Stuart. At each of the former monuments, people have gathered. Most of them are Black. Many of them are still in their church finery.

At the still-standing Lee Monument, I see a familiar face.

Richard Slade is there with his cousin, Chanelle, and her boys.

"Never thought I'd see this day," he says.

In the background, somebody has set up loudspeakers. While we're standing there, Sam Cooke breaks into "A Change is Gonna Come." I was three years old when it hit the charts.

Change came. Partially and eventually.

Marse Robert, when I gaze up at him, looks apprehensive.

AFTERWORD

As in most of the Willie Black mysteries, there is a lot of "real" Richmond in *Monument*. However, some of the events, and sequences of events, have been altered for literary purposes. Many of the events involving interactions between Richmond police and protesters are fictional, such as the arrest of a Black man for wearing a mask into a bank during the COVID-19 epidemic and the killing of Willie Black's abductor. Because so much happened in real time Richmond during 2020, especially regarding the pandemic and the Black Lives Matter movement's role in taking down Confederate statuary on Monument Avenue, it seemed more necessary than usual to point out that this is a work of fiction, and that all the characters are fictional.